A SHAKER

A Bad Hair Day

TWENTY-FOUR NEW SHORT STORIES

EDITED BY L. S. FISHER

www.MozarkPress.com

Published by Mozark Press, www.Mozarkpress.com
© 2012 Linda Fisher
PO Box 1746, Sedalia, MO 65302

Cover design and book layout by H. Ream.

ISBN: 978-0-9844385-7-0

DEDICATION

This anthology is dedicated to the memory of Sonia Todd whose stories and blog brightened our world. May she forever enjoy the glory of heaven.

OTHER TITLES
SHAKER OF MARGARITAS SERIES

HOT FLASH MOMMAS
(A Show-Me Book Award Winner)

COUGARS ON THE PROWL
(Missouri Writers' Guild Anthology of the Year Award)

v

CONTENTS

ACKNOWLEDGEMENTS

We are grateful to every author who submitted a story to *A Shaker of Margaritas: A Bad Hair Day* regardless of whether the story was selected for this edition.

Deepest appreciation is extended to all who proofread and assisted the editor in any way. Mozark Press would like to especially acknowledge Harold Ream for the countless hours he spent on the website and providing technical support throughout the publication process.

INTRODUCTION

The *Bad Hair Day* anthology began with a call for humorous fiction stories about one of those days when life just doesn't go according to plan. In fact, we wanted stories about a day as horrible as a bad perm or hair that turns green, unintentionally. Yet, as in real life, the female protagonist should work her way through the challenging day with humor, stubbornness, and attitude.

The stories in this volume are an uplifting diversion for those days when Murphy's Law rules. We can't always avoid bad hair days, but laughter is truly the best defense.

So if you're having one of those bad days, get out that shaker of margaritas and curl up with *A Shaker of Margaritas: A Bad Hair Day* and let the laughter begin.

L. S. Fisher

FOUR LITTLE WORDS
Mary Ann Corrigan

I spread the morning paper on the kitchen table. April 16th—the best day of the year for me and many other accountants. For the last three months, I'd worked days, nights, and weekends to finish my clients' income taxes. Now, finally, I had time to myself and could do the pleasant things I'd postponed—plant pansies in the front yard, swim in the new indoor pool at the Y, and invite the neighbors for an impromptu happy hour. Ben could help with that. He was on spring break with no classes to teach. Before doing anything else, though, I wanted to linger over the newspaper and coffee.

I looked up as Ben came into the kitchen from the garage.

He grabbed a mug from the cabinet. "Glad you left me some coffee."

"Your appointment didn't take long. What did Dr. James say?"

Ben filled his mug. "Arthritis, not a disc problem. No surgery. That's the good news."

And what's the bad news? I'd have to prod it out of my close-mouthed husband. A bit of paper peeked out from his shirt pocket. "Is that a prescription in your pocket?"

He pulled it out. "Sort of."

"What's it for?" Hemlock, judging by the doomed look on Ben's face.

"Ways to ease the pain. Back exercises twice a day, an anti-inflammatory every six hours, and—" He stirred sugar into his coffee. "By the way, are you working today?"

"I'm working at relaxing." Had he forgotten yesterday was the end of my crunch season? No. He was just trying to change the subject. "What else did the doctor say you should do for the pain?"

He plunked his cup on the kitchen table, sat across from me, and sighed. "Shop."

My jaw dropped. "Well, I believe shopping cures a lot of ills, but I've yet to meet a doctor who agrees. I wonder if Dr. James would write *me* a prescription like that." And if the IRS would let me deduct my purchases as medical expenses. "How's shopping going to cure your aching back? It usually gives you a headache."

He gazed into his mug. "He said to buy a new mattress."

Halleluiah! How many times had I suggested the new-mattress cure for Ben's back, only to have him pooh-pooh the idea? Now, for the sake of marital harmony, I swallowed the four words that every spouse loves to say and hates to hear.

Ben's eyes narrowed. "I know what you're thinking, Jenny."

After thirty years of marriage, he could pick up an I-told-you-so telepathically.

Telepathy works both ways. "I just realized why you asked about my plans for the day. You expect *me* to buy the mattress that the doctor prescribed for *you*."

"Well, I hate to shop, and you love it, but—"

"Nobody loves shopping for mattresses. People do it because they have backaches or bedbugs. Mattress sales guys know how to exploit that. They're so aggressive that even used car lots won't hire them."

"You want to throw me to those sharks and let me fend for myself?"

He had a point. Their pressure tactics would drive him out the door. Then we'd have to sleep on the old mattress forever. He'd groan, toss and turn all night, and keep me awake. "Okay, I'll go buy the mattress, but I don't want to hear any complaints about it."

He sipped from his mug. "You make the world's best coffee, Jenny!"

This compliment out of left field put me on the alert. He was trying to soften my resistance—but to what? I recognized the ploy because I'd recently tried it myself. I'd rubbed his biceps, told him he was the sexiest statistics professor on the planet, and then suggested we hire a housecleaning service. The tactic hadn't worked.

"What do you want, Ben?"

He took off his glasses and leaned across the table so I couldn't avoid his puppy-dog brown eyes. "Dr. James said we have to shop for the mattress together."

I wanted to shop with Ben about as much as I wanted a root canal. I sat back and folded my arms. "Our marriage has lasted this long because we never shop together. It drives me nuts that you buy the first thing you clap your eyes on."

"It drives me nuts that you touch everything and read all the labels."

"It's called comparison shopping." I sipped my coffee. It had turned cold. Dr. James was right. The mattress had to work for both of us. "Okay, let's go shopping, for better or worse."

On the way to the mall, I planned my strategy—keep the sales-clerks far away from him, force him to try out several mattresses, and refuse to leave until we bought one we both found comfortable.

We could see the sign in the showroom window from across the parking lot. Mattress Madness Sale! When we walked into the shop, no salesclerk swooped down on us. They were all busy with other customers. Thank you, Mattress Madness Sale.

Ben stood rooted just inside the entrance, daunted by row upon row of mattress-topped beds. "They're all a lot higher than ours. Did someone slip yeast in them?" He pressed a finger on the nearest mattress as if testing a cake for doneness.

I took out my tape measure to confirm what our eyes were telling us. "Sixteen inches, twice the depth of our old mattress. Maybe the government adopted princess-and-the-pea mattress standards."

Ben grinned. "Perfect for you."

Scoring off me put him in a good mood, which is why I'd fed him that straight line. "So, pick a bed, any bed." My arm swept around the showroom.

He pressed a hand down on the one closest to the door. "This one will do."

"It will do for the palm of your hand. What about the rest of you? Lie down on it. See if it's comfortable."

"With all these people watching?" He gestured toward a knot of customers.

I craned my neck, pretending to check out the showroom's four corners. "I don't see any dressing rooms for trying on mattresses."

"There's a guy climbing onto a bed. If he can do it, I can." He perched on the mattress and, with one foot propped on his knee, untied his shoe.

I pointed to the foot of the bed. "Notice the plastic cover protecting the mattress where your feet go. You can leave your shoes on."

He untied his other shoe. "I can't be comfortable on a bed with my shoes on."

"You want me to fetch your pajamas and teddy bear?"

"Very funny." He slipped his shoes off and glanced around the room like a thief checking for witnesses. Then he lounged back on his elbows and slid into a lying position. "Come on up."

A daunting task. The thick mattress on top of the box springs created a mountain half my height. I hoisted myself up with the same muscles I used to pull myself out of the pool.

The climb was worth it. Way more comfortable than our old mattress. I looked up at ceiling panels that diffused the light and unclenched my jaw for the first time since walking into the store. "How do you like the mattress, Ben?"

"It's good." He bolted upright. "Let's buy it."

Tempting, but a betrayal of my basic principles of shopping. "You have to try other mattresses. They might be more comfortable and cost less." I spotted a man in a slick suit approaching us. "I'll run interference with the sales sharks while you try another mattress."

I put myself squarely in the path of the man whose name tag identified him as the manager. "Hi there. I'd like to buy a mattress, but only if the salesclerks stay away from my husband. He's the one walking around with no shoes on. He's off his meds. I should warn you that your Madness Sale matches his mental state."

The manager smiled. "I'm sure a smart shopper like you wouldn't select a mattress without knowing which is the best buy."

By which he meant the mattress with the largest commission. "Oh, yes I would. My husband gets loud and rambunctious with salespeople. He'll drive away your other customers. So tell your guys to back off. If they do, we'll buy a mattress. If they don't, we won't." An empty threat, at least I hoped so.

Ben liked all three of the mattresses he tried.

After scaling mattresses two and three, I settled on the first one we'd tested. I then had to endure Ben's I-told-you-so, and he didn't use telepathy to transmit it.

The manager swiped our credit card and arranged delivery for that very afternoon. "We can take away the old mattress when we deliver the new one."

Ben frowned. "That seems so final."

I patted his arm. "We'll have a little memorial service for it."

The manager hustled us out the door.

Ben glanced back at him once we were outside. "Did you see how that guy looked at me? You'd think I was a serial killer."

"I didn't notice." I checked my watch. Barely noon. Still time for a swim. "Mission accomplished."

Ben cringed. "Don't say that! It's asking for trouble."

Halfway to the car, I thunked my head. Mission not yet accomplished. "Our sheets won't fit a mattress twice as deep as the old one. We'll have to stop there." I pointed to the Linen Megashop.

Ben grunted. "Not another store."

"We really should replace our bedspread too. It won't hang down far enough with a thicker mattress."

His grunt morphed into a growl.

Inside the linen store, he spotted a sign that cheered him up. "Bed-in-a-bag! That's for us. One-stop shopping on aisle three."

I followed him, pushing a cart. Aisle three stretched out like the grand canyon of bedding.

Ben peered up at the bulging plastic bags poised on floor-to-ceiling shelves. "They look like boulders ready to crash down on us. Your shopping cart isn't big enough for a boulder. We need a hand truck. What's in those bags anyway?"

If he deigned to read a label, he'd know the answer to that question. "They might have some of the sets on display in the back of the store."

Beyond the canyon walls, a line-up of mock beds presented the latest bed-in-a-bag styles.

Ben studied the first made-up "bed," its sleeping area barely visible beneath pillows of all shapes and sizes. "We've been married thirty years and done fine with two pillows, one for me, one for you. Who are these other pillows for?"

"You know very well they're decorative. You've stayed in hotels. They all have extra pillows."

"They also have empty closets where you can stuff the pillows. Our closets are full. What would we do with the extra pillows at night? If we put them on the floor, we'd have to run an obstacle course to reach the bathroom."

I ignored him and pointed out a sign that enumerated the pieces in the ensemble. "Read what's in the boulder bag—comforter, bed skirt, one fitted sheet, one flat sheet, two pillow cases, two throw pillows, one square and one round, two rectangular pillow shams, and two Euro shams."

Ben raised his hand like a student with a question. "Why should I pay for things that even the manufacturer calls 'shams'?"

A smiling, bouncy salesclerk approached us. "Can I help you find something?"

Ben waved a dismissive hand at the bedding displays. "We don't want any of these sham things. Where can we get something for the top of the bed without all this extra fluff?"

She gestured toward the front of the store. "Comforters are in aisle six, coverlets in aisle seven, quilts in aisle eight. And on aisle nine, you'll find some lovely duvets and duvet covers."

Ben poked me with his elbow. "And you wonder why I hate shopping? Too many choices. What's the difference between a comforter, a coverlet, a quilt, and a duvet? It's the same in the dental aisle at the supermarket. Do I want plaque control, whitening, enamelshield, extra fluoride? All I want is toothpaste, for crying out loud."

"I'm sorry, sir, we don't carry toothpaste." The clerk looked a bit less perky now. "MegaDrugs next door has a huge dental aisle."

Ben raised an index finger. "That's my point!"

I gave the clerk an apologetic smile. "Which aisle for sheets? We'll stick with our old bedspread." Until I could go shopping alone.

With the mattress delivery looming, though, we had to buy sheets now. Ben nearly bolted when he saw all the sizes, colors, and patterns on display. I tugged him toward white cotton sheets, but even this narrow category offered more options than we wanted.

I ran my fingers along an Egyptian cotton sheet in an open package. "When I last bought bedding, you could buy either economical sheets with 180 threads per inch or luxury ones with 200 per inch. Now they come in 300, 400, 600, even 800 thread count."

Ben rolled his eyes. "It's totally bogus. Threads per inch. Ha! It's like asking how many angels fit on the head of a pin."

I checked a few price tags. "The higher the thread count, the higher the price." I checked another tag. "Usually, but not always."

"How can you trust those thread claims? Does anyone really count how many threads are in an inch?" Ben whipped out his smart phone to ask the online oracles.

He could spend hours checking one source against another. I lined up four packages of sheets. My CPA-wired brain divided the cost of each package by the number of threads per square inch. I wasn't sure what the results would tell me, but it gave me something to do while Ben researched thread counts.

He held up his phone in triumph. "You use a pick-eye to count the number of threads in an inch of cloth. It's a magnifying glass for textiles. The Good Housekeeping Institute tested nine brands of sheets, and guess what they found? Thread fraud! Some manufacturers claimed a count more than double the actual number."

"And yet, we need sheets." Why did I ever consider shopping therapeutic? I abandoned my principles and fell back on the fastest selection method—eeney, meeny, miney, mo.

With the shopping ordeal over, Ben took me to his favorite lunch joint. He had no trouble choosing one of the menu's fifteen different burgers. I got home too late for a swim, but at least I had time to plant the pansies.

The new mattress arrived just before dinner time, and the old one departed.

I didn't make the bed until late in the evening. The mattress was so heavy I could barely slip the fitted sheet under three of its corners. For the fourth corner, I had to tug the sheet and lift the mattress at the same time. It wouldn't budge. "I need some help here, Ben. The mattress is too heavy for me to raise the corner."

Ben planted his feet and elevated the mattress three inches. Then he clutched his lower back and howled. It took him a full minute to straighten up.

"You're the shopping expert," he said. "You should have known we had to try lifting the mattress before we bought it."

If I'd clenched my teeth any harder, I would have cracked a molar.

"Maybe we can manage it together." With four hands and our combined strength, we succeeded in slipping the fitted sheet over the last corner of the mattress. "Whew! I'm glad we only have to do that once a week."

Ben rubbed his back. "We don't have to change the sheets that often. After a week, all those threads are just getting friendly. How about once a month?"

"That's too friendly. Every other week."

"I don't know if my spine can take a setback like that every two weeks. I wonder if anyone makes a mattress jack."

"I have a better suggestion. We can hire a housecleaning service. They come every two weeks, and they don't just clean the house. They take the sheets off, wash them, and put them back on the bed."

I waited for his usual objection—he didn't want strangers in the house. When he didn't say anything right away, I felt a tingle of hope. Could this mattress have a silver lining?

Ben rubbed his chin. "Sign up the housecleaners. Anything's better than a backache."

Yes! This day had been worth every miserable minute.

Later, when Ben snuggled between the sheets of many threads, a look of bliss crossed his face. "My back doesn't hurt! That old mattress was the problem!"

I couldn't hold it in any longer. "I told you so!"

Leftovers
Carolyn Mulford

No cars were parked in front of Louisa's Leftovers. Good. I wouldn't have an audience when I donated Arnie's abandoned artifacts.

I chose a space between the thrift store and Brigette's Beauty Salon. Hmmm. Little chance of an operator recognizing and questioning me in this old strip mall. The perfect place to get the overdue cut I needed for job interviews, if anyone ever agreed to talk to a laid-off civil servant who had reviewed grant applications.

One grant had gone to the foundation that operated this charity shop to finance programs for abused women. An appropriate place to dispose of my ex's discards. Not that he'd ever hit me. He inflicted boredom, not pain. Until two weeks ago. Then the coward had announced to the world—including me—on Facebook that he was "riding west for the adventures postponed by marrying too young." A photo showed him and a woman sitting on a Harley. She held a map in front of her face. I gave the relationship 2,000 miles.

I popped the Corolla's trunk and gathered up his bowling ball, ukulele, and hiking boots. Elbowing open the glass double door, I stepped into near darkness. Light from the shop's display windows reached a Donate Here sign on an old conference table to my right. No one came out of the cavern to greet me, but a voice murmured somewhere in the back. Were they saving electricity? I put Arnie's toys on the table and brought in the next load—the box with his Zane Grey collection. Had these books prompted him to go West? I hoped the Indians won this time.

I whumped the box onto the table to attract attention. No one appeared. I returned to the car for the last load, a garbage bag full of pants and shirts he insisted had shrunk and a loaded tie rack. I'd given him a tie on each wedding anniversary. Did I really want to let go of those memories? As I debated, a car parked in front of the salon.

Instinctively I ducked my head to hide my face. Enough! He had humiliated me. Off with his ties.

Still...I removed the silver and blue silk tie marking our twenty-fifth anniversary and marched inside with the others. "Hello. Anyone here?"

The lights blinked on. Far back on the right, white hair bobbed along behind the last row of clothing racks. A walking green pencil emerged into the wide central aisle that separated the clothing from everything else. She paused to remove large green-rimmed glasses and wipe her eyes with a handkerchief that matched her dress and pumps. Not a pencil, a praying mantis.

She hurried toward me. "A green blouse. Thank the Lord."

What the hey? Did green make us sisters? "Good morning," I said briskly. "I need the donation form for a tax deduction, please."

She pointed at an old metal government-issue desk on my left. "Top drawer on the right. Is this your first time here?"

"Yes. I don't know your procedure."

She peered at me through thick lenses. "The other volunteer, Thelma, will be here any moment. She'll show you where everything is." She scurried to the door.

"Wait a minute! I'm not—"

"If something you can't handle comes up, ask them to wait for Thelma." She dabbed her eyes again. "Sorry to leave a new volunteer alone, but I have an emergency."

My haircut could wait a few minutes. "I'll keep an eye on things until Thelma gets here."

"Thank you, umm, what's your name, dear?"

"Dorsey, Dorsey Bent." I watched her trot toward a car.

At least I was being useful, and I could find the form and fill it out while I waited. I did that. No Thelma. No anyone. I swiveled around in the squeaking desk chair and studied a time-dulled portrait of a fifty-something woman in a green dress and a young woman in a white dress with a green sash. Both had green eyes. They had to be the late Louisa Magee, an earthy self-made millionaire, and her daughter Allegra, now head of both Magee Industries and the Louisa Magee Foundation.

Time to tour my temporary domain. Being fond of quirky pins, I started with the locked jewelry case by the desk. Entwined necklaces—costume junk—sprawled across the top shelf. Two lovely cloisonné pins—a hummingbird and a cardinal—rested amid clutter on the bottom shelf. Thelma could sell me the hummingbird.

Next came disorganized shelves of assorted knickknacks, everything from a plastic model of the capitol to a pewter cup. An intricate East African Makonde wood carving and a set of Russian nesting *matryoshka* dolls probably memorialized trips abroad. Not valuable enough to go into an estate sale? Not cherished enough to survive a downsizing? Maybe the owners got tired of dusting them.

Where on earth was Thelma? If I didn't get to Brigitte's soon, I'd hit the lunch crowd and risk bumping into someone who'd seen Arnie's Facebook page.

I moved on to the china. I recognized remnants of old but beautiful sets of dishes. My mother-in-law had searched for that sugar bowl for two years. She'd accused me of driving her son out of town two weeks ago, and of tricking him into marriage twenty-five years ago. Was I a big enough person to buy it for her?

Nope. One of the divorce's many blessings would be never spending another holiday at her table. I hid the sugar bowl behind a duck-shaped cookie jar.

The back left corner contained a mishmash—a faded quilt, board games, a Tiffany lamp, a typing table holding four small framed pieces. I picked up the top one, a canvas reproduction of one of Thomas Hart Benton's farm scenes. Lovely. Four dollars. Louisa's Leftovers outshone Salvation Army offerings, but this place stayed in the dark about displaying and pricing donations.

Had I made a mistake when I approved the grant? If the foundation ran its programs the way it did this place, it didn't deserve a grant. I'd taken pride in allocating taxpayers' money effectively. Had I mistaken pigeons for doves?

The sound of a car sent me jogging to the door praying to see a woman in green.

A petite thirty-something woman with long canary-blonde hair opened the back door of a red Lincoln SUV. She wore high-heeled sandals, hot-pink shorts, a black short-sleeved top, and black pearls.

Couldn't be Thelma.

The woman smiled and waved, flashing long hot-pink fingernails. "I brought my quarterly donation. Would you bring the cart, please?"

Cart? "Sorry, I'm not a—a *regular* volunteer. I don't know where it is." I squelched the impulse to explain I wasn't even an *irregular* volunteer. This place had enough problems without my letting donors know it was unstaffed.

"That's okay, sweetie. I only brought a dozen this time. We can carry them in."

A dozen what? Curiosity piqued, I went outside.

She handed me two shoeboxes. When I took them, she piled on two more, and two more. I had to bend my neck to one side to see.

I carried them in and put them on the table. Not a Nike or Reebok in the bunch. Two were Jimmy Choo, those sinfully expensive shoes the women in *Sex in the City* went on and on about. I didn't recognize the other brand names.

I'd expected her to come in after me with the rest of the boxes. Instead she waited by the SUV. She and Arnie thought alike when it came to how "we" did a job. Pointing that out required more energy than complying, so the donkey trotted back to the SUV.

She loaded five boxes in my arms. "Thanks, sweetie." She took the last one and opened the door for me. "I'll go find the pair I need for the gala tonight while you fill out the receipt for the IRS."

I'd given her an inch. That was my limit. "Sorry, I'm not authorized to do that, but Thelma will be here soon."

"Oh, sweetie, Thelma won't be in today. She's playing in the big charity golf tournament."

I swallowed a curse.

The shoe woman sashayed toward the back. "I'm sure you can figure out the form."

I doubted *she* could, but I'd give her a chance to try. Somehow the lid came off a Jimmy Choo box. The shoes were beautiful, and they looked like new. I opened another box and took out a stiletto heel with the upper made of baby-skin soft purple leather. Handmade in Italy. The sole showed no wear.

The woman rejoined me. "Aren't they exquisite?"

I stroked the leather. "How can you give them up?"

"I'm not," she said. "I'm just rotating them."

"I don't get it."

She grinned. "My husband says I buy too many shoes. He refused to allow any more shelves in my shoe closet. So when I crave new shoes, I bring a few pairs here." She held up silver heels. "If I need a pair, I come get them."

Ingenious, but flawed. "Don't other women buy them?"

She smirked and pointed to the purple shoe. "Try it on."

I could see it would barely go over my big toe. "It's Cinderella's slipper, made to fit only your foot."

"What a lovely way of putting it." She beamed.

I put the shoe back in the box and reached out to read the tag on the pair she'd retrieved. "Twenty dollars, please."

Her mouth formed an O and then a pout. "But they're my shoes."

"Not anymore. You donated them and took a tax deduction."

She stuck her nose in the air. "Thelma never makes me pay for them."

I gasped, feigning shock. "Do you realize you both violated the tax law?"

Uncertainty flitted across her face. She touched her pearls as though they were a lucky rabbit's foot and rallied. "Oh, pooh. Nobody checks those things."

"But they do," I whispered, glancing toward the racks as though an IRS agent lurked there. "The foundation received a state grant and now auditors check everything."

Her eyes narrowed. "I don't have any cash. I'll pay next time I come in."

"But the books have to balance every day." I reached for the silver shoes.

She drew them back. "Damn it! I need these tonight."

The victory tasted as delicious as a chilled Snickers. "Louisa's Leftovers accepts Visa and MasterCard."

She produced a twenty, handed it to me, and stalked out of the store.

Putting the bill in the cash box, I noticed a key. Saved! I'd kept my promise. I could lock the door and walk away. A tag on the key said "restrm." I pawed through the cash box and the desk like a dog digging for bones. No door key.

Where could it be? The praying mantis had come from behind the clothing. Retracing her path, I came to a double door bearing an Employees Only sign and went through it. To my left was a small office—a lovely old oak desk with a phone and piles of paper, an ancient laptop on a tray table, and a battered four-drawer file cabinet with a set of color-coded keys hanging from the lock. I grabbed them and turned around to leave. Two long, empty sorting tables stood in front of metal shelves. The closest shelves were so tightly packed with clothing that a mouse couldn't squeeze through. Louisa's Leftovers had become a dump. Literally.

Depressed, I hurried out. The keys weren't labeled, but I had no doubt the green one fit the front door. When I paused at the desk to pick up my purse and tax form, a Boone Dock Retirement Village van stopped out front. By the time I reached the entrance, the bald driver was placing a plastic step by the van's back door. I shoved the green key into the door's lock. It wouldn't turn. I wiggled and jiggled until I hit the magic spot.

"Good morning," called a silver-haired black woman limping toward me with the aid of a four-footed cane. "You must be new. Green suits you."

Three white women of a similar age and mobility—two canes and a walker—followed her. All four smiled. All four wore something green—a shamrock necklace, a floral blouse, slacks, tassels on a cane.

Could one of them be Thelma? No, they had come to shop. Turning them away would be like taking catnip from a kitten. I stuck the keys in my pocket and held the door open. "Welcome, ladies."

The walker woman peered at me through thick glasses. "I'm looking for a nice scarf for a birthday gift today. Thelma promised she'd put some out."

I remembered scarves hanging on a hat tree. "On the aisle half way back."

The driver shut the van door. "See you in thirty minutes, girls."

The four women turtled off to different sections of the shop.

I checked the change in the cash box: one twenty, one ten, two fives, and ten ones. Did Louisa's Leftovers take checks? Well, it would for the next half hour. I listened to the women joke with each other for a couple of minutes before restlessness compelled me to sort the knickknacks. I'd finished two shelves when someone called out, "Five minutes."

I went back to the desk.

The black woman handed me a five and the sugar bowl I'd hidden. "My sister's grandson broke hers. She almost cried. I've been watching for it for months."

"I'm so glad you found it." Delighted, in fact. I cushioned it with bubble wrap and put it in a plastic grocery bag. "You and your friends come here often?"

"Once a week. It's easier to walk in here than the mall. Cheaper, too. And our money goes to a good cause. I give Allegra Magee a lot of credit for carrying out her mother's wishes." She grinned. "We four call ourselves the Leftovers. After this we go out to lunch, and we leave no leftovers."

A yellow car with a red pizza sign on top squealed to a stop out front. A young blond man in a red and yellow T-shirt jumped out and ran into the store. "I got a big job interview in half an hour. You carry dress shirts and ties?"

"Right back here," a cane woman called.

"Thanks, ma'am." He darted to the back.

Guessing the Leftovers would give him all the help he could tolerate, I stayed put.

A silver Mercedes sedan parked beside the pizza car. Definitely a donor rather than a shopper.

The walker woman approached the desk with three colorful scarves draped over her shoulder. "I need the opinion of a younger pair of eyes."

"Of course." I inspected the scarves with care. Only one had no flaws. "This one looks brand new."

"Then I'll take it."

I put the other two back on the hat tree and accepted her dollar bill and two quarters.

"There's our van," the sugar bowl buyer said. "Let's go."

"I want to see how that boy looks in the shirt first," a cane woman said. "It was the only one that didn't need ironing."

The pizza driver plowed toward us through the maze of clothing racks.

Only then did I notice the quizzical stare of the Mercedes' driver, a beautifully groomed woman about my age. She wore a white golf skirt, a green blouse, and a green visor. So Thelma had finally come.

The young man, now in a blue dress shirt, claimed my attention. He held up a black tie with tiny white polka dots and a brown tie with big yellow swirls. "Which one goes better?"

They were equally awful. I studied the anxious face, trying to figure out how to tell him that. His eyes were the same blue as Arnie's. "I have something much better in my car. You pay Thelma"—I gestured to the golfer—"for the shirt and meet me outside."

She shook her head no, but I sprinted out the door and to my car. I met him as he came out the front door and handed that last anniversary tie to him. "This is a gift—to bring you good luck."

"Wow! It's perfect," he said, holding it against the shirt. "But this is a Louis Vuitton tie. Are you sure you want to give it to a stranger?"

"I'm sure. It's a leftover."

The four Leftovers crowded around to admire the tie. The walker woman said, "Take it, son. Luck brought it to you, and luck brings more luck."

"Thanks, thanks so much." He jumped in the car and roared away.

My spirits lifted. At least somebody had a job interview today. I waved good-bye to the Leftovers and went in for my purse and the tax form.

The golfer sat at the desk reading it. She didn't look up. "Suzanne called me to complain that a new volunteer made her buy her own shoes." Her voice conveyed authority but withheld judgment.

"I'm not a volunteer, but I'm the one who insisted she follow the rules. If you'd come on time, Thelma, you could have continued to let her use the shop as her spare closet." I held out my hand. "Please give me my form."

She leaned back in the chair. Green eyes gazed up at me. "I'm not Thelma. I'm Allegra Magee. And you're the Dorsey Bent who approved our grant." She handed me the form. "Is this a surprise inspection?"

"No, no." Amazing that she'd remembered my name. "The state abolished my department, and my position."

"How on earth did you end up taking over here?"

"The older woman who left mistook me for a volunteer and asked me to stay until Thelma came. I couldn't leave the place untended." Since I no longer worked for the state, I said what I thought: "The foundation has a reputation for running outstanding programs. I would never have supported the grant if I'd seen how poorly this place is run."

She swiveled to face the portrait. "I wish I could deny it. It's been a headache from the beginning—half business, half charity, total inefficiency. Mom insisted it could work, and I promised to see that it did." She took a deep breath and swung back to the desk, her face somber. "She never forgot the years she couldn't afford to buy anything new for either of us."

I'd read that in the foundation's documents. It didn't let Allegra off the hook. "What went wrong?"

"I haven't been able to find the right person to run this unholy hybrid. Initially I hired a young marketing whiz, the one who wrote the grant proposal. She quit because the volunteers patted her on the head and ignored her instructions. So I turned management over to the most responsible volunteers." She smiled wryly. "You've seen how well that worked."

I nodded. "Only half a dozen people came in here all morning. I'm afraid you won't have any shoppers, donors, or volunteers if you don't find someone with dedication and the appropriate skills soon." Fearing she might prefer disaster, I added, "Your mother was right: This place could serve those who desperately need a bargain and persuade those who don't to donate and *spend.*"

She cocked her head. "Are you applying for the job?"

"No, absolutely not." I stepped back, disconcerted. "You need someone who knows retailing. I'm not qualified."

She waggled her finger. "Never say that. You underestimate yourself, one of the few mistakes women make that men don't. I saw how you rearranged those shelves. More important, I saw how you treated the Leftovers and the pizza man." She chuckled. "I almost missed my last putt because I couldn't stop laughing about the way you talked Suzanne into paying for those shoes. That's when it occurred to me that whoever had the moxie to face down that overage brat might be the person I've been looking for. What do you say, Dorsey?"

My heart pounded. Should I accept the challenge? Could I afford to work for a struggling nonprofit? If I didn't dare ask about pay, I didn't have the guts to succeed in the job. I forced out, "What salary and benefits are you offering?"

Her eyes turned dollar-bill green. "I'll match your old package and give you an annual bonus based on how much you increase the foundation's income."

Shock kept me silent.

She studied me. "If you say yes right now, I'll throw in a signing bonus: a cut and styling at the best salon in town." She dangled the keys in front of me.

I took them. I'd always looked good in green.

BOMB SQUAD
Betsy Murphy

"*Oy Vey*, what a day!" Joann, not otherwise fluent in Yiddish or even given much to rhyming, pushed some wandering crystals of margarita salt back up to the rim of her glass. That was a large part of the whole margarita experience for her, and she never could see the point of ordering one without the rim dipped in salt.

"Couldn't have been that bad—you're not in jail, the hospital, or the morgue," Susan tittered as she drained her own fuzzy navel and motioned to the bartender for another. Sandy, as the name tag on his burgundy vest announced to the world, had been avoiding that end of the bar all evening. Yes, women his mother's age could be very generous tippers, but there was something about how they looked at him through their bifocals that made him uncomfortable. He fingered the car key in his pocket and for once was glad that he'd taken his mother's advice and parked under the lone streetlight in the employees' parking lot. "I'll have another," Susan announced as he drew near without even waiting for him to ask.

"Yeah, let's just say this has been one for the record books." Joann's tongue darted around the rapidly melting ice as she regarded Sandy's obvious discomfort. "It started out all right, though. We had finally gotten that bit with my granddaughter Jennifer straightened out—you remember, she saw the book I was reviewing on the Madonna-Whore Cults of Montana."

"Oh, yeah." Susan leered as Sandy bent down to pick up an errant coaster another grandmother had accidentally—on purpose—sent flying his way. "Didn't she tell your ex-son-in-law's priest that she'd seen the VM at a truck stop in Billings wearing a tube top last November?"

Joann blushed briefly at the memory. "Father Pat just has no sense of humor. Anyhow, once I explained to him that the book was written by a Baptist about the Mormons, and that I was just reviewing it for my course in Euphemism Science, he settled down a bit. Her suspension ends next week. Anyhow, that was finally behind us when I set out for the bomb site this morning."

"Wait—you were serious about that, then? Because I wasn't sure." The ears of suited men in boring haircuts at a nearby table perked up at the b-word. One excused himself, presumably to go out and warm up the gray Plymouth sedan they had ridden in on.

"Now Susan, you know me better than that," Joann mocked her friend playfully. "Remember how we'd talked about yarn bombing that ridiculous Rush Limbaugh statue down in the statehouse? During National Knit and Crochet in Public Day—hellllooooo?"

"Yeah, but I never thought you'd actually do it. I mean, don't they have cameras pointed on that—uh, thing?" Susan sat up straight just as the suited drinkers relaxed visibly once the term *yarn* had been added to *bombing*. The junior member of the team was deputed to go outside and retrieve the agent who was right now checking his extra clip of ammo while the Plymouth was warming up. "Sounds like a recipe for disaster to me," she added, suspecting that there was something other than buns in Joann's gourmet convection oven.

"Well, as these kinds of guerilla crocheting events go, the logistics were pretty straightforward. True, there's a camera on the bust, but all you have to do is point a laser pointer into the lens, and all it'll register is static."

"Really?" Susan asked in an amazement also shared by the four suited men. "Like the kind you use to play with the cats?" As guardian of three cats of her own, Susan already possessed at least one of these pointers in most rooms of her house.

"Absolutely." Joann sucked down the last of the now thoroughly melted margarita and motioned Sandy for another. "Try it next time you walk into one of those stores that insist on showing off their shoplifting prevention cameras by making you watch yourself coming through the door. At a damn unflattering angle too, I might add." She wiped the last crystals of salt from the corner of her mouth while Sandy mixed her next one. "Anyhow, that's getting a little ahead of the story."

"But what about the security guard watching the tape?" Susan just couldn't let that part go.

"That's why we did the test runs last week. You remember that field trip Jennifer's class took to the state capitol?" Susan nodded. "No trouble at all to slip up to the third floor of the capitol while the little ones were having a tour of pioneer life in the basement museum."

"You chaperones can be worse than the kids!" Susan chuckled as she watched another fifty-something woman baiting Sandy with an obviously expired happy hour coupon.

"Hey, they all got back to school in one piece. Mostly. Anyhow, there we are setting out for Jefferson City in our marble camouflage—"

"Uh, marble camouflage?"

"Hey, you gotta blend in somehow. Besides, you ever been down there? Lots of marble hallways and lots of lobbyists in cheesy outfits. After we all met up, we stopped for breakfast at this little greasy spoon five miles from nowhere, and we got to talking while we were waiting on our French toast and omelets. Julie was saying how much easier things are now that she's no longer strictly a hooker and has gone bi."

"Like bisexual?" Susan nodded her thanks to Sandy who, upon hearing the word *bisexual*, resolved to always, always, *always* heed his mother's advice in the future.

"No, silly—bi-crafty. You know, knitting and crocheting? A lot of us find hooking to be hard on the elbows after a certain age." The table of suited men choked on their faux-hattans after Joann's last sentence. "Lynn said she'd go out to her trunk and bring in the rest of her stash. That must have been what did it."

"Did what?" Susan asked.

"Oh, just got the convoy stopped about half a mile from the restaurant."

"But there's no law against yarn yet, is there?" Susan was incredulous at the thought.

"No, but this one snot-nosed deputy asked about Sharon's collection of #13 circular needles and Julie's double-pointed needles. 'Why do you need so many?' he asked us. Honestly, where do they get some of these people?" The men in suits shifted uncomfortably in their vinyl seats. "Sharon pointed out that TSA even allows knitting needles and crochet hooks on airplanes, along with scissors with blades up to four inches, and that if he had nothing better to do with his time than harass us, she'd call his sheriff and help find him something. Oh, did I mention that I think this deputy's uncle is the same priest who gave poor little Jennifer the hard time? Obnoxiousness must run in that family."

"No you didn't," Susan's head was swimming, though whether it was due to Joann's exploits or the two fuzzy navels she'd consumed was an open question. "So what did he do?"

"Oh, his face got all red—sort of like our bartender's." Sandy was having a trying shift now that happy hour seemed to be merging with the weekly Cougar Club meeting. "But he had nothing on us so he had to let us go. The funny thing was, after about half an hour, we noticed this car following us..." Joann's voice trailed off faintly, as though she were still trying to figure it out.

"What kind of car? Did you call 911?" Susan was agitated and stirring her fuzzy navel with an orange swizzle stick for all it was worth.

"But that's just the thing—it wasn't just one car; it was a Buick, then a Ford, then a Mercury. But they all had tinted windows and very little chrome. It was probably nothing, but it made those hairs on the back of my neck stand up just the same." The suited men tensed, and then relaxed a bit once they noticed that "Plymouth" had not been part of Joann's list. "Anyway, once we got there, we changed into our camos in the back of Sharon's van and went up the service stairs just like we'd planned. Unfortunately, we had some company."

"*Who?*" Susan demanded to know in a volume that made a few of the other patrons turn in their direction.

"Calm down, calm down. At first, we thought it was just like Mall Security or something, but it turned out to be a Homeland Security detail worrying about how we'd gotten in without going through the metal detectors. I thought our goose was cooked at that point, but Lynn spoke up first and pretended to be from way, way out of town '...and why do you have so many doors to this place? We just took the closest one to where we parked, and someone ought to really re-do this parking lot, it's just so confusing. Why are there more men's rooms than ladies' rooms?...' and on and on. The rest of us followed her lead, and complained when they dragged us back down to the first floor and insisted we go through the metal detector."

"But didn't the needles set off the alarm?"

"Nah, we'd left them in the minivans and only took what we needed for the mission. Even brought plastic crochet hooks for the on-site work. We should have brought a plastic coat hanger, though..."

"What did they do about the coat hanger?" Susan asked.

"Fortunately, they just let it through. Must be a lot of coat hangers in that place," Joann mused. "Anyhow, they just x-rayed the duffel bag, thank God. Who knows what could have happened if they'd opened it up."

Joann took a healthy sip from her newly delivered margarita before continuing. "So, back to the third floor we go—to the Hall of Famous Missourians. We had just enough time to set up and yarn bomb the bust, since we'd timed it to coincide with a health care protest outside the capitol to draw security's interest away from the camera pointed at the Limbaugh bust—which we had the laser pointers on, don't forget—and to the armed osteopaths closing in from the west. We had no sooner—" Joann's words were arrested mid-sentence by unified laughter in the bar. Even Sandy was frozen in mid-mixture, eyes riveted on the television set over the bar.

"And in breaking news," the talking head intoned, "earlier this afternoon, the controversial Rush Limbaugh statue in the Missouri capitol was vandalized." The camera moved in on the bronze head and shoulders encased in a lavender hood rendered in a half-double crochet formation which anchored an equilateral triangle, like some angular halo in a parallel universe. "Police are asking anyone who was present in the Hall of Famous Missourians to contact Capitol Police with any information about the vandalism." One quick camera shot back to the unblinking Famous Missourian in his Teletubbies persona and the news resumed its breathless coverage of local volleyball, weather, and traffic jams on the Missouri River Bridge.

Joann looked around the bar as drinkers and talkers resumed their drinking and talking. Sandy's shift had ended, and the suited men were gone. It was all over so fast.

"So, one thing I don't get..."

"What's that, Sue?"

"When they saw it, why didn't security just cut it off the bust?"

Joann smiled. "Two-part epoxy, my dear. It's great stuff."

I THINK I'LL PASS
Suzanne Lilly

"I'm late again," I muttered as I cruised into the public parking garage and swung my truck into a space on the second level. Traffic into the Bay Area had been thick and slow, and I cursed myself for not taking BART. I backed up to an open metal rail, thinking my truck was safer pointing nose out. I put on the parking brake, slammed the door shut, clicked the automatic lock on my key fob, and jogged out to the street as fast as my pumps would allow.

I was no stranger to the city. I barely noticed the graffiti decorated walls and trash fluttering in the gutter as I trotted past. I checked the time on my phone. *I might just make it to my interview on time if I pick up the pace.*

This job meant a career change for me. I'd left advertising after twenty years because I wanted to do something meaningful, somewhere I could make a difference. What better way to accomplish such a goal than as an urban schoolteacher?

I concentrated on breathing steady and calming the butterflies in my stomach as I waited at the intersection for the green light. Madison Public High School, Home of the Wolves, the painted school sign announced as I approached the front of the dilapidated building. I pushed open the metal double doors and stepped to the security desk.

"Purse, phone, and any metal in your pockets on the conveyer belt," a man with hair the shape and color of a gray thundercloud intoned. I obeyed, even remembering to take off my silver locket. I stepped through the scanner.

"Beep!"

The security guard raised his hand in the universal stop sign.

"Do you have anything in your pockets?"

"No, I emptied them."

"Put your hands over your head, please." He held a metal detection wand in a bad imitation of Zeus with his thunderbolt and ran it over my body.

"Beep, beep, beep!" It alarmed as he brushed the wand near my shoes.

"I have metal taps on my heels," I explained. "I put them on to make my shoes last longer." As an ad exec, I could afford to buy expensive shoes. Now, I hoped they would last me through the next few lean years of teaching, hence the reinforced heels.

The security guard touched my ankle and lifted my foot to inspect the heel tap. "You're free to go ahead." He winked at me as if he was doing me a favor. Eww.

I marched down the hall, finger combing my hair before entering the interview room. They were waiting. All six of them.

Whiskey, Tango, Foxtrot? It's a teaching job, not national security.

A man dressed in a navy pinstriped suit and navy embossed tie glanced at his watch. "Right on time." He stood, smiled, and extended his hand. The superintendent, the vice principal, two teachers, a custodian, and a school board member greeted me in turn.

I sweated through the interview, each of the panelists asking a question round robin style. I spouted my idealistic visions for my classroom, my students' achievement, and their futures. My years of interviewing clients and presenting marketing plans paid off. Certainly, I'd won them over.

After the interview, I headed back down the street toward the parking garage, jangling my keys on my finger. I stopped to text a picture of the school building to Dan, my husband.

"Snick!" I saw the glint of a metal blade and my purse strap broke and fell off my shoulder.

"Hey!" I shouted at a kid in a black hoodie, worn jeans, and Converse shoes racing down the street with my purse. I chased him, but half a block later, he disappeared into a dirty alley. I was so not going in there after him.

"Police! Somebody call the police!" I shouted to anyone who might hear me. A man with a shopping cart calmly pointed to the phone in my hand.

I dialed 911 and tramped back to the parking garage while being connected to the police station.

"Where did the incident take place?" The bored voice on the other end of the line told me this was a routine crime to her. After a few more questions, she informed me I needed to come to the station to finish filing the report.

Thank you for that helpful phone call, Ms. Sherlock. My purse will never be recovered.

In my best receptionista persona I asked, "Could you please hold on a moment?" I set the phone down, waved my fists in the air, jumped up and stamped my feet, and raised my head to the sky in a silent scream. I retrieved the phone from the cement bench and put on my receptionista voice again. "Thank you for waiting. Now, if you'll give me the station address, I'll drive right over."

Waving hand signals through the grimy glass of the ticket booth, I got the man inside to give me a pen. I wrote the address and case number on my hand.

"Thank you, Gary," I read his name tag as I returned his pen.

I trudged back up the two levels to my truck. *Could this day get any worse?* I had a lunch date with Dan at 11:30, but it looked like I'd be needing a rain check.

I didn't even notice the dead guy in the back of my pickup truck until I pulled out of the garage. In the rearview mirror, I saw his feet sticking up over the tailgate. I screamed, straightened my legs into steel rods on the brake pad, and leaned on the horn.

Gary raced out of his booth, arms spread wide, yelling, "What's going on?"

I turned off my truck, stepped out, and covered my eyes. Peeking between my fingers, I saw the person's head lay twisted at an odd angle, making it a 99 and 9/10 percent pure certainty he'd taken a trip to heaven. Or somewhere. I just wished he hadn't chosen my truck as his departure gate.

"Who's he?" Gary, the Ticket Booth Guy asked.

"How am I supposed to know?"

I tiptoed closer and peered at his face. Goosebumps shot down my spine and my hands flew back to cover my eyes again. My heart sank.

"He's a teenager."

"Ah-yup." Gary nodded, chewing on the edge of his overgrown mustache. "You sure you don't know him?"

"No, I don't know him!" I hissed. "Check and see if he's dead."

"How's that?" Gary's eyebrows shot up, deepening the wrinkles on his forehead.

"Here." I grabbed a lug wrench from the toolbox behind the cab. "Poke him and see if he wakes up."

"Lady, you're crazy if you think I'm going to poke some guy with a lug wrench. I'm calling the cops." He pointed a gnarly, tobacco stained finger at me. "Don't go anywhere, because I already done memorized your plate number."

For sure. Because I was so thinking of driving through city traffic with a body in my truck bed.

For the second time this day, I tilted my head skyward in a silent scream. Standing on tiptoes, I pointed the lug wrench into the back of the truck and gave a gentle jab to the teen's arm. "Please be alive," I whispered.

No movement. I jabbed again, harder this time. Still nothing. I used the hooked end to lift his arm. It fell back down on the bed with a thud.

"Oh God, oh God, oh God," I whined, and dropped the lug wrench on top of the toolbox. My stomach roiled and the butterflies morphed into a maelstrom, threatening to send my early morning mocha Frappuccino back for a second taste.

An old blue plastic tarp lay folded in the bed of my truck next to him. I yanked it toward me, and tossed it over his body. Doing my yoga breathing, in through the nostrils, out through the mouth, I laid my forehead on the side of the truck, not caring if I got road grime on my face.

No way could it look good for a future teacher to have a dead teenager in her truck.

I really needed this job. I'd left my six-figure salary to go back to school to get a teaching credential. Now I had student loans to repay, and if I took an urban school teaching job, the state would help pay them off. If I got the job. Which I wouldn't, if they smelled a whiff of this fiasco involving a teenaged John Doe in the bed of my truck.

The police arrived about fifteen minutes later.

"Couldn't you have gotten here any faster?" I didn't care if I offended them. I just wanted to get away from the boy in my truck.

Officer Molina reached over the side, lifted the tarp, and placed his hand on the corpse's neck, checking for a pulse. He shook his head.

Officer Olson leaned in close to me. "Ma'am."

I cringed. *Did I look old enough to be called ma'am?*

"The person is dead. There's no need to rush."

I danced my fingers on the hood of the truck, a nervous habit of mine from my early years of piano practice.

Olson gazed at me, drew his brows together, and tapped something on his netbook. "Ma'am, could you please give us your license?"

I rolled my eyes. "My purse was stolen, along with my license and all my credit cards. The kid who ripped me off is probably having a heyday on my tab right now."

"Is this the kid who stole your purse?" He pointed to the body in my truck.

"What?" *They didn't suspect me, did they?* "Of course not!"

"Did you report your purse stolen, ma'am?" Officer Molina asked.

"Yes, I called 911 as I walked back here to my truck from my job interview."

"Do you have the call log number?"

I opened the palm of my hand where I'd scrawled the reporting information in black ink. Sweat had pooled and smudged some of the numbers. I rubbed my clammy hand on my suit skirt and held my palm out for the officer to read. He tapped the number into his computer.

"There's no report on file with that number."

"What do you mean, there's no report? I called half an hour ago!"

The officers exchanged a glance—the one parents sometimes share when a child is misbehaving. Officer Olson spoke slowly. "Perhaps you transposed a couple of numbers."

He touched Molina's arm and pointed to his netbook. They both scanned my face, peered at the screen, then exchanged another silent communication with their eyes.

"What?" I craned my neck, trying to get a glimpse of the screen. Olson closed the netbook as Molina stepped behind me and cinched handcuffs on my wrists.

"What's going on here? I find a dead body and you're arresting me?" My mocha Frappuccino gurgled in my stomach again, increasing the threat of a violent eruption.

"You have the right to remain silent," Olson began. Ticket Booth Gary snapped a phone photo of me being apprehended by our faithful men in blue. After my Miranda Rights, Molina shoved me in the back of the police cruiser.

"What about the dead guy?" I demanded. "Is anyone going to find out who he is and get him out of my truck? Who's going to clean the truck? Because it's certainly not me. I get queasy around blood, and I get the heebie-jeebies just thinking about what I might find back there." Did I mention I babble when I'm nervous?

Officer Olson gave a heavy sigh and looked at me. "Please, ma'am. Exercise your right to remain silent. It will make it easier for everyone."

This was just grand. Grander than grand. Royally grand.

They drove me to the local precinct, photographed me, finger-printed me, and booked me.

"Why am I being arrested?" I asked the officer processing my paperwork. Without a word, she handed me a black and white photo of a woman who looked just like me, except for the fact she was having a worse bad hair day than I was. Her wild mane of frizz stuck out in all directions. Her description matched mine in her height, five foot four, and weight, which I decline to share, and her age, which shall also remain confidential.

"You're wanted for aggravated assault and drug trafficking." The officer pointed an acrylic nail at a line of text below the picture. "This has been a long time coming, Julia."

"But that's not me!" I don't usually shout, but this situation warranted a loud outburst. "My name's not Julia. I'm Darinda Locke. I've never aggravated assaulted anyone, or however you say it."

Although I did want to aggravated assault that small time hoodlum who stole my purse today.

"Mmhmm. I'm sure your purse didn't have any drugs in it either, when you handed it off." She grabbed my elbow and led me to a bench. My earlier anger quickly drained away and mortal fear replaced it.

"Wait! Don't I get a telephone call or something? They always get a phone call on *CSI.*"

She steered me toward a wall of phones and pointed at one. "Make it count."

Dan picked up on the first ring. "Hello?"

"Thank goodness, you picked up!" At the sound of his voice, my legs turned into wet noodles. I gulped down a breath and in a quivering voice told him about the panel interview, the purse snatching, the dead body, and now my newly revealed criminal record.

"Slow down." In my mind's eye, I pictured Dan pacing and holding a hand against his forehead. I placed my fingers over my trembling lips and gulped another breath. I had to keep myself from crying, or worse, getting hysterical.

"Darinda, you're babbling."

I nodded.

"Where are you?"

"I'm at the police station."

"Which one?"

"I don't know." My voice hitched. The man next to me pointed to a sign on the wall. The Mission Station.

"I'll be right there."

"I love you so much," I whispered.

I hung up the phone and the officer escorted me back to the bench to wait.

I took several deep breaths until my racing heart slowed down. I tried to find something positive in my situation.

Thank goodness for small things. At least I'm not stuck in a cell with some hooker.

No sooner had the thought materialized than it was shattered by the clop, clop, clop of acrylic platform shoes on the tile floor. A woman with dark hair plastered in waves, sculpted into an art deco hair helmet sat down next to me. Her eyes raked over my maroon silk suit, silk blouse, and matching pumps.

"If you're in here for embezzling money, honey, all I have to say is, you should've bought some nice clothes with the dough."

I could feel myself coming down with fish face disease. My eyes bulged, my mouth opened and closed, but no words came out. After several long seconds, I found my voice and my dignity. "What's wrong with my clothes?"

She inspected her nails, painted green and pink to match her tiny spandex skirt, then examined me up and down again. "What's right about your clothes?"

"At least I'm not wearing something that lets my hooha hang out." I emphasized hooha with my classic headshake.

She smiled, the glitter in her lip-gloss glinting in the fluorescent lights. "Maybe you should. Then the popo might let you go a little sooner." She imitated my headshake.

I crossed my legs and leaned away from her. That didn't stop her from wanting to chat.

"What are you in here for, honey?"

"They think I murdered a man."

Miss Hooha stretched her long legs out and crossed her ankles. "That just goes to show how ignorant these popo are. I can take one look at you, and know you wouldn't kill anyone. You're the type that probably picks up a spider and takes it outside, rather than step on it."

"Thank you." *Wait a minute. Did I just thank a working girl for saying I'm not a killer? And how did she know I take spiders outside? Is it that obvious I'm a softie?*

"Listen, honey, is this your first time here? You're a virgin?" She laughed, a throaty laugh that told a tale of one too many cigarettes and who knows what else. Something squirmed in my stomach.

"You'll be outta here in no time."

"They have a picture of someone who could be my twin. Someone who's wanted for aggravated assault. That's why they think I did it." I hated the way my voice sounded like a fifth grader sent to the principal's office for disrupting class.

"Oh, honey, as soon as they run your prints you'll be cleared." She pointed over my shoulder. "You have a visitor."

Dan clasped my arms and pulled me close. "Darinda?"

"Oh, Dan!" I nestled myself in his arms, my hands still in cuffs. He kissed me hard.

"Don't worry, Darinda." He held my face and riveted his eyes on mine. "I'll get you out of this."

"Now ain't that sweet?" Miss Hooha patted her rock hard hair helmet.

"Come over here, Candy." An officer gestured to her. "We've got your paperwork ready."

"TTFN." Miss Candy Hooha waggled her pink and green fingernails at me as she clopped on her acrylic heels to the officer's desk.

"New friend?" Dan grinned and nodded her way.

"Just get me out of here. Please."

"The cops told me the CSI crew is already at the parking garage collecting evidence. They won't find anything to connect you with the crime, and they'll have to let you go."

Relief flooded over me as I leaned against his strong, sturdy chest. "I hope so. How in the world did this happen to me, on a day like today?"

"Would another day be better?" Dan's sense of humor never failed to make me laugh. I giggled, earning a glare from a desk clerk.

Officers Olson and Molina arrived, accompanied by a man wearing a black jacket emblazoned with CSI in reflective letters. Molina took out a key and unlocked my handcuffs. "It looks as if you're free to go," he said.

If he thought that was going to satisfy me, he was out of his mind. "That's it? No apology? No explanation?" I rubbed my wrists and shook my hands. "I suggest you tell me what happened."

CSI guy said, "Apparently the victim was grinding the rails in the parking garage, something the kids are warned not to do. He fell from the third level railing, and unfortunately landed in your truck. We found his skateboard under another vehicle. There's no sign of foul play or injury, other than what would be expected from a twenty-foot fall. He broke his neck when he fell, and that was the cause of death."

My hand covered my heart and a moan of compassion escaped my lips.

Dan whistled. "Do his parents know yet?"

"We're notifying the next of kin now."

I turned to Molina. "What about the aggravated assault and drug trafficking charges?"

Molina shuffled on his feet and cleared his throat. "Yes, well—"

Olson cut him off. "Mistaken identity, ma'am, for which we apologize. The woman on the wanted list bears a striking resemblance to you."

"Apology accepted. But please find her soon, so I don't have to worry about my face showing up on *America's Most Wanted*."

"Yes, ma'am." He handed me my keys and my phone, which immediately rang.

The vice principal of Madison Public High School congratulated me. "Ms. Locke, the interview panel would like to offer you a position as a math teacher at our high school."

I smiled at Dan. As much as I needed this job, I didn't need it so badly that I wanted to risk my life every day. Or be reminded of that poor skater.

"Thank you so much for the offer," I answered. "However, after the morning I had, I think I'll pass."

FLUFFO VERSUS CHARLOTTE
Cathy C. Hall

Fluffo was not a bad bunny. But it would be a stretch to call the rabbit that resided in the Taylor home, "good."

So when Charlotte Taylor took him out of the cage every morning, she was very careful. Unfortunately, at 10:31 on this particular Saturday morning, she was not careful enough. Fluffo bolted from her grasp, the rabbit's claws gouging chunks of skin from her right forearm.

"Spit!" she shouted. Charlotte knew little ears were right behind her.

It was the little ears—and the sweetly pleading mouths that went along with them—that had coerced Charlotte into bringing home the bunny in the first place. Her children had wanted a puppy, but Charlotte thought with three kids under the age of five, she'd better start with something easier. Like a cute, fluffy bunny.

And Fluffo *was* cute. He was little, too, being a dwarf rabbit. But there was nothing easy about that bunny. At that precise moment, Fluffo darted beneath the couch. Three sets of eyes peered under the sofa. One baby voice grunted; two high-pitched voices called his name.

"Here, Fluffo. Come here, Fluffo!"

Charlotte sighed, holding her throbbing arm. Bunnies do not come when called. But that didn't stop the kids from constantly, yet futilely, calling him.

"Fluffo! Fluffo! Here, Fluffo!" Her oldest reached an arm under the couch—then yelled.

"Oh, Joey!" cried Charlotte. "Did Fluffo bite you?"

Bunnies also bite. But so far, Fluffo had only bitten Charlotte.

"No-o-o-o," said Joey. Joey desperately wanted to keep the family pet. So he often covered for the hairy brute.

Charlotte carefully examined her son's finger. It appeared puncture-free. But Fluffo took advantage of the opportunity and escaped past her.

"Oh, Lord," she moaned. Fluffo had left a wet present on her new, sand-colored carpet.

Charlotte had researched rabbits before she added Fluffo to her brood, but she supposed she must have skipped some important parts. She'd read that they could be house-trained, but apparently, that process was trickier than it looked. She'd also read something about rabbit aggression, but the dealer she'd contacted had been adamant that once Fluffo had been neutered, he'd be gentle as a lamb. Either lambs weren't that gentle, or Fluffo was some sort of mutant rabbit.

She spied a white tail behind the curtains and quickly yanked them back.

"Gotcha!" she hissed, dive-bombing for the bunny. But Fluffo was very fast. She'd missed that bit in her research as well.

"Uh-oh, Mommy," said her daughter, Emmy. "You got your boo-boo on that." Emmy pointed to the white curtains where now, specks of blood dotted the left panel. Charlotte must have pressed her arm against the material when she was trying to corner Fluffo.

"Ooooh, that rabbit," she muttered through clenched teeth. "Watch out, honey. Mommy needs to get a chair."

Charlotte stomped into the kitchen to grab a chair so she could reach the curtain rod. She'd have to clean that curtain now, or the blood would leave a stain.

If Tom were here, he could deal with the bunny. But Charlotte's husband had other plans for *his* Saturday morning.

"What are you doing up so early?" she'd asked. The clock next to the bed blinked 7:05.

"Golf," he whispered. "Go back to sleep."

"I'm up now," she said, stretching. "Golf? Since when do you play golf at 7:30 on a Saturday?"

"Since my buddy, Kent the accountant, asked me to join his foursome."

"Kent the accountant," she said, sitting up.

"It's the perfect time to talk finances, hon. I have to think about the economy. My assets."

"*Your* assets?" She raised her eyebrows.

"*Our* assets, honey. You know that's what I meant." He stuffed his wallet in his back pocket. "We need to maximize our assets."

"So what am I supposed to do all day while you're out there 'maximizing our assets'?"

Tom leaned over and gave her a kiss on the forehead. "Oh, you'll think of something," he said.

Charlotte didn't have time to think of anything except that rabbit. She knew it was probably her imagination, but she thought she could hear him chewing off the legs of the dining room table as she dragged a chair over to the window.

"Whatcha doing, Mommy?" Joey stood on the right side of the chair, Emmy on the left. Baby Mark had toddled back into the kitchen, and she watched helplessly as Mark made it to his kiddie table and grabbed the box of cereal. It tipped over on his head.

"Mommy's getting this curtain down, so watch out," she said. She pushed up against the rod, but it wouldn't budge. She pushed again, and still, the rod held firm.

"It's not coming down," said Emmy.

"Yes, I know, sweetheart. I just…need…one…" Charlotte put all her strength behind one more push and the rod popped out of the bracket, up into the air, and fell back down on her face. The wooden pole hit her directly above her right eye.

"Yay!" said Joey. "You got it!"

She got it, all right. Charlotte could feel a lump forming on her brow. She may have seen actual stars for a second or two.

"There's Fluffo!" cried Emmy.

Charlotte groaned as the bunny hopped over the white curtain, leaving paw prints behind. She couldn't be sure what the bunny had been into, but it appeared to be a mixture of cereal crumbs, wood shavings, and rabbit poop.

She gathered up the yards of curtain and headed to the sink. She dumped the panel on the counter; she needed the stain remover that was on the washing machine. Upstairs. She turned around and cringed.

"Oh, Mark," she said, scooping up the baby. Little bits of what she fervently hoped were cereal and *not* wood shavings, or worse, clung to his mouth. Out of the corner of her eye, she saw Fluffo, quivering at his water bowl, *inside* his cage!

"Shut the door. Shut the door!" she yelled. "Joey!"

Where the heck was Joey? she fumed. She took a step toward Fluffo's cage and swoosh! She slipped on a pile of soggy cereal, but managed to hold Mark upright as she skidded across the floor.

"Mommy, are you okay?" asked Joey, casually sauntering into the kitchen.

Fluffo bounced by her, heading *out* of the kitchen. She watched his tail swish by her face.

"Mommy's fine," she said through gritted teeth. She set Mark on the floor and stood up, but it hurt to put weight on her left foot. *Terrific*, she thought. She'd twisted her ankle.

Charlotte hobbled over to the sink where the stain on the curtain waited.

"Joey, stay right there and make sure your brother does not put a single thing in his mouth."

She grabbed the bottle of dish detergent—her ankle hurt too badly for her to go all the way up the stairs to fetch the stain remover now—and squeezed. A yellow trail shot across the curtain, over the counter and onto the floor.

"Argghhh," she said. She grabbed a wet dishtowel, scrubbing furiously at the floor, then raised the cool towel to the goose egg that had formed on her forehead. Her aching head started to feel better, until the soapy suds dripped into her eye.

"Ow, ow, ow," she said. She leaned over the sink, and cupped cool water, splashing her eye till the stinging abated.

"*No!*" said Joey behind her. Mark screamed and burst into deafening tears.

"What in the world?" asked Charlotte, squinting through her bad eye.

Joey was holding Mark's tiny hand in a death grip.

"Mommy!" wailed Mark, right before he walloped Joey with his free hand.

"*Ow!*" yelled Joey. He grabbed Mark's other hand as well.

"Stop it, Joey," said Charlotte. "Why are you holding his hands, anyway?"

Joey started to cry. "You told me not to let him put anything in his mouth, and he keeps trying to suck his thumb."

Charlotte took a deep breath. "It's okay, sweetie, he can suck his thumb."

Emmy walked into the kitchen. "I found Fluffo," she said. "He's in the office."

"*Noooo!*" screamed Charlotte. She limped out of the kitchen, down the hall, and through the office door. Fluffo was poised to strike, three inches away from seven electrical cords. Cords that powered everything techno in her world.

Charlotte had read an entire paragraph about bunny-proofing a house, which had included something about protecting cords. But she'd laughed out loud at that idea. After all, she had three kids and had never needed to kid-proof her home.

"Okay, rabbit," she said softly. The rabbit was seconds away from being Fricasseed Fluffo. "It's okay. Don't do anything stupid." She took a tentative step. Fluffo sat, his whiskers twitching. And then he chomped down on the nearest cord.

"*No!*" cried Charlotte.

"Hey, where is everybody?"

"Tom!" Charlotte called from the office. "*Get in here!*"

Tom stood in the open doorway of the office, three children crowding behind him. Fluffo dropped the cord, completely unscathed, and hopped over to him. Her husband reached down and picked up the bunny.

"Poor Fluffo," said Tom. "Has Mommy been fussing at our good, little bunny?"

"*Good* little bunny?" hissed Charlotte. "If you knew what that rabbit did today...look at my arm! And the curtains are ruined..." Charlotte's voice broke. "And this knot." She pointed to her head. "You should feel it. And the carpet stain...and Lord only knows what that rabbit's been eating. Or what your youngest son's been eating. And I tried to catch him, Fluffo that is...but now my ankle..."

Charlotte's shoulders sagged, and she struggled to hold back the tears.

"Aw, it's okay, honey," said her husband. He held up Fluffo as if the rabbit were a talking puppet. Then he squeaked out, "You just had a bad hare day."

The kids laughed at their dad's joke, though Charlotte was sure they didn't get it. Her husband turned around, bowing to his kiddie audience, and then, before she knew what came over her, she kicked him. He was bowing and his...asset was right there, in front of her. And so, she'd kicked him. Not hard, but sudden enough that Fluffo flew out of her husband's arms as his grip loosened from the jolt.

"Get him, Daddy!" yelled the kids.

"Shut the front door!" yelled her husband.

The chase was on again.

But not for Charlotte. She limped to the stairs, careful not to put too much weight on her swollen ankle. She thought a nice long soak in a hot tub might help her maximize what was left of *her* assets.

Besides, Fluffo was not a bad bunny. Judging by the ear-piercing shrieks she heard behind her, Charlotte guessed her husband was discovering what a good little bunny Fluffo could be.

NO-HAIR DAY
E. B. Davis

I stood in front of the powder room mirror, my hand frozen in mid-air clutching the blond wig that I was about to fit over my unlovely pate. A man armed with a knife had entered my home through a screen door I'd failed to lock. His intrusion shattered my enjoyment of this "off" chemo day in the regiment. I held my breath. Wasn't my no-hair day bad enough without some jerk-off home invader?

He passed by unaware of my presence. I watched him in the mirror, his head turning from side to side, as he walked forward into the family room past the staircase. Athletic shorts, black T-shirt, tattoos down his arms, and high-topped sneakers. He could have come straight from the basketball court, but the knife in his hand told me he had another game in mind. I jammed the wig on my head and peered out the door, which was ajar.

Why me? The question I'd asked myself every day for the last six months since my ovarian cancer diagnosis. The lack of answers rankled. My bald head resulted from Taxol—one of my chemotherapy drugs. I resented cancer, and now I resented this intruder. How dare they disrupt my beautiful life? Like on my chemo days, which took nine hours and left me exhausted, I felt like crying. My life had become surreal—my time—precious. Spending it with some lunatic wasn't on the schedule.

Maybe he'd take some stuff and leave. Since I was close to the front door escaping to my neighbor Carla's house, across the street, was my best choice. I crept out of the powder room in the direction of the screen door when reality smacked me and chilled my bones. My sixteen-year-old daughter, Jenny, slept upstairs in her room. Summer vacation started today. I'd forgotten she was at home while bemoaning my fate. Mothering Jenny had taken a backseat to my diagnosis. My heart rate zoomed as I assessed the situation.

Protecting my child, putting myself between the man and Jenny, and getting her out of the house without alerting him were my priorities. A quick swivel reversed my direction. I scooted toward the staircase checking to make sure his back was turned. I got as far as the second step.

"Where are you going, lady?"

Doctors poked and prodded me with futile questions since my diagnosis. No wonder cancer patients developed black humor as a survival tactic. It came so easily now. How should I answer his question? Just checking to make sure there were fresh sheets in the guest room? Getting the key to our safe for your convenience? I answered him with silence and continued up the stairs.

He ran over and grabbed my arm.

My other hand remained on the handrail. I pulled back to resist. He wasn't a large man, but his goateed face looked thirty years younger, a few years older than Jenny. Before my diagnosis, I'd gone to the gym three times a week and lifted weights. Chemo had weakened me, but I managed to twist my arm out of his grasp, lean into the railing and use the height from the third step to snap my foot into his chest. As he flailed from the blow, he grabbed my hair. The wig pulled from my head. His eyes widened, and he uttered a squawk staring at the wig in his hand before falling backwards into the lower hallway.

I ran up the stairs as Jenny stumbled out of her room still full of sleep, and I envisioned the toddler she'd once been. I grabbed her arm. "Quick! There's a man, an intruder, downstairs. Let's go into the master bathroom."

"What? Are you serious?" she asked, but then we heard pounding on the steps.

I pushed her in front of me. Once in the bathroom, I slammed the door shut and locked it, doubting it would stop him for long.

"Do you have your cell phone?" Jenny asked.

"No. Do you?"

"No. What are we going to do?" she asked me, her voice a panicked whisper.

"The first thing I'm going to do is get you out of here." I surprised myself with my determination and shoved open the bathroom window. "You can get out onto the front porch roof, then scoot into the valley between the main house roof and the garage. Hide there, but if a car passes, wave and yell to call the cops." As I worked to remove the screen in the window, the man pounded on the bathroom door.

"Open the door, ladies," he said. His voice wasn't loud, which surprised me. Perhaps he'd invaded others' homes before and had perfected a routine.

I ignored him and put my hand on Jenny's arm to propel her out the window.

She resisted. "I'm not leaving you, Mom."

"Oh yes, you are," I said, and pushed her toward the open window. "You can get help."

"No." Jenny turned to face me in a boxer's stance. She had grown to her full height, taller than me by two inches.

I looked up at her as if she were crazy. "Of course you're going. Staying is nuts."

"Ladies, open the door before I bust it open." The intruder sounded irritated, as if we'd failed to follow his script. I ignored him again.

Jenny squared her body, her feet aligned with her hips. "No, you're always pushing me away. I'm not leaving."

"This isn't the time to defy me. On Friday night when I want you home before midnight—defy me then, not now."

"This isn't defiance—it's demand."

"What do you mean?"

"You know damn well what I mean."

Why did she sound like me? I wasn't sure what she was saying, but I knew it had nothing to do with the current situation. "I want you safe."

"I want you safe, too," Jenny said, echoing my words.

An abrupt bang resounded against the door. "Open the door, now," the intruder said. The quietness of his voice unnerved me. He was more insistent this time.

Anger flashed over me. How dare he? In the last six months, new demands had been thrust at me that I'd never wanted, resented, but couldn't deny. Juggling chemo, while maintaining a normal life for my husband and daughter, was wearing thin. The twit at the door had no idea his demands were last on my list of priorities.

"Jenny," I said, using my most authoritative mother voice, "go now."

"No. You can't order me away anymore."

"I will break this door down," the intruder said.

"Oh, shut up," I yelled back. "We're having a discussion."

"What?" Incredulity seemed to color the intruder's question.

I ignored him. He had no idea that I faced death every day. I was only concerned for my daughter, who wasn't complying to my wishes.

She faced me looking angry too. "You haven't let me go with you to any of your chemo appointments."

"Do we have to discuss this now?" My disbelief at her poor timing must have been apparent.

"Yes."

"Honey, you don't want to go with me."

"Yes, I do."

"In the first place, it's boring. In the second place, it's awful. I don't want you around all that—sickness and death."

"You pushed me away. We should be fighting this together. You've pushed Dad away, too."

"I'm not. I'm trying to protect you. My friends can take me to and from chemo. Your life should be normal."

"My mother has cancer, and I'm supposed to act as if nothing is wrong?"

We faced each other, arms crossed against our chests. "Yes," I said, aware that my answer sounded stupid.

"Open the door, now!"

Jenny and I turned toward the door simultaneously and yelled, "No."

"That's crazy, Mom. I'm not going to pretend everything is normal. I won't live in denial even if you are."

Was I living in denial? No, I wasn't in denial. I was totally and absolutely furious about having cancer. Jerry, my husband, adjusted with a quiet determination I had yet to muster. My response wasn't productive, the professionals told me. One of the nurses had recommended that I go to a support group. I'd frustrated the counselor by refusing to meet the challenge of chemo. Resenting cancer made me its victim, a status I needed to lose, she said. I was supposed to become proactive in my treatment, which would boost the effectiveness of the chemo.

She designed visual exercises in which I was supposed to evoke my inner warrior. What inner warrior? There were no Valkyrie women in my ancestry. It was all make-believe, pretending to decide who would die on the battlefield as if survival were my choice. The counselor wanted me to conquer the cancer by slaying the cells using the chemo as my weapon. I was flunking support-group therapy.

Yesterday, the lady receiving chemo in the hospital bed next to mine said I should look at the hair loss as a way to experiment with hats, as if without chemo I would have missed a great opportunity, then she winked and donned a black, fuzzy fedora worthy of Marlene Dietrich. I turned away at her prattle as she patted my arm. The only opportunity I'd missed was punching her.

Why did everyone make me mad? I should be appreciative and well adjusted. I felt like a rebellious child and looked away from my daughter as tears formed in my eyes. "Okay, maybe I haven't accepted my diagnosis. I don't want to die, and I don't want you to see me die. I'm angry that I may hurt you, and it's not my choice at all."

"See, that's the problem, Mom."

"I don't understand."

"No, you don't."

With another blow to the door, the intruder said, "You bitches are dead meat. Open the door or I'll knock it down."

His goateed face appeared in my mind. "By the hair of your chinny-chin-chin?" Sarcasm worked for me.

"What? That pisses me off." He must have remembered his fairy tales.

Like I cared about his emotional state. It was obvious he didn't have a gun or he would have used it by now. "Go steal some stuff, why don't you?"

"That's not why I'm here."

What the hell? "So why are you here?"

"Two reasons. The first is your pot."

"Pot? What pot?"

"Everyone knows people who get chemo have prescriptions for pot—good pot."

The nausea removed the extra sixteen pounds I'd accumulated, a pound per year, since I bore Jenny. I felt lousy, but I loved the result. The doctors said I was more than welcome to a prescription for Marinol, a drug containing THC, which would reduce the nausea but also get me high. Being caught up in my own drama was bad enough. Being a bad example to Jenny broke the rules in my motherhood manual. Sure, there are exceptions to the rules, and Jenny would forgive me. But what if I didn't win this fight? Would my daughter remember me as a whacked-out, stoned mother—her final memories for the rest of her, I hoped, long life? No way, wasn't happening.

"I don't smoke pot. I don't want my daughter to have some whacked out pot-head for a mother."

"You didn't take the pot?"

Contempt or ridicule? Either way, he thought I was an idiot. Who cared for his opinion? He suffered from false information. Doctors don't prescribe marijuana.

"Oh, for crying out loud," Jenny said to the intruder. "I know who you can buy it from. Let me give you the kid's name and phone number. There's money in the top drawer of my bureau. Go buy an ounce."

I turned to Jenny amazed, but she ignored me, opened the cabinet doors and took out appliances, placing them on the countertop.

"What? We're going to do our hair?" I said, knowing I had no hair.

"No. We're not doing our hair."

She plugged in all three curling irons I'd bought her. After using the first one for a week, she claimed it pulled her hair. I bought a Teflon coated iron the next time, but it performed with lackluster results. The third one was smooth and chromed. It worked fine— finally. I watched as she took out my old electric rollers. I hated those damn things. The curlers got so hot they burnt my fingers when I tried to roll them. And after I'd put a few into my hair, I always burnt my hand on the uncovered, hot rods as I selected the next roller.

"So what are we doing?"

"Demonstrating positive action," Jenny said.

"What?"

She nodded toward the door and whispered, "We'll burn him when he tries to get us. Look for anything else we can use."

I had no intention of fighting the young man. "That's ridiculous."

"No, it's not. Why won't you fight?"

"I shouldn't have to."

"Well you do. 'Shouldn't' doesn't have anything to do with it." Jenny glared at me.

Evidently, I frustrated my daughter as well as the medical team, counselor, and the intruder. No sounds came from behind the door, which worried me. What was he up to? I hoped he had left, but then I heard a noise.

"What's that?" I said to Jenny.

She walked over to the door and assessed the noise. "Sounds like he got a crowbar, maybe from the garage."

I heard a splitting sound. The cheap hollow-core door was cracking. "You said there were two reasons you were here. What's the second reason?" I asked the intruder.

"To kill you," he said matter-of-factly.

"Why?"

"With two kills, I gain leader status with my gang." He laughed.

With all the other problems I faced, the intruder's presence had taken a backseat to my irritation. Now, fear arose, and I felt my stomach quiver. Jenny and I looked at each other. We'd surmised the same thing. His manner was too calm and determined, making him an effective enemy. This reality preempted cancer and threatened Jenny.

Like everything else out of control in my life, my inner warrior, the one the counselor tried to get me to summon, arose. I grew a foot in height and developed muscles like Hulk Hogan. I gritted my teeth, lowered my head, and prepared for battle. No one hurts my daughter.

I whipped open the cabinet doors. Underneath the sink, I kept cleaning supplies—spray tile cleaner, spray ammonia for mirrors, baking soda for dental appliances, and vinegar for the shower doors. From helping Jenny with science projects, I knew combining baking soda with vinegar would cause an explosive, frothing reaction, and I took them out, mixing them in a squeeze container I used for lotion when I traveled, and shut the applicator before the mixture escaped. Jenny grabbed the pail holding her old bath toys. She took her squirt gun and filled it with ammonia.

"I have a good aim," she said, with a nasty smirk she threw toward the door.

I heard the door crack again and saw the hinges skew.

"There's Carla," Jenny said, from her view of the window.

Carla's car pulled up in her driveway. As she got out, I yelled for her to call the cops. Her mouth dropped, and she ran into her house. The bathroom door gave way.

The intruder pulled out a knife and grinned. "The cops won't get here in time to save either of you."

Jenny lifted her squirt gun and pulled the trigger. Ammonia streamed into his eyes. He dropped to his knees, bent over, covered his eyes with his hands, and howled. The knife clattered onto the tile floor.

Jenny bent over to get the knife.

"Careful, pick it up by the blade," I said, contrary to my normal admonishment. "His fingerprints are on the handle."

She took my advice and threw it out the window. We'd find it later.

I ripped two curling irons off the counter, yanking the cords out of the outlet, and hit him in the neck with the hot irons pressing them against his skin. He yowled in pain, writhed up on his knees, facing us, grabbed at the irons, and burnt his hands. Jenny stuffed hot curlers down his athletic shorts. The netting around his privates held the curlers like they were made for the purpose. He grabbed his crotch, which pressed the searing curlers into his privates, a result he hadn't considered.

Jenny took the curler appliance from the counter, dumping the rest of the curlers so the hot rods were bare. When he let go of his crotch, she slammed the hot rods into his chest, toppled him over backwards, and then straddled him while branding him with the rods.

I grabbed my hair dryer and wound the cord around his ankles securing his legs.

"You really ought to let us wash the ammonia from your eyes before they're permanently damaged," I said.

He opened his eyes, and Jenny leaned back to give me a clear shot. I squirted the baking soda/vinegar solution at him. It erupted out of the container, smacked his eyes with a velocity and an acidity I appreciated. Elementary school science rocked. Jenny and I had loved the exploding volcano project.

His mouth dropped, as if he were dumbfounded that anything we could inflict would damage him. The kid was arrogant and ignorant—typical, young male.

I took out the portable clothesline and extracted the cord. Jenny knew I wanted to tie his hands so she lifted up on her knees and flipped him over. As his face started to slam onto the tile floor, he tried to protect his face by carrying his weight on his elbows. I yanked one arm back, and Jenny took hold of the other. She held both of his wrists together as I tied his arms behind his back with the cord. His face crunched into the tile. I heard the pop of his nose. He screamed.

Seeing him trussed, squealing like a pig, I said. "I'd quit the gang, dude. You're one of the three little pigs, not the Big, Bad Wolf."

A siren screeched in the distance, getting louder as it came down our road. Carla came out her front door and directed the cops to our house. I yelled to the patrolmen to enter through the screen door and come upstairs.

The police took our statements and found the knife in the front yard. One of the patrolmen noticed the intruder's injuries. "What did you do to him?"

"Just gave him some beauty treatments," I said.

"Nothing women don't go through every day," Jenny added.

The patrolman rolled his eyes. After they left with the punk in their custody, Jenny and I sat at the kitchen table.

"I'm sorry," I said, "I didn't mean to push you away."

"Two can fight better than one, Mom. We've got the entire summer. By the time I go back to school, you'll be finished with the chemo, recovered."

I admired her positive stance and felt affirmation in her belief. "Yes, I'll be cancer-free," I said. My conviction wasn't false bravado. My warrior wouldn't fail me now.

"Tomorrow I'm coming with you to chemo. If you need pot, I can get it for you."

I shook my head at my Valkyrie daughter and was about to wave my finger in her face, but I stopped and saluted. "Yes, ma'am, commander. We'll fight this together, and we'll win."

TWENTY-FOUR HOUR BUGS
Theresa Hupp

On a hot and fetid July night, Connie Pearson lay in bed, her stomach roiling. Her husband George snored beside her. He insisted on opening the bedroom window, even when the daytime highs were in triple digits. Now Connie sweated on clammy sheets.

Or maybe it wasn't the heat making her sweat. Maybe she had the same stomach flu George had two days ago. For twenty-four hours, he whined miserably, as most men do when they are sick.

When the worst of his illness passed, he wanted to eat, as men are also wont to do.

"How 'bout I make you a piece of toast?" Connie asked.

George nodded. "Make it two."

"Do you want eggs with that?" She was being snide, but George took her seriously.

"Two. Scrambled. And maybe some bacon."

Now, at the recollection of slimy eggs sizzling in heavy bacon grease, Connie's stomach rebelled. She rushed to the bathroom and vomited.

She had the flu.

The rest of the night passed in a daze. She sweated. She shivered. She moaned. She puked.

George snored.

When the alarm went off, Connie didn't move. "George," she whispered. "Wake up."

"Huh?" George lurched to his elbows beside her, shaking the mattress.

"No," she groaned at the motion.

"What's wrong?"

"I'm sick. You'll have to get the kids to day care." Jason was five, and Erin, two. They needed constant supervision in the mornings.

"Unh," George responded. He was not a morning person. But he staggered to his feet. With every thudding step he took across the room, the bed shook again, until Connie felt like a dory in a hurricane.

"Okay, kids, heave out," George called when he reached the hall-way. Connie ran to the bathroom. "Heave" had been an unfortunate word for George to use.

Connie made it back to bed and lay in a stupor, only vaguely aware of the children babbling as they dressed and went downstairs to eat. At one point, she heard George shout, "No, no, Erin! Don't pour juice on your cereal."

A colorful image of Lucky Charms floating in a brew of milk and orange juice popped into Connie's head, and she hurried to the bath-room again. Where she saw a spider behind the toilet. A big, black spider, the kind she called "sewer spiders," because they climbed up from the drains on hot summer days.

She opened her mouth to scream, which was a mistake. She clamped her hand over her mouth and reeled to the sink.

"George," she croaked, after her nausea subsided, "George, I need you."

"I'm kind of rushed," he said. "Can't you take care of yourself?"

"There's a spider," she said. They had an agreement—George killed the spiders, and she dealt with roaches. Her six-foot-two husband went white at the sight of a roach. And she got the heebie-jeebies when she saw a spider. Connie thought she had the best of the deal—roaches were rare in their house, and spiders were frequent.

George sighed, but dug an old tennis shoe out of the closet and entered the war zone.

Connie curled in the bed in a fetal position. She heard stomping in the bathroom. George came out holding the shoe high. "I missed," he said.

Connie waved her wrist. It was the only protest she could make in her weakened condition. "What if I have to throw up again?" she asked.

"Use the kids' bathroom. We're leaving now," George said. "I'll call you later."

When the rest of the family was gone and the house was still,

Connie called her office. "I'm sick," she rasped into her secretary's voice mail. "Flu." She hung up.

Connie shook with chills until her whole body cramped. She puked again, using the kids' bathroom, as George had suggested. By now, she was in the dry heave stage, exhausted and sore.

On her third trip to the kids' bathroom, a brown spider sidled out of the corner and into her line of vision. If a mother screams in the bathroom, but no one hears, does it count as fear?

Her scream certainly didn't faze the spider, which scuttled behind a basket of bath toys in the corner. A brown recluse, she was sure. Connie knew from experience that their bites festered and left red pits in her skin for weeks. In her current state, the spider could devour an entire limb before she shook him off.

Both bathrooms infested. What was she supposed to do?

Connie stood up, her legs quaking. She wasn't sure if it was her illness or panic. Should she deal with the arachnids now or later? What if she had to throw up? She could use a sink again, but who knew when another spider would creep out of the drains? She would have to clear out at least one bathroom.

She went into the master bath. No sign of the earlier arachnid there. But that didn't mean anything. Connie knew it was lurking.

She went into the kids' bath and picked up the toy basket, holding it as far away from her as possible. The brown spider ran out on the floor and hid behind the toilet. She could see it, but she didn't think she could get at it. Not with her legs still quivering.

Bug spray. If she sprayed the bathrooms heavily enough, the spiders would die, or crawl back into the woodwork. She would feel safer if she knew they were puking their guts out like she was.

But the bug spray was in the basement. Two flights of stairs down. And back up.

Connie's arms and legs shook as she put on her robe and slippers. She glanced in the mirror before heading downstairs. She looked as bad as she felt—hair stringy and greasy, face red and blotchy, back hunched like Quasimodo. No wonder George had left without a good-bye kiss.

Connie clung to the stair rail and stumbled her way from second story to main level, shuffled down the hall, then down another flight to the basement. At the bottom of the basement steps, another huge black spider waited.

She shrieked, as her slipper slid on the last stair. She landed on her rump beside the spider. "Go away! Go away!" Connie screamed, flapping her arms in a panic as adrenaline overrode her aches and pains.

The spider obediently scampered away, and Connie pulled herself up to sit on the stairs, her head on her knees. The nausea waxed as the adrenaline waned. She moaned a long slow moan. When she thought her stomach could handle it, Connie peeked out of one eye looking for the spider. Gone. Whereabouts unknown.

Connie tottered to her feet and went to find the bug spray. George kept it back in an unfinished area of the basement on a high shelf behind some tools, so the kids couldn't get to it. The biggest spiders in the house lived in that part of the basement. Connie wasn't eager to stick her hand above her head scrabbling around for the spray can. But she didn't want to climb a stepladder either. So she scrabbled. Her fingers latched onto an aerosol can, and she pulled it down.

Raid. She could hear the bugs in the old TV ad scream, "Raid." She hoped her bathroom spiders would scream like the ones on television.

Connie hugged the can of Raid close to her chest and limped back upstairs. Her rear was bruised from her fall, every muscle ached, and her stomach still rumbled. But now she was armed.

When she reached the upstairs, Connie held the spray can out at arm's length and rushed into the kids' bath. "Yah," she cried, as she spewed insecticide in all directions.

The brown recluse ran out from its lair behind the toilet and shriveled in an ugly death. She thought she did hear it scream as its eight legs tightened into cramps worse than hers.

Emboldened, she marched into the master bath, where the first sewer spider still hid. She sprayed until the Raid can sputtered, but didn't see any movement. Surely, it was dead. No bug could survive that blast.

Connie coughed at the scent of insecticide. Coughing made her puke again. But after this episode, she finally felt a little better. But weak.

Connie stumbled back to bed, and slept.

The phone woke her shortly before noon. "It's me," George said.

"Uh," Connie replied.

"Still sick?"

"Yeah. You woke me up."

"Sorry. Just checking on you," George said. "I gotta go to lunch now. Big client shindig. At McCormick and Schmick's. I'll probably have the crab."

Connie thought of crabs scuttling, all their legs moving at once. That made her think of spiders. She moaned.

"Sorry, babe," George said. "I know how you love crab."

"Not today," Connie whispered.

"I'll get the kids tonight. Maybe bring home pizza." George rambled on for a minute, but Connie didn't listen. "Take care of yourself," he ended. "Bye, now."

Connie couldn't sleep after George's call. Maybe she should try some tea. She put on her robe and slippers again, and hobbled downstairs. She took the teakettle off the stove and turned to the sink.

There in the white Corian sink sat another brown recluse. And Connie was out of Raid.

Necessity helped her sluggish brain kick into gear. "I can boil it," she said. She had used that technique before. But how could she fill the kettle when the spider occupied the sink? She found a large Pyrex measuring cup, filled it in the laundry room sink—thankfully not infested—and stuck it in the microwave on "High."

When the water boiled, Connie tiptoed over to the sink. "Die, you bastard. Die!" she yelled as she poured the entire contents of the Pyrex on the spider.

Its legs splayed out, it kicked once, then slid down the drain. For good measure, Connie turned on the hot water and the disposal. That spider would not bother her again.

Worn out after the battle, Connie filled the kettle and made tea. When it had steeped, she sank onto the family room couch and sipped. Her stomach flipped once, but then quieted as the hot liquid soothed her bruised intestines.

After an hour of quiet on the couch, Connie felt better. She stared calmly as another spider sauntered across the floor. When it had reached the middle of the room and had no easy escape, Connie stalked up behind the pest and ground it into the carpet with her slipper.

Another arachnid bit the dust. True, Connie left the entrails on the floor for George to deal with later. But she had killed this monster with her own strength, using no external tools—no Raid, no water.

Connie smiled for the rest of the afternoon. Her stomach felt better. She wasn't ready for bacon and eggs, but she was vanquishing the bugs. Flu and spiders, they couldn't keep her down.

SNIPS OF SCANDAL
Jodie Jackson Jr. and Caroline Dohack

The earthquake rolled through at 6:09 a.m., four minutes after Remington Ford presented an artillery of identification to prove who she was, where she lived, and where she was registered to vote: voter ID card, driver's license, natural gas bill from Union Electric, empty prescription bottle, Missouri Press Association membership card.

"And a few other things in here," Remington said, still digging through her bulky black purse. "Need more?"

She considered dumping the entire contents on the table where chief precinct judge, Vernon Brooks, was crosschecking each item with the list of registered voters. Remington flipped open her compact and quickly glanced to see if the zit on her forehead was adequately hidden.

"The addresses on this bill and this driver's license don't match up, young lady." Vernon Brooks summoned the other three election judges to huddle over the mismatched proofs of identification to decide whether their local newspaper reporter could cast a legal and binding vote.

"This will take forever," Remington mumbled

Clara Beth McKenzie, the bun-headed matriarch of Seven Hills Baptist Church, examined the driver's license, puzzling over the change from the reporter's long, lustrous locks in the driver's license photo to the short, spiky hairstyle she now sported.

"Your hair ain't the same as in this picture," Clara Beth said.

Then the ground shook.

"Ooh." Clara Beth squealed, putting her hands to her blushing cheeks. "That's a good 'un. That was more of a pulse than a shake."

The New Madrid seismic fault's latest slip seemed to gently lift the ground with a wave of energy—no more than a few seconds—typical for rumbles that were followed only by aftershocks of imaginative embellishment among the residents of Jewel Box. The women in the Elks Lodge chirped and chattered about the quake, each making reference to "The Big One." Remington put out a hand and pleaded for a ballot.

"Oh, that's right, hon." Vernon Brooks handed Remington the Scantron form and a Sharpie. "I'll bet you write a big ol' story for tomorrow's *Jewel*."

"Something like that," Remington said.

"Where the hell is Ford!" Douglas Garrison shouted at no one in particular. The young reporter had ignored his demands to "cease and desist" from any stories that represented County Prosecutor Jeb Nichols in an unflattering light. The copy Remington filed before leaving late the night before focused on a seemingly dramatic decrease in the number of child molestation cases that had been prosecuted since the county commission shepherded Nichols into office four years earlier. Remington's sources strongly hinted that at best Nichols neglected his duty; at worst, he ignored it.

The story—or what little of it she read—brought Jana Garrison to tears.

"That girl just hates Jeb, and he's such a good, decent man," Jana, the newspaper's proofreader and crossword-puzzle author, told her publisher-editor husband. After comforting his wife for a full hour, Douglas wrote a terse termination letter to Remington. The letter was folded and tucked behind the John Deere calendar tacked to the corkboard by the desk where Douglas penned op-ed columns and handled circulation matters.

The Jewel was Remington's first non-college newspaper gig. She longed for a shot at covering news that didn't involve coon dog calling contests, fairs dedicated to warm season grasses, or the Pitch-It Fall Festival, which focused solely on how far one could throw a household appliance. The election season had seemed like an opportunity for her to show off her reporting talents, but her boss didn't seem to like where they were taking her.

Douglas Garrison pecked away at his keyboard, writing for the umpteenth time that Jewel Box was "rattled but not shaken." He copied and pasted from a dozen other stories the background of the great earthquake scare of December 1990 when climatologist Iben

Browning predicted the New Madrid fault would produce "The Big One." It hadn't, but the residents of Jewel Box were always ready for the day an earthquake would put them on the map—or wipe them off it. Douglas pressed a Post-it Note onto the side of his monitor: "Call Browning."

"I'm heading over to The Mane, puddin'. I think that will help me feel better. And probably somebody needs to remind Cicada to update her earthquake wall," Jana Garrison said as she passed. "Oh, and Iben Browning's been dead twenty years."

Remington slid her ballot into the automated counter when Cicada Phillips stepped in with about a dozen other voters.

"Hey, Remi! You get yourself one of those 'I Voted' stickers?"

Remington peeled the backing off her sticker and pressed it onto her chest.

"There. That says I'm a good citizen," she said.

Vernon Brooks "shooshed" the women and shot a scowl their way. Cicada pantomimed the motions of popping a zit.

"Gross!" Remington hissed, just loud enough to draw another scowl from the senior precinct judge.

"Let me vote real quick, and then we'll walk over to the shop," Cicada said. She leaned toward Remington and whispered, "Maybe get another of those stickers to cover that thing between your eyes."

Remington frowned and self-consciously brushed her bangs forward.

"Don't worry," Cicada reassured her, "I'll put my micro-derm training to work to get you fixed. But in the meantime, you really should ask Vernon for another sticker."

"Not funny," Remington mouthed as she stalked out of the building.

Rather than walk three buildings down to Cicada's shop, The Mane Attraction, Remington was going to drive two blocks to her reserved spot in front of *The Jewel*. As she backed up and squinted into the late autumn sun, she felt a jolt when she bumped into the Jewel Box police department's new SUV. Police Chief Sam Fuller crawled out of his ride and met Remington at the rear of her car.

"Hey, Sam, guess I was in a little hurry there." Remington rubbed her left hand at the spot where her car made contact. "A little ding. Sorry about that. I can cut you a check next week when I get paid."

"I suppose there's no harm," Fuller said, "but I can't ignore you not wearing a seatbelt."

Remington cocked her head toward the officer and blinked. "You're kidding, right? I was just going to *The Jewel*."

Fuller was friendly enough when he was off duty, but when it came to carrying out the law to its very last letter, he was all business.

"'Fraid not. Better grab your license and proof of insurance."

"Sam, you are kidding, right? It's me. Remington."

"Don't care if it's you Mel Gibson," he replied. "License and insurance. Now."

Even in the face of multiple infractions, Fuller couldn't resist taking a crack at Jewel Box Mayor Mel Gibson. The longtime incumbent was running for his sixth term unopposed, but still dotted the little town's lawns and vacant lots with signs touting the reelection of "The other Mel Gibson."

Remington felt her heart race and imagined that blemish growing into a Cyclops-esque orb. She couldn't find her wallet.

"I think my license and insurance are in the Lodge here," she said. "Just let me step in and get it."

"License and insurance must be on your person. Proof of insurance must be maintained in vehicle at all times."

Fuller wasn't budging. He wrote out three tickets: seatbelt violation, operating a motor vehicle without a valid driver's license, and failure to maintain financial responsibility.

Cicada left the Elks Lodge and saw Jana Garrison waiting at the front door of The Mane Attraction. Jana, a fading beauty, always paid in cash and typically wanted the works—especially if Angelina Jolie was on the cover of that week's *People* magazine. Still, her pushy demeanor and backhanded compliments made her minutes spent in the salon feel more like hours.

Cicada welcomed her first customer of the day and flipped on the lights. She enjoyed Jana's predictable reaction: a quick, deep breath, and exclamation about the spectacular scene that unfolded. Recessed track lighting mounted on the foyer walls brought Hollywood to life in cinematic fashion. Full-size cutouts of Marilyn Monroe, Audrey Hepburn, George Clooney, and others, along with an array of movie posters promoting everything from *Gone with the Wind* to *Gone in 60 Seconds*, adorned the walls and ceilings. Ultimately, Cicada planned a "walk of fame" to mimic the sidewalk stars in Hollywood. Jana repeatedly offered to get that project started by paying for a star for her favorite—Angelina.

"I really like what Angie's doing with her hair these days," Jana said. While Cicada prepped her work area, Jana browsed the "Little Jewel Museum," a display of glass cases in the middle of the shop where items that crossed The Mane's path were exhibited. For instance, Neil Armstrong dropped off a rock he'd found. John Wayne once stopped by to sign a cowboy hat. Ted Williams donated a baseball. Glenn Campbell brought in a handful of rhinestones.

Jana thought the exhibits cheapened the Hollywood experience, because Neil Armstrong was only a man who lived in Moon, Oklahoma; John Wayne was a farmer down in Doniphan; and Ted Williams was a regular in stage productions at Central Methodist University in Fayette. Glenn Campbell, though, was *the* Glenn Campbell. Mayor Mel Gibson had a variety of personal items on display as well. The more famous Mel Gibson did not.

"What are you thinking today, Mrs. Garrison?" Cicada sprayed a few puffs of lavender air freshener.

"I just need some extra body. Maybe some highlights, too, I suppose. But there's something you're forgetting."

Cicada shrugged.

"The earthquake wall, puddin'. You need to keep up."

Of course. Merged into one wall with movie memorabilia was a narrow map showing the region between St. Louis and Memphis. Every verifiable seismic movement above 2.0 on the Richter scale was recorded with a red pushpin. In the seven years Cicada owned the shop, she'd stuck hundreds of pushpins into the wall. Larger pins represented the massive, river-retreating quakes of 1811 and 1812.

"Just like Southern Cali," Jana sighed. "This will just have to do until I can get there."

"You gonna do commercials or real acting?" Cicada knew her customer would talk about it anyway.

"Oh, I'll probably not get out there." For once, Cicada thought, Mrs. Garrison demonstrated perceptible pain instead of pompous pretentiousness. "But I'll stay sharp, and until a real hairstylist gets hold of me, this will do."

Cicada gritted her teeth. So much for feeling Jana Garrison's pain.

"You vote this morning, Mrs. Garrison?" Cicada asked, examining Jana's roots. "Not much suspense, like usual."

Jana straightened her back in the swivel chair. "Except to know who's behind the foolish attempt to change prosecutors! Write-in on the ballot? What are we, a bunch of hillbillies?"

"Don't know," Cicada replied.

Cicada often planted the seeds for spirited conversation, but refused to join in when the topic touched politics or religion. When she just couldn't stand to bite her tongue anymore, she called Remington Ford. It was the details pieced together from Cicada's conversations with her clients that fueled Remington's pending article about Jeb Nichols' failure to prosecute child molesters.

Jeb Nichols had been a gift from the county commissioners during the last election, when then-prosecutor, Kit Stephens, had the temerity to introduce a ballot initiative to make the county prosecutor a full-time, benefits-eligible position. When the commissioners altered the wording on the initiative to emphasize the added cost to the county, Stephens successfully sued to have the initiative wording restored to be consistent with that of the other initiatives.

Incensed, the commissioners endorsed Nichols, a personal injury attorney, who did the bulk of his work from an old laptop at Casey's General Store, one of the few venues in town with free Wi-Fi. He had no experience outside of dubious civil litigation, but the commissioners promised him a hefty salary—even greater than the one Stephens had requested—if he would take the job.

Remington had it on good authority—a sheriff's deputy Cicada sometimes dated—that Nichols refused to present information on suspected child molesters to the grand jury that he convened once a quarter. "Insufficient evidence" was always the rationale, regardless of how thorough the officers were in their investigations.

Remington's article on Nichols—written against the order of Douglas Garrison who insisted, instead, that Remington write an update on Mayor Gibson's spider bite—presented information that police had interviewed two unnamed witnesses who had given statements about being abused some years earlier—by Nichols himself. Garrison knew about some old allegations against Nichols, but the rumors died off and Nichols later represented the Garrisons when Jana hurt her back when her car was T-boned by a wealthy developer from Sikeston. The case was settled out of court. The day Jana Garrison was in the attorney's downtown office to sign all the paperwork—about a year before Nichols became the darling of the county commission—Douglas Garrison received an anonymous phone call.

"The only reason your lawyer isn't in jail is because the star witness changed his story. Kid perjured himself. No case. Discredited all the accusers." The caller hung up.

"All the accusers." Douglas heard those words echo even now, but he'd gotten to know Nichols, and Jana was especially fond of the prosecutor.

Douglas had made himself perfectly clear regarding the types of stories that would appear in *The Jewel*. Remington said she had the court documents and several sources willing to speak on the record, but when she showed them to her boss, he declared, "Horse crap! This is a family paper. We don't smear the reputations of upstanding citizens. You think you're so smart just because you went to J-School, but I don't think they taught you anything."

The editor heard his reporter come in and log on to her computer. He glanced again at the termination letter, even as "all the accusers" again reverberated through his mind. Douglas shook his head and scratched his chin. He preferred that Remington focus her talents on community life, toting her dinky Canon PowerShot around town to take pictures of teenage boys posing with dead turkeys, fair queen competitions, and the occasional albino opossum. No, her muckraking just wouldn't do.

He cleared his throat. "Remington, I need to see you."

By 8:00 p.m., the votes were already counted, and Jeb Nichols was re-elected to another four-year term as county prosecutor. Remington had been in the swivel chair farthest from the front window of The Mane since just after six. She'd walked around in the rain for an hour before coming in to tell Cicada that she'd been fired.

"Fired me, just like that. Told me I had a lot of talent, but a lot to learn," Remington reported. "Earthquake, car accident, this damn zit..." Her eyes started to fill with tears. "And Jeb..."

"Oh, quit your blubbering. I went ahead and emailed your story to the *Southeast Missourian*," Cicada said. "I gave them my number."

"You what?"

"That'll teach you to leave your laptop open around here."

The phone rang. A newspaper carrier in front of the hair salon opened a newspaper machine and deposited a bundle of *Jewels*, positioning the top copy to face the street, "Prosecutor survives challenge" emblazoned across the top of front page. A drop headline declared, "Voters speak, Iben Browning still waiting."

Cicada handed the phone to Remington. "It's for you."

Remington Ford told *Southeast Missourian* managing editor, Robert Trapp, how she investigated the story. It was the same information Douglas Garrison was reading after opening the envelope he found under his keyboard. Trapp had talked to investigators himself and was ready to run the story on one condition: Remington had to reveal the anonymous sources. They could remain anonymous and be ID'd in the story with pseudonyms to protect their identities. "I have to know. Gotta be sure this is legit. You also need to tell me when you can start work," Trapp told her.

"You've got an opening?"

"No, but I'll make one." He insisted again. "I need to know your sources."

So, she told him.

Fifteen years ago, two half-sisters found themselves bounced from county to county by the state's foster program. One of their stays had been in the home of a young St. Louis attorney, Jeb Nichols, and his wife, Suzy, who felt it was their Christian duty to "look after the orphans and widows." Suzy had been a wonderful foster mother, but there was something off about Jeb.

There were times he was too angry with the foster children, but also times he was too affectionate. Suzy tried to brush it off as too much job-related stress.

That is until the night she had to take Jeb to the emergency room after a strange teen named Cicada clipped off Jeb's left earlobe with a pair of manicure scissors. When asked why she attacked her foster father, Cicada said she didn't want his greasy hands on her anymore. Family Services stepped in and interviewed the rest of the children, most of whom also reported incidences of abuse.

The trial lasted a week. Five children ranging from age nine to sixteen testified against Jeb, but the youngest recounted some details in a manner inconsistent with the rest of the witnesses. The judge declared a mistrial. Jeb walked, but Suzy filed for divorce, and the children were split up and sent to new foster homes.

Years later, Cicada relocated to Jewel Box and opened a small salon. She did her best to put what happened in St. Louis behind her, but it all came back when she ran into a familiar face at Casey's. She avoided Jeb as best she could—no small task in a town the size of Jewel Box—but when she started to hear word of wrongs going un-righted, she decided it was time to expose him.

"But because of the victims' ages, those court documents will be sealed. How can I know this is true?" Trapp asked.

Remington stopped, stumped. "I personally know this is true."

"That's not good enough for me," Trapp said.

"What's the hold up?" Cicada mouthed.

"Proof," Remington answered.

"That's it? Well, here," Cicada said, pushing aside a few jars of blue liquid to reveal a hinged jewelry box. She lifted the lid, and a tulle-skirted ballerina twirled to the mechanical strains of "Swan Lake."

From the box, Cicada produced a rusted pair of manicure scissors and what looked, at first, like a bit of dried apricot.

"A little shriveled." Holding the specimen between her thumb and forefinger, she examined it in the light. "But, it'll fit him like a missing puzzle piece."

Cicada pulled back the shades and watched Jana Garrison pounding on her car door, trying to open the locked door in the pouring rain. Inside *The Jewel*, Douglas Garrison chatted on the phone with the police chief, then recalled all of the newspapers that had just been delivered. He put a second press run on hold and raced out the door with his camera.

The new *Jewels* came off the press just before midnight and the replacements went in the machine in front of the hair salon where Cicada and Remington soaked up the dark silence. A tired, elderly voice accompanied a tap at the front door and Vernon Brooks shuffled in, trying to close a clumsy umbrella. Soft amber light illuminated the newspaper machine and a new front page with the headline, "Prosecutor arrested." There was even a photo of Police Chief Sam Fuller leading Jeb Nichols to the police department's new SUV. Remington's ding—and byline—were in plain sight.

"Guess I got it a little better than I thought," she sighed.

Mr. Brooks reached out to offer Remington her wallet.

"Left this behind this morning, little lady. Nice story. I told you you'd get a big one." He smiled and left.

"Now you've got your license," Cicada teased.

"And this," Remington said, retrieving a photograph from the wallet. The rough-edged photo showed two little girls—sisters—ages six and thirteen. "We sure were cute back then, Cissy."

Cicada teased again. "I'm still cute. As for you…"

She brushed Remington's bangs back over the zit. "Well, it's a start," she said.

THE FANDANGO TANGO
C J Clark

It was a steamy, humid night in Magnolia, Mississippi, when Rose Tiddlemyer put her hands near her breasts and with an *oomph* hiked up her bustière. "Damn this thing. I don't know how anyone keeps one up. If it slips while I'm dancing, I'm going to look ridiculous," the seventy-eight-year-old silver haired grandmother said. Her slinky cerise satin gown showed every curve of her supple body. Unable to wear a slip, as it would show through the thigh-high slit, she hiked her hosiery affixing it to garters she had shortened with safety pins. Her matching cerise sequined shoes glittered dazzlingly although they pained her feet terribly.

She looked at the clock on the dressing room wall—8:15. Where was her partner, Hap? Nervously, she paced, balling her hands into fists, chewing off the lipstick she had just applied, while looking at the clock every thirty seconds. What would she do if Hap didn't show?

Five minutes later, a knock on the door sent her rushing to open it. Startled to see Hap's disheveled appearance and distressed face, she asked, "Hap, where have you been? We've got five minutes or so before we're on. Hap, are you all right?"

Hap replied in a distressed, agitated voice, "I'm fine…I think. I had an accident."

"Oh, no." Rose interrupted. "Was anyone hurt?"

"No, no one hurt. I ran into a stop sign. And it wouldn't have happened at all if it wasn't for my grandson," he said as he prepared to change clothes. "I was taking him home when his damn snake got loose. I thought I felt it creep up my pant leg, and I lost control of the car."

"Oh, dear. Did you find it?"

"That's the damnest thing. I don't know where the hell it went to. I know I shouldn't have taken the time to look, but…"

"Well, you're here now. If you're sure you're all right...hurry, will you? We haven't much time. And this damn bustière won't stay up." She grabbed at her boobs, shimmied, trying to hike the thing up again.

Just then, a stagehand knocked on the door. "Farquire and Tiddlemyer up next."

"You think you got problems. I've only got one hook and eye holding on my cummerbund, and I just discovered the button holding up my suspenders is hanging on by a thread," her partner said, as he threw on his tux jacket. He paced the floor, looked at the clock on the wall, practiced the two-step, and announced, "I'm ready. How about you?"

"Hap, I know it's our first competition, and we're not spring chickens. That's why we're in the Silver Slippers division. What can they expect of us at seventy-five plus?" She refreshed her makeup, then pressed her fingers to her hair before shooting it with another jet of hairspray.

Coughing, flailing his hands in the mist of spray, he spouted, "Do you *have to* keep spraying that toxic junk? You look fine. Although, I've never seen a grandmother with a slit to her—ahem—regardless of her figure."

A knock on the door announced the two-minute warning.

"Shall we?" Hap asked, gallantly extending his hand.

Confident and poised, they stood in the wings. Hap polished his shoes against his pant legs and Rose nervously smoothed imagined creases from her dress while awaiting the announcer's intro, "...and last, but not least, Hap Farquire and Rose Tiddlemyer."

A round of applause welcomed them to the dance floor.

Automatic smiling faces were flashed in spite of hurting feet, too tight undergarments, and general anxiety. Cole Porter's "It's De-Lovely" began as the couples started their slow-quick-quick rhythm for the Quickstep.

Suddenly Hap made an unrehearsed move. He plunged Rose into a dip whereupon her pasted smile crumbled. The safety pin burst and the garter dangled at an awkward angle. *Retch!* Her nylon stocking ran from thigh to knee. She prayed no one would notice. As if that weren't bad enough, *twang,* one of the garters gave way. Startled, she wondered: *will it show beneath my dress*? *Twang*, another one let loose. Rose could feel her nylon stocking slipping inch by inch. Could they finish the dance before it puddled around her ankle? She tried to hold her thighs together, but it hindered the quality of her performance. Courageously she smiled, then made a funny face as she felt it slipping…slipping…*oh dear, I hope the judges don't see this*. By the time the music ended, her stocking pooled at her ankle; Rose minced off the floor like a Japanese geisha.

"At least that dance is over," she sighed as they returned to their dressing room to prepare for the next set, and Rose replaced the nylon.

"Now let's see our couple do the Tango," said the announcer.

Rose and Hap strolled to an open spot on the floor taking their dance stance as "La Cumparsita" began to play.

"Now don't be afraid to twist and jerk me," she said. "I can take it."

As they began the *caminata,* that walking, stalking movement with a quick pivot to turn back, Rose's foot turned and she stumbled. Righting herself, she discovered she'd broken the heel off the sequined pump. Gracefulness fell by the wayside as Rose limped unevenly through the next couple of steps. When the perfect opportunity arose, she gaily kicked off both shoes not realizing that now the slit gown dragged on the dance floor. In seconds, the excess material had twisted between her legs, throwing her off balance. A heap on the floor, quick thinking Hap did all he could to save face. He spread his legs and in an Apache dance move, he flung Rose between his legs. Unfortunately, at seventy-seven, his legs didn't spread well, or Rose wasn't as slim as he thought. Just then, the impact of the accident hit. A loud snap. Hap doubled over as his back went out. But the pain was too much, and the next thing he knew he was on top of her.

"S-S-S," Rose chattered incoherently as her eyeballs grew large.

"No need to swear. Give me a sec to recover," whispered Hap.

Opening her mouth wide, her face contorted, and a scream rent the air, "*Snake!*"

Hap looked around, and sure enough, there was Elmer, his grandson's garter snake, slithering over his shoulder. Swiftly grabbing the thing, he flung it away. Pandemonium broke out. Screeches and screams filled the air. Several women fainted.

"Eek! Get it off of me! Get it off!" others yelled.

"Don't fling it over here."

"Snake! Snake!"

"Get it someone."

Audience members turned into a jumble of chaos as women scrambled, or jumped up on seats, and men turned every which way. The judges stood up trying to figure out what was going on.

"Got it!" someone hollered, holding the harmless snake by the head, dangling it in the air for all to see, before removing himself to the exit door.

As quickly as it had begun, the audience and judges regained their composure.

Meanwhile, embarrassed beyond belief, Hap and Rose clumsily managed to get up. Hap grabbed the hem of her dress in his hand. By doing so, the skirt hiked up to expose Rose's cellulite thighs.

Whirling her like a matador's cape, the tension was too much. *Twang, twang, twang, twang.* Rose felt all four garters spring open. With her skirt so short, she felt certain everyone could see her undergarments. One stocking crept lower…lower…and the movement of her feet accelerated the condition. *Dance. Dance. Ignore it.* Gliding across the floor, her nylon stocking trailed behind her. The other had come off somewhere on the dance floor. The garters jangled like gyrating Cobras. Humiliated, they ended the dance, hastily retreating off the floor.

The illustrious judges: LaVonda of Magnolia's Magnificent Mansions House of Design, Zendal Sales, an upcoming entrepreneur from Atlanta, Georgia, and Willow Songbird of the *Magnolia Monitor* newspaper, huddled together in deep conversation.

Moments later, the masters of ceremonies, Dolly Varden and Bubba Craddock announced the winner.

"Tonight's winning couple is number 27—Rose Tiddlemyer and Hap Farquire—they have shown us all how to be good sports."

The applause was thunderous.

Rose smiled and walked barefoot to the podium carefully holding up her dress. The bra cups in the bustière were now in her diaphragm giving her an odd shaped chest. Hap stood, half bent over, beside her accepting the trophy.

"I'd just like to say—"

A picture of how they must have looked crossed his mind. Bursting into laughter, the hook and eye on his cummerbund separated, and it slid to the floor. As he leaned over to retrieve it, *fling!*, the suspender button broke loose. The loose strap flew up smacking him in the face.

Rose, being a true Southern lady, maintained her charm, with a slight giggle she furled her hands in the air, "Ah well, the show must go on."

SUNDAY AFTERNOON
Mary Laufer

A piece of ash fell from the sky and drifted into Sharon's backyard. Shriveled and crisp, it looked like burnt paper to Sharon. She reached out and tried to catch it in midair, but it floated past her and landed in the grass by the swing set.

"What's that, Momma?" Sharon's little girl jumped off her swing, pigtails flying, and bent down to pick up the mysterious object, but it disintegrated between her fingers, covering them with a film of soot. She held up her hand for her mother to see.

Sharon frowned. "Don't wipe that on your shorts, Lindsay," she said, but then her concern shifted to what might be burning. She took off her sunglasses and scanned the forest along the horizon. A swirling plume of white smoke rose above the pine trees, and Sharon's Sunday afternoon boredom was immediately replaced with panic. She ran to the patio and yelled through the screen door, "John! The woods are on fire!"

Inside the house, the television blared as a sports announcer gave a play-by-play account of the football game. A pass had been intercepted; the Dolphins were still in the lead.

"John, come see this! There's a forest fire!"

Sharon's twelve-year-old son, Jacob, pressed his nose against the screen. Finally, her husband, a short man with a potbelly and red hair, slid open the screen. "Can't it wait until the commercial?" He peeked over his shoulder at the commotion on the television inside, and then shook his fist in the air. "Go! Go! Yessss!"

"Will you look this way for one second?"

John turned around. "What in God's name is the problem?"

"I told you before that I smelled smoke," Sharon said, "and you acted as if it were my imagination."

"I thought you were accusing me of smoking again."

"No, that's not the kind of smoke I meant." She pointed toward the woods. "What do you make of that?"

John blocked the sun with his hand and squinted toward the woods. He shrugged. "It's probably a small fire at the landfill."

"It's too close to be the landfill," Sharon said.

"Well, it's far enough away that it's not going to hurt us. Stop acting like Chicken Little." He returned to the game.

Sharon fumed. *"Chicken Little?"* It was brush fire season in Florida! They'd had no rain in weeks! Even the cypress trees were showing signs of drought.

Sharon followed her husband inside. "If you're not going to report the fire, I will!" As she was punching in 911, a helicopter passed over their roof. Its chopping blades drowned out the commentator's voice as he discussed a five-yard penalty.

Sharon watched out the window as the helicopter headed toward the woods. As soon as it was out of hearing range, the faint wail of a faraway siren took its place. She set the phone down. "See! It *is* a forest fire!"

"Sounds like it's being taken care of," John said from the recliner, his eyes fixed on the TV.

Nearby on the couch, Jacob was hypnotized by the men in shoulder pads and helmets. One of the players kicked the football, and the rest broke from formation.

The siren grew louder. Sharon couldn't see any trees along the horizon anymore, only thick smoke. If there were any animals left in the swamp, the fire would surely force them out.

She opened the screen door. "Come inside, Lindsay."

"But I hear a fire truck! I want to see it."

"You're not going to see it from there. Come in and look out the front window."

Lindsay scurried past her into the house and climbed on a stuffed chair near the front window. "I can't see it," she whined.

"I'll take you out in a minute." Sharon picked up her sunglasses and announced into the family room, "We're going out to see the fire truck," but neither John nor Jacob acknowledged her. John lay sprawled in his recliner with his hands clenching the armrests as if the chair were a vehicle transporting him to another world, a world of quarterbacks and touchdowns. Outside, the sports commentator's voice that Sharon had just left blasted through her neighbors' open windows. Lindsay skipped ahead on the sidewalk along Satinwood Circle, stopping once to admire a chalk drawing, another time to point out a mound of fire ants.

"Stay away from the ants," Sharon said. "You know how you break out in hives when you get bit."

Lindsay tiptoed around the ants and they continued on, passing several one-story stucco homes similar to their own, each crammed so close to the one on either side that Sharon had a difficult time keeping an eye on the smoke in the woods behind them.

A small crowd had gathered on the corner. "Marty's here!" Lindsay exclaimed. She ran up to a brown-haired boy wearing a Batman shirt and a red baseball cap. His mother, a tall woman in khaki shorts, said hello as Sharon joined them. Everyone looked toward the Cypress Crossings entrance, where a fire truck was parked on the roadside, its red lights flashing.

Sharon turned to Marty's mother. "Am I crazy to be worried, Nicole? John said I was acting like Chicken Little."

Nicole let out a laugh, and then saw that her friend was serious. "You'd be crazy if you weren't concerned. Everything's tinder-dry right now."

Sharon brushed the hair out of her eyes. "And the wind is picking up. Maybe we'd better wet down our lawns when we get home."

"Is John watching the game?" Nicole asked.

"Are there alligators in Florida?" Sharon joked. "I take it Duane is camped out in front of the TV, too. We heard it when we walked by."

Nicole sighed. "It's so loud, I can't stand it! He didn't even hear the sirens. The house could burn down around him, and he wouldn't know it."

"Did I ever tell you that I went into labor with Lindsay on a Sunday afternoon? Of course, John was preoccupied with football. I tried unplugging the damn television to get his attention, but he just plugged it back in again. Thank God, Lindsay took her time coming."

Nicole whispered, "We deserve more than this! We should have affairs on Sunday afternoons."

Sharon glanced around the corner at their neighbors. Not a single man was in the group. "Do you really think we'd be able to find men who aren't watching football?"

"You're right. Nix that. We'll have to make do with what we have. How about you and I go to the mall and pick out some really slutty lingerie? Maybe we can lure our husbands away from football."

"Yeah, that'll happen!"

The women laughed. Another siren wailed and a longer truck clamored through the subdivision entrance and came to a stop. Four firefighters bounded out, unfolded the thick hose and hooked it to a hydrant.

Marty pulled at the side of his mother's shorts. "Lindsay says her daddy started the fire with his cigarettes."

Sharon raised her eyebrows. She shook her head at Nicole, and then put her hand on Lindsay's shoulder. "Your daddy didn't start the fire."

"But he said that you said he was smoking!"

Sharon bent down beside her. "I guarantee your daddy was too busy watching football to sneak off to the woods for a smoke."

The flames swiftly pushed beyond the margin of the woods, and gusts of wind fanned the fire, randomly igniting new patches of grass that flared up and crackled. The smoke wafted toward them, and Lindsay began to cough.

"This isn't good for your asthma," Sharon said. "We'll have to go back."

"But Momma!"

"Honey, it's time to go. Say goodbye to Marty."

Everyone said "Bye," and they started home. They hadn't gone far when Marty squealed behind them. Sharon turned to see huge flames leaping out of the smoke. For a moment, the two firefighters at the front of the hose were obscured. Then they reappeared, still poised with the hose, and retreated, backing closer and closer to the road.

Sharon's skin prickled. The wildfire was spreading through the field like lightning. At this rate, it was only a matter of minutes before it spread to the palmettos that fringed the sidewalks along the main road. If the palmettos caught fire, the trees and shrubs around the entrance were next. Her heart racing, Sharon picked up Lindsay. "The fire is out of control!" she yelled to the women on the corner. "It's almost to the entrance!"

"They'll send more trucks," someone said.

"I'm not waiting for them!" Sharon ran down their street, barged into the house, and flew down the hall into the family room. "John!" she shrieked. "We have to leave! The fire is going to block the entrance!"

John gasped, and she thought that he understood, but he stared straight ahead at the television. One of the players with a dolphin on his helmet was running with the ball. The other team chased him across the turf.

Sharon set Lindsay down. "John! We don't have much time!"

"Huh?"

"I saw the fire! It's going to block the way out!"

"You probably saw the red lights on the fire truck."

"I saw flames! Jumping flames!" Her arms flailed as if she could still see the fire in front of her. "We have to go now, while we can still get the car out!"

John took a sip of his beer, and then reached for a handful of popcorn from a bowl on the end table. "Calm down. The firemen are out there, aren't they?"

Without warning, Lindsay began a coughing fit. Sharon heard whistles at the end of each cough, the kind of wheezing that in the past had quickly progressed into a full-blown asthma attack. She rushed to the kitchen, found Lindsay's nebulizer, then rummaged through a drawer for the jar of bronchodilator medicine.

"I'm taking Lindsay away from here!" she said to her husband as she held the nebulizer mask over the girl's face. "Are you coming with us?"

"The second half just started, and I…" His voice trailed off.

Sharon recognized her husband's evasive tone, the sheepish look. "And what?"

"I have a bet on this game."

"*A bet*? You're gambling now? How much of a bet?"

John didn't answer.

The fire was getting closer with every second that passed. Sharon wished she had a whistle to blow or knew the referee's hand signals that always stirred her men to action. With hands on her hips, she planted herself in front of the television. She spoke like she did when she sounded out letters with Lindsay, pronouncing each word distinctly. "You-need-to-come-with-us!"

"Get out of the way!" John yelled, motioning vigorously with the remote control.

Sharon winced, stepped aside, and redirected her attention to her son, who lay on the couch unfazed by his parents shouting. "Jacob, we're leaving in one minute! Go wait in the car for me!"

The boy blinked, finally comprehending what was being asked of him, and glanced at his father, who continued to watch television. "If Dad's not going, I'm not either!"

Suddenly John sat up in his recliner and sprang to life. "Why didn't the ref call pass interference? His hands were all over him!"

Jacob stood on the couch and yelled, "Are you blind, ref? It was right in front of you!"

The two of them jumped up and down as if they were exercising with a video.

"Challenge the call!" John told the man standing on the sidelines.

"Watch the replay!" Jacob hollered.

Sharon let out a cry of agony, "I hate football!" and looked around for something to throw, picked up the plastic bowl from the end table and slung it at the TV like a Frisbee. The bowl crashed into the screen, popcorn flew in the air, but neither the bowl nor the screen shattered. As if in response, fans in the stadium stood up in the bleachers.

"They reversed it!" John yelled. He and Jacob danced around and cheered.

Popcorn crunched under her feet as Sharon reached for Lindsay, who now sat on the carpet chewing kernels. Sharon lifted the girl into her arms, grabbed the nebulizer, and headed toward the garage. Halfway there, she hesitated and looked back at John and Jacob.

If only she had taken her iPhone outside with her and recorded the fire so she'd have an instant replay to show them! "You're making a bad call!" she cried. "You're gambling with your lives!" She hurried to the car, strapped Lindsay into her booster seat, and zoomed out the driveway.

In the short time she'd been at her house, the blaze had doubled in size, widening its path and sweeping toward the entrance. The high grass on both sides of the main road was on fire now, as well as the palmettos that grew along the sidewalks. Surges of dense smoke swelled around her car as if it were an airplane flying through waves of clouds. Sharon drove slowly, her foot riding the brake. "How much farther?" she asked herself. "I can't see more than a foot in front of me!"

A burnt stick struck the windshield, embers glowing along the end.

Lindsay shouted, "Daddy's cigarette!" The stick blew off as the car moved forward.

"No, honey. It was just something that fell down from the sky."

A piercing scream filled the car. Sharon wanted to cover her ringing ears, but she had to keep her hands on the steering wheel. "Stop it, Lindsay! Why are you screaming?"

"The sky is falling!"

"What?"

"The sky is falling! That black thing fell down by my swing and then Daddy called you Chicken Little and now pieces of the sky are falling again."

"The sky can't fall! The wind is just carrying away burnt sticks and ashes from the fire." Sharon thought, *Oh, my God. Is that what I sounded like to John?* For a few moments, she felt a little foolish, as if she had overreacted, until the smoke shifted and she had a glimpse of the inferno that ravaged the field. "It's karma," Sharon said. "This is what I get for boiling those poor lobsters last night."

Another fire truck screeched in, its lights showing her the way out. Sharon pulled over to let the truck pass and then made a beeline for the exit. She continued a few miles until she came to a Kmart on the outskirt of town and turned into the parking lot. She and Lindsay got out of the car and looked into the distance. The sky was red over the treetops. Brown smoke billowed upward into a tall column.

"Will the fire kill the ants?" Lindsay asked.

"What?"

"Will the ants die?"

"I guess so." *They probably won't die at all,* Sharon mused.

They'll just go deeper into the ground and come up later somewhere else, like husbands' bad habits.

"Good," Lindsay said. She was quiet for a minute. "What about Daddy and Jacob? Is our house going to burn down?"

"No, sweetheart," Sharon said with feigned calmness. "The firemen will put out the fire. Daddy and Jacob will be all right."

Two more trucks whizzed by, their sirens and horns rattling her nerves. Sharon took her cell phone out of her purse and called their home phone number. It rang four times before the answering machine picked up. "Hello, you've reached the Conner residence. We can't come to the phone right now..." Although she was still infuriated with John, the sound of his voice comforted her. It gave her hope that the house was still there, that he and Jacob were still lounging in the family room while the firefighters battled the blaze around them. "Look!" Lindsay said. "What's that?"

Sharon looked up. A strange-looking aircraft flew over them. "I think it's a special plane to help put the fire out."

Half an hour later, as they waited in the car, she called home again. This time she heard a click and then a recording, "We are unable to connect to this number. Please try again later." She felt a pang in her heart.

A small voice came from the back seat. "I have to go to the bathroom."

Like a zombie, Sharon walked through Kmart's automatic doors with Lindsay. After they used the restroom, Sharon bought Lindsay a pretzel, but she couldn't eat anything herself. She pushed a shopping cart up and down the aisles in a fog. It wasn't until they were in the checkout line that she noticed what her daughter had tossed into the cart: four storybooks, two coloring books, a box of markers, a Barbie doll, several packages of Barbie clothes, and a small jar of bubbles. Sharon had only ten dollars in her purse; she absently charged everything to her credit card.

When they came out of the store, the fire was still burning. Sharon read Lindsay's books aloud and helped her take off Barbie's dress and put another one on. "These outfits are too sexy for little girls to play with," she said. They tried out all the markers in the coloring books, and then blew bubbles. Eventually her daughter fell asleep.

After four hours, the dark clouds trailed off and the sky began to clear. When a fire truck rumbled by in the opposite direction, its siren muted, Sharon started the car's engine and headed home—*if there's anything left that I can call home*, she thought.

She saw refugees assembled in a church parking lot. Sharon stopped the car and unbuckled her daughter out of the booster seat. They moved through the people and searched for familiar faces.

"Marty!" Lindsay said, and Sharon spotted Marty's red baseball cap. His mother and father stood beside him.

"There you are!" Nicole said. "Where'd you go?"

"We went shopping and bought some sexy outfits," Lindsay said.

Nicole's eyes got big. She nudged Sharon with her elbow. "You didn't waste any time, girl!"

"They're outfits for Lindsay's Barbie doll!" Sharon insisted. "I took Lindsay to Kmart to get her away from the smoke. Listen, have you seen John and Jacob?"

"No, but don't worry. The entire subdivision was evacuated. Some were even airlifted by helicopters."

Sharon was not reassured. "My guys would never leave on their own. How did you pry Duane from the game?"

"I flipped the circuit breaker," Nicole said.

"And she poured beer over my head," Duane added. He touched his hair, which was a sticky mess.

An ambulance attendant who was wrapping a boy's arms with gauze had overheard them. "They might be at the Red Cross station over at the high school," the woman said.

Sharon got back in her car to go to the school, but turned on impulse when she came upon what was left of the Cypress Crossings sign. A man in fire gear ran into the middle of the street and held out his hand for her to stop. "You can't go down there, Ma'am. No one is allowed past this point. You'll have to turn around."

"But I think my family is still at our house!"

The man's eyebrows came together. "They didn't get out?"

"I don't know. I can't find them! Please let me through!"

"Tell me their names, and I'll check the evacuation centers for you." He detached a radio from his belt.

"John and Jacob Conner. Their last name should be Football. They couldn't tear themselves away from the game."

"I hated missing the game myself. How did it turn out?"

Sharon rolled her eyes. *Was he kidding? He honestly thought I was watching football while waiting to find out if my house had burned down?*

Lindsay spoke up. "We didn't watch the game. We tried on sexy outfits instead."

An amused grin came over the man's face.

"She has asthma. I had to get her away from the smoke," Sharon explained. "My husband wouldn't leave—he had a bet on the Dolphins."

"Oh, you're Dolphin fans? You can go on through," he said and waved her on.

Honestly? Sharon sped down the main road of the subdivision. The palmettos along the sidewalks were charred stumps. Where the field used to be, there was just blackened ground, like the surface of a dead planet, and beyond that, skeletons of pine trees.

"It's karma," Lindsay said, looking out the window at the stark landscape. "This is what I get for putting toys in the cart when you weren't looking, Momma."

An armadillo ambled in front of them, and Sharon swerved around it. She made a right on Satinwood Circle, drove down the street and passed one scorched house after another. They all looked the same, mere shells of concrete block. One, two, three, four, she counted. The next smoldering foundation must be their house.

"Daddy and Jacob!" Lindsay cried and Sharon's heart stopped.

At the end of the cul-de-sac, John and Jacob wandered around in circles like displaced animals. Without saying a word, Sharon got out of the car. She ran to Jacob and hugged him close. His clothes were darkened with ash, but otherwise he appeared unscathed.

John still held the remote control. When his eyes met his wife's, she expected remorse, an apology, something.

Instead, he lifted the remote in the air and shouted, "We won!"

WATER, LIKE THE CAMERA, ADDS TEN POUNDS
Sioux Roslawski

What began as a way to save a measly five dollars turned into a million dollar memory…or at least what *could* have been a picture-worthy memory, if only cameras were capable of telling lies.

Having given up decades ago on growing anything resembling flowing Farrah Fawcett tresses, Maggie wore her hair short. And straight, since she ended up with third-degree burns whenever her fingers clutched a curling iron. When the steel-gray patches got too brazen, Maggie would buy a box of hair dye and do it herself. She was a regular DIY type of girl when it came to her hair.

This incensed her hair stylist. The only Russian working at the salon, Larisa tried to lull Maggie into submitting to getting her hair professionally colored. Maggie weighed the options: spend fifty dollars on Larisa's workmanship or stay at home and simply squirt stuff onto her head and the walls and the floor for seven dollars instead? She resisted the lure of Larisa's proposing an expensive pro dye job.

But Larisa persisted. She tried to bamboozle Maggie with the sounds of balalaika music in her little hair-littered corner. A pot of borscht simmered on a hot plate, and the movie *Dr. Zhivago* played on a continuous loop. Could the intensity of Omar Sharif's burning eyes—black as onyx—batter down her cement-hard resolve? No, she continued to decline Larisa's offers to let *her* get rid of Maggie's gray, so the sly hair stylist tried a different tactic.

How about a pre-cut shampoo? That, of course, would add another five dollars to the salon bill. Since Maggie's hair-cutter proved to be a formidable and crafty opponent, she had to become wily—Larisa was as sharp as her clippers…

Making appointments on Saturday, when Maggie could shower and immediately head to Larisa, ensured that she arrived with damp hair. "A shampoo?" the hair expert would ask hopefully when Maggie stepped into the salon, herding Maggie toward her sink.

"No, thanks—I just washed it," and she'd ruffle her locks to emphasize the still-wet strands.

And it worked. That is, until a packed weekend and a busy week resulted in Maggie having to make an appointment with Larisa right after work on a Wednesday.

Maggie packed her shampoo and a towel into her bag, along with her lesson plans, and went to school that morning. *After the students are dismissed, after my curriculum meeting, after all the other teachers leave the building, I will be able to wash my hair, and I have the perfect place to do it: the faculty bathroom,* she thought. It was small, but private, with a locking door, thanks to an old deadbolt.

After all, why would I want to answer a bunch of questions about why I'm washing my hair at work? If I wanted an audience, there's the huge sink in the students' bathroom I could use. A spacious, circular affair made of shining stainless steel, with enough room for a child to swim. Huge, yes. Private, no. So, Maggie decided on the teachers-only toilet.

Because the staff restroom was so small, it was equipped with an extremely tiny sink. After all, this was not a room to luxuriate in—not a place to spend some "alone" time reading the newspaper while perched on the throne. This petite potty room was situated in an alcove, right next to the nurse's office—a kind of afterthought. It was as if some bumbling architect had said, "Look, we have four square feet of floor space here and nothing to do with it. How 'bout putting in a bathroom?" It was small enough that if a person stood in the middle, they could raise their arms and reach any of the four walls without even moving.

But despite its lack of spaciousness, this glorified closet *was* useful. Teachers rushed in with only a few minutes to spare before they were due to pick up their students from PE or Art. It was big enough to get the normal bathroom business done, but there was certainly no room to do much moving around—stand up, flush, pivot, and wash hands. It was graced with a basin barely big enough to engage in any thorough hand washing, but Maggie figured with some clever maneuvering, she could get all her hair splashed, sudsed up and rinsed off.

So after her meeting finished, Maggie headed down the hall to the staff restroom. She had to tilt her head sideways, cram it carefully under the faucet, and wash one side. Before she switched sides, Maggie had to maintain the same angle of her head in order to pull it up and out.

Did I get under the faucet from the left side or the right this time? she asked herself more than once. The normally so-simple process became something she had to concentrate on. It was crucial that she get her head out of the sink the identical way she got it in. Like a soldier retracing steps across a minefield, if Maggie switched things up, it could be hazardous.

In the home stretch, she was almost finished rinsing the soap off when the unthinkable happened.

She tried to pull her head out using the left-side escape route, and then the right. No luck from either direction. Several more attempts resulted in the same conclusion: Her head was stuck. The silver-toned spout was holding her head hostage.

And almost immediately, sweat dampened the raggedy T-shirt Maggie had donned to douse her hair. The faucet jutted out way too far into the miniature porcelain tureen to allow her head easy access.

It doesn't make sense. If my head had the room to get in here, it should have the room to get out. In Maggie's mind, it was logical. But with each fruitless tilt of her skull, she became a bit more panicked. Even attempting to pull her head straight out, without angling it, resulted in nothing. Groping around—blindly—for the knobs, Maggie managed to turn the faucet off.

Okay, calm down. There has to be some sort of clever thing that perhaps Dan can think of, she thought. Dan, the night custodian, was somewhere in the building. It was just impossible to know exactly where he was at the moment. *Mopping the upstairs ramp? Sitting in the janitor's office reading the newspaper? Hiding in some classroom watching TV?* Maggie had no idea where he was, but she figured she should send out a distress signal…and quickly.

"Dan. Hey, Dan. I'm kind of stuck here in the bathroom." It was a tentative plea for help. Nothing.

For the next thirty-five minutes, Maggie alternated between yelling, and making a racket with backward mule kicks to the door. Finally, she heard Dan wheel the vacuum cleaner back into the nearby supply closet.

"Who's in there?" Dan had finally heard her.

"Oh, thank God, Dan. It's me, Mrs. Gann. I'm stuck in here."

"What do you mean, stuck? Did you fall down? Did you hurt yourself?"

"Uh, not exactly... My head, it's stuck. In the sink. And I can't seem to get it out."

Dan pulled on the door. "Dead bolted," he said, "There's nothing I can do. I'll have to call the fire department. Those guys will be able to get you out of there in no time." Maggie started to protest that calling 911 was surely *not* the next step, but Dan had already trotted away. A methodical, plodding man, Dan kept focused on whatever task he was accomplishing. He kept "blinders" on, so as not to get distracted, and some frazzled teacher was not going to succeed in sidetracking him, that was certain.

So Maggie waited, alone. She figured that as fond as Dan was of shows like *Cops* and *Law and Order*, he would probably wait at the front door to let the fire department in, his face smooshed against the glass door in anticipation. By now, her T-shirt was soaking wet, just like her hair, and her aching bent-over back was a chiropractor's dream come true.

I'm never going to live this down. Is this ring-dang-doo worth five dollars? And I was worried about being laughed at for washing my hair in the bathroom sink. Everybody's going to pee their pants laughing over this one, she figured.

From the moment she heard the fire truck's siren, until her rescuers clomped down the hall, Maggie fretted. She'd seen fire fighters hatchet down a door in movies and television shows, but that probably wouldn't work in this case. The door was metal, and besides, she was stuck too close to the door. *Maybe I'll have to spend the rest of my life in here, hunched over the sink*, she thought sheepishly. *One good thing, I won't have to worry about my overdue report cards if I get relegated as a permanent bathroom fixture. And all the stomach crunches and sit-ups...I won't have to worry about doing any more of those, either, if I'm stuck here the rest of my life,* which made Maggie grin. A little.

"Ma'am? How are you doing in there? It's the fire department."

Ma'am? she shuddered. *At what age did I become a ma'am?*

"Please call me Maggie. I'm sure you don't remember me, but I see you guys every time we have a fire drill. And I'm fine, considering I've had my head stuck in this sink for over an hour. The only thing that is injured is probably my pride."

"Ma'am, don't even think about it. I'm Captain Rhodes, and we've seen some pretty bizarre things in our line of work—people getting stuck is something we handle all the time."

"Well, you guys can't chop down the door to get me out. I'm less than two feet away, so what *are* you going to do?"

She could hear one of the firemen chuckle. The captain continued. "No, we're going to use a hydraulic tool for this job. It'll stretch the doorframe apart, and then all we have to do is lift the door out of the way. It works kind of like the jack you use on your car— but sideways. It'll be a breeze."

And easy it was. All Maggie heard was creak-creak-creak—it sounded just like the carjack her husband used—and in less than ten minutes, the fire department had the door completely gone and set up against the wall nearby. With a couple of well-placed taps of a hammer, they had the sink broken—the porcelain fell in a few large chunks, without a single bruise or microscopic cut to Maggie's head. "You guys are good," Maggie gushed.

Straightening up, she stretched her back, trying to work out the kinks in her spine. As she turned around, Maggie caught sight of what she was in the middle of.

Seven men. Not all of them were young, but they were all in decent shape and looked even more muscular in their heavy gear—the bulky jackets, fireproof pants, and boots. Surrounded by so much testosterone, Maggie thought of a way to salvage the situation. *Perhaps I can keep from becoming the butt of everybody's joke,* she plotted.

"Guys, can you hang on for just a second? You were my heroes tonight. I'd love to get a picture before you go." Without waiting for a response, Maggie hurried down the hall to her classroom to get her camera.

One of the men agreed to snap the photo while Maggie stood in the middle of the firemen. After she thanked them, and after they clomped down the hall heading back to the truck, Maggie planned what she was going to say when she showed off the picture of herself, shoulder to shoulder with six hunks. As she clicked on the button to look at the photo, she gasped.

There *was* a circle of six muscular men. They were definitely drool-worthy. But in the middle of them was somebody who looked suspiciously like Christopher Walken. Maggie's grayish hair had dried while she was hunched over the sink—in a wild, haphazard style—and after she was extricated from the porcelain prison, she'd nervously finger-combed her hair straight back from her forehead. And her oversized T-shirt was not camouflaging her flab any longer. It was still damp and clinging to the rolls of Maggie's muffin top in an unsightly manner.

Maggie decided the picture was something she needed to keep to herself, perhaps with the hair scribbled out. Maybe in this case, a thousand words would be better than a picture. Since the camera refused to lie, Maggie would have to fill in with some fibs, and in *her* version, she looked ravishing. And all six of the firemen leered at her.

Gladly, she'd shell out the five dollars for a shampoo the next time she needed a haircut. And while Larisa massaged the soapy bubbles into her scalp, Maggie could tell her about when the firefighters had to break the door down to rescue her—how when they caught sight of her incredible beauty, they argued over who would get to carry her out of her porcelain prison.

Now that's *a memory worth holding onto*, Maggie thought, and smiled…

THANKSGIVING WITH A TURKEY
Harriette Sackler

Suzie tried to focus her bleary eyes on the bedside clock before answering the phone. Seven thirty in the morning? A holiday morning? Only one person on earth would have the nerve to call her at this hour.

"Mom, what the hell is wrong with you?" she croaked into the phone. "What can be so damned important that you feel compelled to wake me in the middle of the night?"

"Suzie, stop being so melodramatic. You act like you're the second coming of Sarah Bernhardt. What a career you'd have on the stage!"

"Well, I've learned from the best, haven't I? Now what do you want?"

"I wanted to be sure that you don't forget the stuffing and pumpkin pie you're bringing for dinner, that's all."

"Don't worry about me doing what I need to do, Mom. You'd be amazed at how capable I am."

"Good, Miss Big Advertising Executive with no respect for her mother. And by the way, I've invited that nice young man, Harold, to join us. His parents are on a cruise, so he doesn't have any place to go for Thanksgiving. It's the least I can do for him. After all, you're dating."

Suzie was about to go ballistic.

"I'm not dating that guy. I went out with him once just to get you off my back. It was one of the most boring evenings I've ever spent. I can't believe you've managed to ruin what might have been a bearable Thanksgiving. I'd have a better time if I just stayed home, thanks to you."

"Oh, Suzie, will you stop with the theatrics? It won't kill you to be civil to that young man. He's quite a catch, after all. An accountant, nice looking, and he loves his mother. I'll expect you here at three."

Suzie couldn't fall back to sleep after the phone call was blessedly over. It was too much to expect that this day would be different from any other when it involved her mother. It seemed that Diane Robbins' sole passion was to micromanage her daughter's life. No matter what decisions Suzie made about her education, career, home, or clothes, her mother felt compelled to take issue with her. The best times of Suzie's life were when she was miles away from her mother, like when she spent summers at a sleep away camp in Maine, or when she decided to go to college in Boston rather than stay in Manhattan as her mother wanted her to do.

Suzie Robbins knew her mother was toxic—a woman who gave no thought to how her caustic words affected her daughter. As an only child, she had always borne the brunt of her mother's endless criticisms, barbs, and meddling. After all, there wasn't anyone as defenseless as an only child. As far back as Suzie could remember, her father had spent long hours out of the house, always working. When he happened to be home, he zoned out, ignoring his wife's incessant complaints and sarcasm. Suzie didn't understand until she was in her late teens, that this was his way of coping. Why he didn't just divorce his wife was anybody's guess.

When Suzie landed a position with a large Madison Avenue advertising firm and proceeded to work her way up the executive ladder, Diane wouldn't even acknowledge her daughter's success. Instead, she dumped on Suzie for not pursuing a degree in teaching, a job that would offer lifetime security. And, as Suzie liked to point out, at a fraction of the salary she now made.

And when Suzie bought her beautiful Riverside Drive condo overlooking the Hudson River, her mother berated her daughter for undertaking such a large mortgage commitment instead of renting. After all, Suzie would be able to retire from the world of work when she married. A good catch would provide her with a house in the suburbs and all the creature comforts she could ever want.

And, of course, her mother knew what was best when it came to choosing a husband. Only a doctor, a dentist, or an accountant would do. Maybe a lawyer, if he graduated from the right school. Certainly not one of those losers who got his degree at Brooklyn College and wound up as an ambulance chaser in some rotten neighborhood.

Diane never missed an opportunity to "fix her daughter up" with marriage candidates who were the sons, nephews, or family friends of women she knew from her apartment building, the supermarket, the hairdresser, or anywhere else she spent her time. Suzie avoided these blind dates whenever she could, but every once in a while, she got caught in her mother's trap. Then she'd be forced to spend a miserable evening until she came up with a polite excuse to end the torture.

Suzie had fantasized many times of throwing her mother off a bridge or pushing her in front of an oncoming subway train. But, truth be told, she just couldn't do that to the woman who had given her life. Had Suzie possessed more backbone, she'd sever her relationship with her mother. Certainly, there were career opportunities in other places—California, New England, the Midwest, or Alaska—maybe even Hawaii, but damn it, Suzie was a New Yorker. She needed another way to silence the wicked witch.

Suzie finally dragged herself out of bed and went into the kitchen to make coffee. She always thought more clearly with caffeine coursing through her veins. It was time to send her mother a message she couldn't ignore. Get out of my life!

Almost an hour passed before Suzie realized that she was still sitting in the kitchen staring off into space. As she was well aware, her mother could not abide human weakness. When it came to choosing a suitor for her daughter, Diane would eliminate any possibilities demonstrating any type of perceived shortcoming. The kernel of an idea was forming in Suzie's head, but one detail eluded her. Something to do with her dinner with Harold. Something he said. What the hell was it?

Suzie closed her eyes and thought back to that evening. They'd been seated in a midtown Chinese restaurant. While sipping their drinks, Harold had regaled her with stories about his adventures as an IRS tax auditor. He derived a great deal of satisfaction catching poor terrified low earners in tax return errors. As if a few extra bucks squeezed out of a struggling family would make a difference to the country's economy. Suzy could barely contain her revulsion and boredom.

When the waiter came over to take their orders, Suzy asked for a chicken chow mein combination plate, and Harold requested an order of spare ribs and beef with mixed vegetables. As the waiter turned away, Harold asked that the chef not put any mushrooms in the dish. "They really don't agree with me," he said.

That was it! That's what Suzie was trying to remember. The piece of information that would allow Suzie to send Harold on his way and send her mother a message she couldn't ignore.

Suzie rummaged through her pantry and found a can of sliced mushrooms. She removed the casserole dish of chestnut stuffing that she'd prepared the night before. After cutting the mushroom slices into tiny pieces, she added them to the stuffing. She smiled when she thought of her friend Nancy, who broke out in red, lumpy hives whenever she ate overcooked shrimp. And Eddie, from down the hall, who went dashing for the restroom whenever he inadvertently ingested milk products. It wasn't funny, of course, but nothing that couldn't be rectified in short order.

She wanted to see Harold's reaction to the stuffing. Hopefully, it would be just uncomfortable enough to encourage him to excuse himself and leave her parents' apartment. And then good-bye, Harold. Her mother would be appalled to think of her daughter with a man who suffered from a condition as loathsome as allergies. And, to top it off, Suzie would let Diane know unequivocally that she would never darken their doorstep again if she was ever forced to endure another minute with one more of her mother's flawed choices of suitable husband material.

The car service delivered Suzie to her parents' apartment building in Queens at three thirty. She instructed the driver to pick her up at eight. She didn't want to stay a moment longer than she had to, but it would have been unwise to leave before helping clean up after dinner. That would just give her mother more to complain about.

"There you are. I expected you here at three."

"And Happy Thanksgiving to you, too, Mother. Had I considered that traffic would be so heavy, I'd have left earlier."

"Well, as my Uncle Max used to say, 'common sense is not so common.' And that certainly is true in your case, Suzanne."

"Mother, you certainly are a joy." Suzie was ready to turn around and march out the door.

"Stop being so touchy and go inside and say hello," Mrs. Robbins ordered.

Suzie gritted her teeth, put a smile on her face, and went down the hall to the living room, glad for the moment of being out of her mother's sight.

"Hello, Daddy, Happy Thanksgiving. Hello, Harold." She walked over to her father and planted a big kiss on his cheek.

"Suzie, dear, Harold has been sharing stories about his fascinating experiences as an IRS auditor. It's so comforting to know that our government has such dedicated people ensuring that no error in tax computation goes unpunished. After all, every nickel counts."

Suzie stifled a guffaw at her father's sarcasm, which seemed to elude Harold, judging from his self-satisfied expression. Looking at this nondescript man, she just couldn't fathom her mother's motivation for trying so hard to bring them together. It wasn't that he was physically grotesque or evil; he was just so painfully boring and limited. She'd rather remain unattached for her entire life than ever have to settle for a guy like him.

"Well, if you'll excuse me, I'll go help Mom in the kitchen. I'm so looking forward to a leisurely Thanksgiving dinner." Yeah, right, leisurely Thanksgiving torture.

At five, they gathered around the food-laden dining room table. The mouthwatering smells of roast turkey and all the accompaniments made Suzie's stomach rumble in anticipation. Her mother insisted that Suzie and Harold sit opposite each other, so that it was virtually impossible for her to avoid looking at him.

As her father carved the turkey at the head of the table, her mother, at its foot, passed around dishes of sweet potato pie, stuffing, home baked rolls, string bean casserole, and cranberry sauce. Her father kept up a constant stream of chatter to lighten the atmosphere.

Harold was so busy stuffing his face with food that, blessedly, he couldn't say a word.

"So, Suzie, when do you leave for Europe?"

"I'll be leaving on December fifteenth, spending time in London, Rome, and Paris. My client is a couture design house that wants our agency to familiarize itself with European fashion trends before we implement its multi-million dollar advertising campaign."

"It sounds like a good opportunity for you. Will you have time to sightsee while you're over there?" Suzie's father had a strong interest in European history and was well read on a number of related subjects.

"Definitely, Daddy. Any particular books you'd like me to keep an eye out for?"

"Your father doesn't need any more books, if you please. I feel like I'm living in the middle of a public library. And, to tell you the truth, I think it's very inconsiderate of you to go on a trip during the holidays. Your place is with your family."

"I'm sure you'll do fine without me, Mom. And since when do I need to be here for the holidays?"

"Well, you know your father and I…"

A horrific sound emanated from Harold. Suzie shifted her gaze to him just as he grabbed his throat. His faced turned a bright red and his eyeballs bulged until Suzie thought they were going to pop out of their sockets. His mouth opened in a silent scream, and he seemed to have lost the capability to draw breath. He tried to rise from the table, but as his chair overturned, Harold dropped to the floor, writhing.

Suzie and her parents stared in shocked silence and, then, as if in unison, began screaming.

"Oh, shit, he's choking on a piece of food," Suzie yelled and quickly leapt up to run around the table to administer the Heimlich maneuver, something she'd learned in a college first aid class and never thought she'd have to use. She could barely raise Harold's upper body from the floor or wrap her arms around his portly middle. One, two, three, pull. One, two, three, pull. But no chunk of lodged turkey shot out of his mouth.

"Call an ambulance. Now!" she yelled, as she let Harold's head drop to the carpet. As disgusting as the prospect seemed, she proceeded to administer CPR. It just wouldn't be right to let him die in her parents' dining room. She wasn't that cold. She tilted up his chin and took a deep breath. Okay. Puff, puff, puff. Then she put the heel of her hands below his breastbone. Push. Push. Push. Again. Nothing!

Luckily, paramedics arrived in record time and relieved Suzie of her attempts to force air into Harold's lungs. They quickly smacked an oxygen mask onto his now purple and swollen face and gave him several injections of who knew what, all the while in contact with the hospital's triage physician via radio. When they'd transferred him to a stretcher, they wasted no time in rushing him to the waiting ambulance. Suzie was given the okay to ride up front next to the driver while Harold received emergency care behind her.

Suzie's heart was pounding so violently that she was sure the medics could hear its loud thumping. She was drenched in sweat, even though she prided herself on maintaining her cool in most circumstances. Except, of course, in any interactions with her mother. If Harold kicked the bucket because of the damn mushrooms she put in the stuffing, then she'd be a murderer, a felon, a capital offender who would spend her life in the Big House, possibly wasting away on Death Row. She wondered if her mother could be charged as an accomplice. After all, if she would only have left Suzie alone and not hounded her to the point of desperation, none of this would have happened. Mitigating circumstances. Wasn't that what it was called?

Even in her current state, Suzie had the presence of mind to pull out her cell phone and call her car service. She told them that her plans had changed, and she would call them later in the evening with instructions about where and when to pick her up.

Yeah, right, she thought, *if I'm not getting a ride to jail in a police cruiser.*

The next few hours were the longest of her life, that is, except for the time she spent with her mother and the date she'd had with Harold. She turned off her phone after the twelfth call from Diane, who blamed Harold for collapsing in her dining room and ruining Thanksgiving dinner.

Finally, a doctor came into the waiting room and called Suzie's name. On wobbly legs, she walked over to him to hear what she assumed would be the news of Harold's demise.

"Ms. Robbins, I'm Dr. Fitzhugh. I was told that you accompanied Harold Kline here in the ambulance."

"Yes, yes, that's correct, Doctor. Harold was celebrating Thanksgiving at my parent's house when he collapsed."

"Well, I'm pleased to tell you that he's out of danger now, but he did have a very close call. You see, he suffered from an episode of anaphylactic shock, which is a severe reaction to an allergen. For instance, you often hear of people who react to bee stings in a dramatic way unless they're quickly injected with epinephrine."

There it was. Instead of just breaking out in hives, that damned Harold had to nearly die because of a few mushrooms in the stuffing.

The doctor continued. "Obviously, he didn't take his condition terribly seriously, or he would have worn a medical alert bracelet or carried an epi pen with him in the event of an allergic crisis."

That idiot, Suzie thought. *How dare he be so stupid?*

"An epi pen? You know, my parents would have put Harold's coat in the bedroom of their apartment when he arrived. Might he have had an epi pen in it? And, by the way, what exactly is that?"

"Oh, I'm sorry, Ms. Robbins. Of course, there's no reason for you to know if you don't suffer from this kind of problem. An epi pen is an emergency injectable containing a dose of epinephrine to be used at the first sign of a severe reaction."

"I see." Suzie said. "Do you know exactly what Harold is so allergic to? There were no bees flying around the apartment at the end of November."

"We were able to ask Mr. Kline when he finally regained consciousness. He told us that he's severely allergic to mushrooms, which happens to be a common allergen."

So I really did almost kill him, Suzie thought. *I guess the good Lord was watching over me tonight. And, watching over Harold, too, I guess. Score one for the Greater Power.*

"Wow," Suzie murmured. "I've heard of people breaking out in hives from eating something they were allergic to, but not almost dying."

"It's only a matter of degree, Ms. Robbins. Now, I must get back to my patients. It's been a busy night."

"Thank you so much for your help, Doctor. Can I see Harold now?"

"I'm sorry, Ms. Robbins. Mr. Kline was so traumatized by this event that he expressed the fear that if he ever saw you or your family again, he would be reminded that he almost lost his life while having dinner with you."

Ha! Part of the mission accomplished. No more Harold!

"Well, I can understand that. Would you wish him the very best from our family? We're so sorry that this terrible accident happened."

As the doctor walked away, Suzie sat down, pulled out her phone, and dialed the car service. She asked to be picked up within the hour and taken back to the city. Talk about bad hair days! She hoped she never had another one as dramatic as this. At the very least, it ended well. Harold was now a thing of the past, at least figuratively, and she wouldn't be spending the rest of her life living in a cell.

But now, she had to deal with her mother. She picked up her phone once again and waited for Diane's irritating voice to come on the line.

"Suzanne, we've been waiting in a panic. Why didn't you answer your phone when you knew it was your mother calling?"

That was the main reason not to answer the phone, Suzie thought.

"Mom, I wanted to call you as soon as I had something to report." She went on to explain all that the doctor had told her. She ended by conveying Harold's sentiments about ending contact with her family.

"Well, of all the nerve," her mother snapped. "As if I'd ever want him back in this house! Why, wasn't he a sight, gasping and gurgling all over my dining room floor! And how were you supposed to know he was allergic to damn mushrooms? Were you supposed to be a mind reader? And, by the way, I do have to say that the stuffing was delicious."

Suzie was stunned, not by her mother's caustic words about Harold, but that she had actually complimented her. Talk about once-in-a-lifetime experiences. Tonight had been filled with them.

"Now listen to me, Mom," Suzie pleaded. "Please, do not play matchmaker again. I'm perfectly capable of forming my own relationships. I beg you to let me make my own choices."

"Nonsense! I'm your mother and only I know what's best for you. Even if I was caught by surprise by that Harold's stupidity. By the way, Martha Atkins, the retired teacher in my Zumba class, has a nephew, a doctor, who just moved to New York from Oregon…."

SECOND LIFE
Karin L. Frank

Mrs. Peterson parked the car in front of the beauty salon, shoved a few quarters in the meter, and thrust the door open. Raucous music blared from the radios of cars passing in the street. Mrs. Peterson closed the door to the salon hurriedly, cutting off the irritating sounds. "I know I'm late," she said and threw her hat and purse into a chair.

"I can still squeeze you in," Nancy, the beautician who had been doing her hair for several years, said. "It's no problem."

"That's wonderful," Mrs. Peterson said. "That'll make it the first thing today that hasn't been."

She climbed into the chair and proceeded to tell Nancy all the incidents that had gone wrong with her morning.

Nancy listened, said nothing, and did her usual best not to get soap or water into Mrs. Peterson's eyes or mouth. "You want the usual rinse, Mrs. P.?" she asked at the critical moment.

"Of course, why wouldn't I?" Mrs. Peterson allowed just a hint of sarcasm to edge her voice. After all, she was the customer.

"Just checking," Nancy said. She allowed just a hint of stoic restraint to flatten her voice. After all, she was the reliable professional.

"Naturally, dear."

Neither of them paid any attention to the labels on the bottles on the counter.

Mrs. Peterson was just succumbing to the soothing balm of hands washing and rinsing her hair when Nancy, shrieked, "OMG, OMG, OMG, Mrs. P, you're purple."

Heretofore as unfailingly polite and unflappable as Mrs. Peterson herself, Nancy now seemed bent on cramming the knuckles of one hand down her own throat. In the other hand she clutched the just-removed towel to her chest. "I must have picked up the wrong bottle of coloring rinse."

Mrs. Peterson stared into the mirror. She had expected the usual faint sheen of blue that made her gray hair sparkle as though it was silver. Instead, her hair blazed out from the mirror in scintillating shades of purple.

Dismay and anger burbled up into her mouth, the yin and yang of a case of heartburn. She opened her lips to scold, to berate Nancy for adding to the stack of irritants that had spoiled her day.

And giggles erupted.

She covered her mouth with a manicured hand, but bursts of laughter escaped, scurrying away from her.

"That's a most unusual color," she said when she thought she could form a sentence that wouldn't break up into skittering mice.

Mrs. Peterson thought of herself as a pillar of society. She didn't hesitate to tell everyone that she had a staid personality. She had gotten an education, she said, but thankfully in a totally innocuous subject, English Literature. She had married William Smithson, right out of the dental college, and raised two children, Bill Jr. and Katie. The boy was now a high school English teacher, soon to be promoted to principal. The girl had chosen medicine. She was now a family practitioner.

But that color...Mrs. Peterson has seen it in the pages of a gardening magazine once. It shone from the blossoms of a French hybrid lilac. She had desired an entire row of them to adorn her front lawn. But the bushes had been priced at over one hundred dollars each. Her husband's practice had not been flourishing yet. The children had been small and their care expensive. The house was not yet stocked with all the items of furniture and cutlery that a house needed. She had refrained.

Over the years, she had forgotten.

Now that color glowed out of the mirror, incandescent, exuberant, regal. A blush of well-being suffused her heart.

She smiled.

One of the younger beauticians wandered over. "It does look nice on you, Mrs. P.," she offered. Her short bob, displaying a rainbow of neon colors, stood out from her scalp like the quills on an aroused porcupine.

"It's a different me," Mrs. Peterson said. She stared at the woman in the mirror and lifted one hand as though to introduce herself. She couldn't complete the gesture. The hand dropped to her lap.

"You've become your own avatar," the spiky-headed beautician whispered in her ear.

"Avatar?" she mused. A thin *crema* of pleasure formed on the surface of the warmth flowing outward through her arteries. She knew it would spill over as more giggles if she let it.

The youngster kept babbling on about the Internet and how an avatar was a personality one could adopt for a virtual reality.

Virtual reality, my ass, Mrs. Peterson thought. *I'm not gonna waste this on any reality but the old meat and potatoes one.*

She was instantly gladdened by the realization that she hadn't said anything out loud. And startled by the unfamiliar diction of her phrases.

I never even think words like that, she thought. *Does the hair color have some magical property? Can I really be another "me"?*

"If you like the color I can leave it, Mrs. P."

Mrs. Peterson thought about it.

She stood.

Mrs. Schmidt, the owner had come over. "I'll make you a cup of cappuccino," she said. She stared at Mrs. Peterson's hair. The fingers of her right hand plucked at the buttons on her blouse. "You just relax in one of the nice padded chairs by the window." She bowed Mrs. Peterson away from the mirror and toward views of sidewalks and parking lot. "Decide what you want to do."

Mrs. Peterson let herself be ushered away. She accepted the cup of steaming milk and roasted coffee. She leaned back in the overstuffed chair. Nancy and the quill-crowned one hovered. Mrs. Schmidt watched from behind the main counter.

This is how queens are treated, Mrs. Peterson thought. *She had never been treated like a queen.*

Images flooded her mind.

She saw the young people at college to whom she'd never dared to speak. They had been the different ones, the ones who dressed unconventionally and babbled among themselves about wild and unfamiliar subjects. They had fascinated her, but she had remained aloof.

She saw places she had never visited. Her family had sent her on the Grand Tour for a graduation present. But she had wanted to experience Africa, Asia, or South America. Sometimes she still watched the Travel Channel alone in the house after Bill had gone to bed.

"What is that color anyway?" she called out to Nancy.

"It's Passionate Purple, Mrs. P.," Mrs. Schmidt replied. "It's very popular with the younger dating crowd."

"She means with the hotties, Mrs. P.," the rainbow-hued porcupine explained. "Ladies who are out to snag young hunks use it a lot."

"Do they?" Hotties and hunks, eh? Such titillating epithets.

"Such imaginative names the cosmetics companies paste on their products," she told Mrs. Schmidt.

Mrs. Schmidt's upper lip twitched into a smile and then subsided. "It helps to sell them."

Mrs. Peterson finished her cappuccino.

She returned to the hair styling chair and permitted Nancy to snip and comb and fluff. "Mark that bottle of hair rinse with my name," she said. "I don't want any more surprises next month."

Nancy smiled. "Absolutely, Mrs. P." She wrote Peterson in big caps with a magic marker across the label of the bottle.

The porcupine grinned.

Mrs. Schmidt sighed and rang up the bill. The cash register tinkled a snappy tune.

As the door to the beauty parlor closed behind her, Mrs. Peterson spied a sign across the street. Ballroom Dance Class and Salsa Club, it read. And beneath that, Learn All The New Latin Dances.

She had never noticed that sign before.

"Hum," she mused. Salsa. Rumba. Tango even. Dancing might be fun.

She crossed the street and approached the storefront dance studio. As she opened the door, the music burst out at her. She stepped into it as though she was stepping into her morning spray of perfume. It settled on her clothes like the scent of lilac that she wore.

Scintillating, she thought. *Like the new color of my hair.*

"Would you like to try a free lesson?" a young woman asked. She stepped out from behind the counter, all grace and long legs.

"Yes. Yes, I would."

"Here's John. He teaches our introductory lesson," the young woman said. "Will he do?"

John approached. He was also all grace and long legs.

"He will do very well," Mrs. Peterson agreed.

"We'll go into the small studio," John said in a melodious voice. "We can hear only our own music in there."

Our own music, she thought.

He took her hand and led her into a small empty room with a very large window. The hardwood floor gleamed. He flipped a wall switch and music flooded the room.

"Shall we try the rumba? Rumba's always a good place to start."

Mrs. Peterson nodded assent. She let him clasp her around the waist.

"It's a lovely day," John said, making conversation as he swept her out into the middle of the room.

"You don't know the half of it," Mrs. Peterson said.

"And I really like your hair. What is that color?"

"Lilacs in spring. French ones." She gave her senses over to the music and let her giggles envelop them.

"*Ooh la la,*" John said.

MAKING NEW TRACKS
Linda O'Connell

"It's Halloween, and I've always felt like I've been hiding behind a mask," Trish said. She and Rosie, next-door neighbors and best friends, sat at Rosie's kitchen table nursing coffee and their bruised egos. They were both in the midst of ending their turbulent, long-term marriages and ditching their cheating husbands.

Before Rosie had married and settled down to live under the king's twenty-year control, she'd had a colorful past and sexual history. Trish had been, and still was a bed-dud; she lived vicariously through Rosie's storied past. Rosie had been a free spirit, an actual Go-Go dancer when she was single. Back then, if a whim hit her, she'd go with it. Trish could tell Rosie was ready to go again, on the verge of a whim.

"Time for a complete overhaul. We can be anyone or anything we want to be. I want a new look, and I can't afford the salon treatment. If you'll frost my hair, I'll give you a home perm," Rosie chirped. "I want blonde highlights and you've always wanted curls. Let's do it—a new look."

They laughed at the sight of one another. Trish had a hundred perm rods dangling, and Rosie looked like a porcupine wearing a rubber cap. When it was all over, they were both overdone. Rosie had a crown of granny-white hair instead of frosted blonde layers, and Trish's hair was a bonnet of ringlets.

"At least my ears don't poke out anymore and make me look like a wing nut," Trish said when she looked at her giant pouf.

"Don't worry, it'll relax in a few days, and girlfriend, we need to start relaxing a little, too." Rosie finger-combed her hair and tried to blend the contrasting colors. "It's okay. It's time for a change. People change, you know?"

How well Trish knew. Jack had moved on before he'd moved out, and he was still making her life miserable delaying court dates and dallying. She was exhausted from living in limbo. She had a part time job, limited skills, and no sheepskin. She still had her figure, but she didn't believe the women's magazine articles stating that she was supposed to be in her prime. Sounded like as much bunk as, "Your high school days are the best days of your life." In high school, when most girls were testing limits, makeup, and fashions, Trish was a plain Jane conservative dresser who hung on the periphery and never quite fit in with any group. While others were dating around, she was hitched to her jealous steady boyfriend via his initial ring on her third finger. Not much had changed.

"Rosie, do you know that my hair has been the same lifeless drab for years? In school, I'd poke pink plastic picks in brush rollers and sleep on them, but in the morning my hair would bush out like an overgrown yew. Then an hour later my hairdo would wither and fall flat. Couldn't make up its mind, just like me. I've hated my straight hair as much as I've despised my straight-laced life. I'm glad I did this."

Still officially hitched to the kid she'd married at eighteen, Trish felt like she had grown up and Jack had only grown older. She had always been reliable; everyone depended on her stability. Now, she had no one to depend on but herself, and she felt a multitude of emotions. Change was coming her direction like a wisp of wood smoke on the evening breeze. Autumn had crept up on her like the crow's-feet around her eyes. Winter's wrath trailed close behind. She'd always been a nervous Nellie.

Trish answered the phone at 7:30 p.m. "Did you get rid of your candy yet? Listen, dump it all in the next kid's treat bag." Rosie cackled her signature rat-a-tat laugh. "Turn off your porch light and throw on your one-piece, silk, leopard-print lounging suit, and I'll wear mine. My brother's bartending tonight, and he invited us to drop by in costume. He also has a band tonight. I say it's about time we did our own trick-or-treating again. What do you say?"

"Oh, wow! I still have that picture of us dressed like Miss Piggy and Kermit the Frog when we went out that Halloween with the kids. We got more candy than they did that year."

"Yeah, that was then and this is now. Don't you think it's our turn to have a little fun?" Their teenage kids, like their fathers, were out doing their own thing.

"Oh, why not?" Trish was ready to break her self-imposed rules.

It had been years since Rosie had been in a bar, and Trish had never been. She had an occasional wine cooler at home, but she lectured her son and daughter endlessly about booze. Her heart pounded at the thought of stepping out…out of her role as housewife and mother. Tonight she was slipping out of her goody two shoes and tripping into the unknown.

She grabbed her mascara and eyeliner, blackened her nose, and drew cat whiskers on her cheeks. Then she painted her lips fire-engine red. She zipped her leopard-print lounging pajamas up to her chin. Rosie rang the doorbell. Trish clomped to the door wearing her daughter's oversized fuzzy house slippers with fake claws. Immediately her eyes were drawn to her friend's plunging neckline and excessive cleavage. Rosie twirled around on her spike heels and shocked Trish when she grabbed a black tail, fashioned from a leg of pantyhose, swung it and purred. Trish gaped at Rosie's streetwalker makeup and outfit.

"I can't do this! I look like a goofy stuffed animal compared to you."

"Yes, you can. You look fine. Let's go have a little fun like our soon-to-be ex-husbands who, you can bet, are out doing worse than this."

Trish spewed a few "what ifs" and Rosie countered each one. They were a sight to behold as they trotted to the car. The meowing and howling catcalls started as soon they entered the little neighborhood bar. Rosie was back in her comfort zone, reliving her youth, her brother supervising. They sat on high barstools against a mirrored wall. Trish was wound as tight as the ends of her curly hair.

The place was crammed with revelers, standing room only. When a slow song came on, Trish weaved her way to the bathroom, and Rosie headed to the dance floor. Trish returned and observed two middle-age guys standing in front of her. She watched as they scouted for some action. The last thing she wanted was another man in her life, and she made certain that her body language indicated as much.

Trish had never liked drawing attention to herself, and she felt stupid dressed in her dumb costume. Engrossed in a song, she sat back. As she crossed her right leg over her left, she nudged the guy standing directly in front of her. She clasped her hand over her mouth when her furry house slipper stuck to the seat of his pants like a piece of felt to a flannel board. She yanked her foot back using both hands. Her face blazed red, and she shouted an apology just as the music stopped.

"Bob's my name, what's yours? By the way, I like your way of introduction and your costume." He winked and extended his hand. Trish wanted to slink out the door.

"Umm, my name is Trish. I am so sorry. That was a complete accident, I assure you."

His buddy, who must have been his brother, said, "His name isn't Bob; it's really Ed. It's Edward. We call him Eddie."

Gee, Trish thought, *why didn't I think to use an alias?*

Bob-Ed-Eddie elbowed his buddy, "Shut up!" He looked back at Trish and said, "My name is Robert Edward."

"Then why do I call you Ed, Eddie?" His partner punched him in the arm.

The band struck up another song. Eddie-Bob leaned in and asked Trish to dance. She smiled politely and shook her head, no. He persisted.

"Despite that shoe trick, you look like a nice lady. You have natural curls? What's that unique perfume you're wearing?"

Trish was ready to kick him again, hard, if he sniffed her neck. He didn't have a clue as to how to approach a woman, and Trish didn't have the heart to tell him the truth. She wanted to say, "I *am* a nice, still-married lady. My unique scent is home-perm solution, and unlike my friend, the sex kitten over there, this wild-haired cat is not on the prowl."

Getting Rosie out of the bar was like trying to brush tangles out of teased hair. All she wanted to do was dance-dance-dance. That night the women celebrated, not just the end of their respective marriages, but the beginning of their own empowerment.

"I was afraid to go out tonight. Rosie, I've been afraid my whole life—afraid I wasn't a good enough mom, always afraid Jack would walk out, and tonight I was afraid he would walk in and find me out.

But you know what? It did me good to step out of my comfort zone and see how the other half lives, even if half of them were dressed like clowns."

"Or acted like clowns." Rosie rat-a-tat laughed. Trish and Rosie entwined arms as they sashayed to the car. Consoled by their own strength and determination, they convinced themselves of their capabilities.

Rosie spoke softly. "Until tonight, I hadn't realized how I've completely lost track of who I am. I love to dance. I haven't danced in years. You hear me? *Years*."

"I know what you mean. I don't think I've ever had the chance to find out who's behind this smiling false face," Trish admitted. "His wife, their mother. Who am I?"

"Hey, that stuffed-animal-look with your curls becomes you," Rosie teased, running her fingers through her own mountaintop of snow-white hair.

"Leopard Lady, it's time we seized the moment and leave those tomcat husbands behind. Make tracks. New tracks," Trish said.

"After tonight, I'd say we're on our way!"

ALICE ON PEABODY STREET
Rosemary Shomaker

"Mary, do you have any meat tenderizer?"

"Well, um, yes," Mary said as sweat dripped from her cheek onto the phone. "It's nine thirty in the morning and eighty-five degrees already, Alice. How can you think of cooking?"

She wiped her drenched face roughly with her glove and saw the hand pruner, trowel, and spade design darken with sweat. She was annoyed by the heat and irritated by Alice's call; they had met at community association activities and a few cookouts, but they were only passing acquaintances. The phone's ringing had startled her, and with uprooted English Ivy vines in both hands, answering the phone had been a chore. She had released the ivy to grab the phone and jammed her hands into her cargo shorts adding yet another rip to the too tight, college-era shorts.

"Are you premeditating some culinary challenge for dinner or something?" Mary asked, and then fumbled the phone, dropped it, and saw it swallowed up by the invasive weeds. As she bent to search for the phone, the clothespin holding her hair flopped against her temple holding only one damp clump; she felt the rest of her loosed ponytail as a slippery hank on the back of her neck. Mary found the phone and brought it absently to her face, thinking how mahogany brown her wet hair looked.

So, perspiration has a gray masking effect on hair, Mary thought. Then, half hoping she had disconnected the call, she said, "Sorry. I dropped the phone."

"The meat tenderizer. Uh...uh...can you bring it over right away?" Alice asked.

Oh, for God's sake. Why was papain so critical to Alice now? Sun-blonde, petite, cheery Alice. Come-join-me-in-my-fairytale Alice. She expected everyone to drop his or her business and skip along the yellow brick road with her.

"Mary, I really need it," Alice said in a thready voice.

Wait, Mary thought. *This does not sound like the normally upbeat Alice.* The wavering frailty in Alice's voice registered, and Mary made the non-cookery connection. "Did you get stung by a bee? Where are you, Alice?"

"Wasps I think, or yellow-jackets," Alice sighed. "I'm at home."

"Are you inside? Are you allergic to wasps? Shall I call the rescue squad? Can you get to a neighbor's house?" Mary's rapid-fire questioning kept pace with the clomping of her red gardening shoes as she dashed across her deck, through the back door, and into the kitchen.

"No, I'm not allergic. I think the tenderizer will do the trick. And Benadryl." Then Alice added weakly, "Can you come over now? My neighbors are all elderly; I didn't want to bother them, but I knew you'd be home."

"Sit down and drink some water; I'll be right there. Call back if you feel any worse."

Guilt and worry charged Mary. Alice really did have a problem, and Mary was sorry that she'd been snippy with Alice and dismissive of her phone call. She turned to see that leaves and other yard detritus had detached to the floor with her every step; some still clung to her knee-high athletic socks. The mess heightened her already anxious mood.

Mary threw open cabinet doors and rifled through her cooking and baking supplies. Ah-hah! Meat tenderizer! She tossed it on the counter. She saw the baking soda. Wasn't that a home remedy for stings? Was it baking soda or baking powder? She dropped both to the counter and swiped it all into a plastic grocery bag. She detached her hair clothespin, hung her head in the sink, and sprayed cold water over her face and head as much to cool as to clean herself. Blotting her head with paper towels, she headed out of the utility room door, reaching for the first aid kit as she left.

An oven-quality rush of heat hit Mary's face and burned through the tears in her shorts as she flung open the car door and sat down. Upon ignition, the car's digital thermometer showed a ninety-three degree interior temperature. Pressing the air conditioning button and maxing the fan achieved no cooling goal. The resulting commercial-strength oven blast, however, did complete her melting process. The blast took her breath away and forced her eyes closed. She felt Bikram hot yoga-like sweat completely wetting her body and the car upholstery. The windshield fogged up, too. The digital panel informed her that the humidity was sixty-seven percent; the time was 9:55 a.m.

She recklessly backed out of the driveway, narrowly missing the Absher's mailbox. Mary knew that her intense perspiration was not accompanied by the usual focused centering of hot yoga class, and that she'd better get hold of herself. Her anxiety, guilt, and regret were mixing into a panic. She'd heard stories of allergic reactions to stings; she knew one mother who carried several EpiPens in case of her child's severe reaction. Why she was so concerned about Alice was a mystery to Mary. She hardly knew Alice. Maybe it was a premonition.

Mary braked in place, opened the windows, took a breath, shut down the AC, and then proceeded toward Alice's side of the neighborhood more calmly. Two blocks down Garrison Street, seven blocks along Bullfinch Lane, and a right on Peabody Street; she'd be there in five minutes.

Her morning English Ivy eradication project would have to wait until she assessed Alice's condition. She didn't think Alice had any insect allergies; Alice had said she wasn't allergic, right? Oh, why had she told Alice to drink water? If she was having an allergic reaction, her throat might tighten up or close!

At 10:07 a.m., Mary burst in to Alice's living room yelling, "Don't drink the water!" Alice gasped, and Mary ran to her, convinced she was convulsing. "Your throat! Can you swallow?"

"Mary! You startled me! What? Oh, yes, I did drink the water; was that wrong?" Alice responded, still wide-eyed. "You look different than you did at the Anderson's cookout last Saturday. What happened to your hair?" She patted the sofa indicating Mary should sit.

Realizing her red clogs, white socks, grungy shorts, and holey T-shirt were definitely not her J. Crew summer socializing self, Mary said, "Ugh. Sorry. I was gardening." She must look horrible and, cringing at her wet underarms, smell unpleasant, too. Mary sat, but not too close to Alice.

Alice, moving closer to Mary, said, "I think the drink of water did me good." Pulling plant debris from Mary's hair, she continued, "I'm sorry I called you, Mary; I can see you were busy. I can probably get old Mrs. Baxter over here to help me now."

Mary looked intently at Alice. Her clothes were straight; her hair was in place. The clock showed 10:12 a.m.; more than thirty minutes had elapsed since Alice called. Maybe she was okay. "I'm already here, and I brought some medicine, so let me see the sting."

"Thanks, Mary. I do feel a bit wrung out," Alice said, and she lay back on the sofa and raised a washcloth to her shoulder.

Mary followed Alice's motion, and her eyes widened at the host of stings on Alice's arm and neck. "Holy cow, Alice! You did get stung!"

"Yeah. I woke up early and decided to work in the yard before it got too hot. I was trying to dig out two small dead azaleas by the fence. A few bees crossed my vision as I jabbed the shovel at the loose roots. I swear I felt six stings at once, Mary, and then I panicked and began doing the jump-run-slap anti-insect dance." Alice seemed grateful to have an attentive sounding board, and Mary needed to hear the details so she could decide what to do next.

"I ran in the screened porch, took off my hat, and smacked away those that flew in with me. I locked myself in the half bath, threw some washcloths in the basin, and ran some cold water.

"The cold cloths felt good on the stings. I thought I was calming down until something flew into the window screen and panicked me again. I had visions of swarms of yellow jackets attacking through the window, so I slammed it down and locked it. I didn't even look to see what had struck the screen.

"When I stood and looked in the mirror, the sight of these welts on my face and neck unhinged me. I must have come in here and sat down because the next thing I remember is talking to you on the phone. Did you bring the tenderizer?"

Well, at least Alice is lucid, thought Mary. Her speech and state of mind were sound. A call to 911 seemed unwarranted.

Alice continued, "I went to the kitchen for a glass of water after we talked, and I sipped about half a glass before I saw seven or eight wasps on the floor—I must have swatted them off when I dashed through the kitchen."

Mary emptied the bag on the coffee table and opened the first aid kit. Alice's pale blonde hair looked perfect as usual, swept back from her face with a mother of pearl barrette behind each ear. Inconsistent to the flawless look, however, was the puffiness of Alice's face. This, and the red swellings on Alice's face, worried Mary.

"No tenderizer. First, swallow these two Benadryl."

Alice swallowed the pills, and then leaned back on the couch pillows. She was wheezing, and her eyes looked unfocused. Mary got a wet washcloth from the bathroom—that floor was another graveyard of yellow jacket bodies—and dabbed the stings she saw on Alice's face, arms, and neck.

"Are you in pain? Can you get your breath?" she asked Alice as she applied hydrocortisone cream to the stings.

Alice did not answer. She just watched Mary attending to her welts.

"Okay, that's it, Alice. We are going to the ER."

Mary had noticed Alice's socks and sneakers in the bathroom, but it wasn't until Alice stood that Mary saw red patches on Alice's legs and feet. Some loose slippers by Alice's front door would have to serve as footwear. Mary helped Alice gather her purse and keys, and they headed out the door. A clock chimed the half hour.

Alice proceeded automatically, almost unconsciously, and this distressed Mary. Before she locked the house, though, Alice did grab a Washington Nationals baseball cap and hand it to Mary. Mary put the cap on Alice's head as they headed down the sidewalk, but Alice stopped her and placed the cap on Mary's head instead.

Mary settled Alice in the passenger seat, partially reclined with the sun visor down and windows opened. The vehicle was again an oven, even from this short time in Alice's driveway. She had to get air moving through the car to "de-bake" it. She cranked the AC and fan on high and left the windows open. She removed the Nationals cap to ventilate her head and to keep it from flying out the window.

At the main entrance to the neighborhood, a funeral procession held them up for three cycles of the traffic light before Mary could turn onto Parkside Street and head toward the hospital. The delay gave Mary the opportunity to check on Alice. She closed the car windows, sealing in the cool air and suppressing the roadway noise.

"Alice, how do you feel now?"

"Not great. Swallowing is difficult."

Mary no longer made Alice talk. She tuned the radio to quiet classical music and, once the procession cleared, sped down Parkside. Alice relaxed somewhat against the reclined seat and breathed more easily for the ten minutes it took to arrive at County General Hospital's emergency room.

Hospital signs led Mary to a lane in front of a massive sliding door with a pergola-like concrete overhang. A white-uniformed young man appeared on her left.

"ER patient?" he asked. At her nod, he raised his hand toward the sliding doors and out came a blue scrub-attired tall man pushing an empty wheelchair. The driver and passenger doors opened simultaneously.

From the right, Mary heard, "Hi. I'm Eric. Can you move into this wheelchair? I'll help you."

Into her left ear, the white-attired man said, "Your keys, ma'am."

Alice was exiting the car and being helped into the wheelchair. Mary sat, unmoving and uncomprehending.

"ER valet, Ma'am. My name is Michael," the man at her side said. "Your car will be safe in the north valet lot until you need it." His smile was reassuring. "This allows you to go into the ER with your, um, sister? Your friend?"

Mary gathered her purse and her wits, and then stepped out of the car handing her keys to Michael. While following Alice and Eric, Mary mused, "ER valet? No wonder medical costs are so high!"

Eric parked Alice at the ER reception desk and left. A woman in soft pink scrubs was asking Alice questions, so Mary moved to hear.

"Bee stings? Trouble swallowing? Breathing?"

"Yellow-jackets," Mary corrected.

Another pastel pink woman went behind the desk, and she and the other pink nurse worriedly conferred. Eric reappeared at the end of the counter and answered some of their questions. They were too far away for Mary to hear.

The first pale pink woman said, "We'd like to get you back into an exam room. Can your friend give us your personal and insurance information?"

Alice, powered by Eric, was already rolling as she handed her purse back to Mary. Mary thought she heard a faint "yes" from Alice, but she'd been swept away so fast that Mary was unsure.

Mary stood at the reception counter rifling through Alice's wallet for an insurance card and answering name and address questions. She scanned the waiting area and saw several tired looking men and women and two children staring at the ER television. Either Alice had managed to one-up them in the ER triage sequence, or they had family or friends already in the ER treatment rooms.

The wall clock read 11:30 a.m., and the questions about Alice had ended. Mary was again unsure of procedure. Should she wait in this dreary area? Go farther into the ER to find Alice?

Pink woman said, "Go on back to find your friend. First door on the left."

Standing in this doorway, Mary saw stainless steel counters in the middle of a large brightly lit room. Curtained cubicles populated the room's perimeter. Scrub wearing and lab-coated people zigzagged among the counters, cubicles, a far set of double doors, and the very doorway in which she stood.

A purple-clad lady urgently approached Mary. "Are you hurt, dear?"

Mary looked at her dumbfounded. The woman led her to a chair, and as Mary lowered herself, she saw her reflection in a glass panel. Her hair was askew in the mini coils of an air-dried old perm. Her shirt was sweat-stained and torn. She was still wearing the outfit from this morning when she was pulling weeds. The baseball cap was in the car.

"I'm looking for my friend," Mary said,

The nurse pointed to the scratches and dirt on Mary's legs and arms and grabbed some Betadine and gauze.

"No, no, really. I was just gardening. I'm here with my friend, the bee sting lady."

Shaking her head, the woman pointed to a nearby cubicle. Mary could see the person in the bed. It was an oxygen-masked Alice; eyes closed, an intravenous line in her arm.

"Alice?" she asked in a quiet voice. At no response, Mary gasped, "Oh, God!" and rushed to her side. "Are you okay? Why the IV?"

"They inserted that as soon as my fanny hit the bed. They've taken my vitals and said that Dr. Carter will be with me soon." She grasped Mary's hand.

They sat silently holding hands for several minutes, waiting for Dr. Carter.

Alice, eyes closed, roused herself to say, "You caused quite a stir out there. I guess you look more like an emergency room patient than I do." She then opened her eyes and grinned. "There's a brush in my purse. Could you please brush your hair?"

Mary found the brush and stepped into a bathroom she had seen on the solid wall two cubicles away. Three minutes later, she was back, refreshed, cleaner, and more kempt. She'd even managed to tidy up her torn shorts and ratty shirt. Both Mary and Alice looked up at the sound of a strong, calm voice.

"Ms. Satterwhite, I'm Dr. Carter. Good news. Your body is responding properly."

"Oh, thank goodness. Dr. Carter," Alice said, and then added, "this is my friend Mary."

"Pleased to meet you," he responded automatically with a nod to Mary, and then continued, "Ms. Satterwhite, you are not having an allergic response. Your body is producing histamines to attack the sting sites. Your weakness is because of the rush of energy to your wounds and away from regular body functions. The IV is for hydration, and we will dose you with antihistamine and ibuprofen. I'll check on you in forty minutes, and if all is well, you may then go home."

Alice signed seven documents and was officially "released" soon after one o'clock. Eric wheeled her out the huge sliding doors while Mary dug through her purse for her car keys.

"Your coach awaits, ladies," Eric said as Michael swung the car under the portico.

Mary laughed when she saw her keys dangling from Michael's hands; only then after the flurry of the day's activities, did Mary remember the hospital valet service.

Michael and Eric seated Mary and Alice neatly in the already air conditioned car, and with good-byes all around, Mary drove away from the emergency room.

"I can't thank you enough, Mary," Alice said. "I'm so relieved to be feeling better, and who knows what would have happened to me if you hadn't come to help."

"I'm glad all that is over, Alice. You'll have to destroy the yellow jacket nest tonight, you know."

"No way, Mary. Tomorrow I'll spray the hive. When I get home I'm having a big glass of wine and staying inside the rest of the day."

"No, you are not. The doctor said to avoid alcohol. Your body is flooded with antihistamines and painkillers. Besides, you've got to poison the nest while the yellow jackets are dormant at night. They live in a ground nest, not in a tree hive like bees or under the eaves like wasps."

"How do you know this stuff, Mary?"

"I guess the same way you know how to be pleasant and get people to help you. It's my nature. Tell you what, when I drop you off, you stand on your screened porch and direct me, and I'll mark the place in the yard where you were attacked. I can come by at dusk with some Malathion and destroy the nest for you.

"But first I want to go home and yank out some more ivy; I can't waste this lovely getup!" Mary laughed and looked down at the beleaguered appearance that had alarmed an emergency room nurse.

"It's a deal, Mary. If you clean up before you come over and appear like the Mary I remember from the Anderson's cookout last month and not like a wild dreadlocked woman in apocalyptic clothes, I'll even buy you dinner at Charlie's Café." Hesitantly, yet smiling, Alice continued, "You know, Charlie's is right next to Southern States. They are open until seven. Would you help me pick out a few bushes to replace the dead ones I've begun to dig out?"

Mary smiled, too, knowing that tomorrow she'd be planting those bushes for Alice.

Thus the seeds of friendship are sown and grown. An emergency room visit and a bad hair day are examples of shared experiences that can become the basis for the supportive companionship integral to weathering the trials, travails, and ordinary errands of life.

THE MAGGOT WRANGLER
Steven Clark

Cammie's green eyes sharpened as she crouched, seeing Trudy creep up to the dark form in the brush.

"Ollie," her voice trembled, "is it you? It's been weeks. Ollie? It's me. Trudy."

Cammie readied her container.

Trudy bent down. "Ollie, I love you."

Flemming was behind the main camera, and he pointed to Cammie—*maggot wrangler.*

Cammie hurried to the body while the camera was on Trudy. She opened the container, and shook it. Maggots sprinkled out like sick oregano over the dummy's face; makeup did a great job of turning it into a putrified corpse. The maggots squirmed into the eye sockets and mouth like it was a convention and the gaping orifices the bar. Cammie had been saving these little buggers up. Cammie crouched back out of camera view. Flemming motioned for the handcam, and Turk moved in, catching the maggots on his close-up lens. There would be several cuts. Cammie knew Flemming was a quick-cut man.

Flemming's finger aimed at Trudy. She looked down at the corpse. Her eyes popped and she screamed. Screamed again. Hands to her ears. Another scream, and she fell down, ranting and rushing down the scrubby hill.

"Cut!"

The set came to life. Trudy stopped and looked up, waiting for makeup to dust her off.

Flemming looked at Turk, whose jowls spread in a wide smile. "Print."

Cables, cases, mikes, and all the flotsam of showbiz were packed up and loaded. "Okay," Flemming shouted, "scene fifty-eight. Let's move, people."

The scene was a mile away, and Cammie went to collect the maggots. Turk called her.

"Hey, I got the number for you."

"Great. You're sure?"

"Yeah, man. It's a green light. *Evil Maggots.* They start shooting in three weeks, and I glanced at the script. It's like *Gone With the Wind* for maggots. They even get to talk."

"Cool," said Cammie. When you are a maggot wrangler, you have to network like everyone else.

"And get this," Turk grinned, "it's big budget. They're shooting two weeks in Brazil."

Cammie's oval face beamed. "I could do with a few days in Rio."

Trudy walked up, smoking a cigarette.

"How do you work with those damned things?"

Cammie shrugged and slouched like a vet. "It's what I do."

She'd done a lot, and it took two years just to break into the studio. In her badass tank, wrinkled OD shirt, skimpy khaki shorts, and hiker boots, she looked like a maggot wrangler. Like she was on call from a gig in the jungle. The bustle on the set was frantic, since they had to wrap in three days or go over budget. That meant a visit from the suits, and nobody wanted that.

Cammie stuffed the number in her pocket and turned to collect the maggots. Then her face twisted in horror. One of the techies rushing to the next set cut his ATV too close to the dummy and ran over it.

"Hey!" Cammie screamed and went to the dummy. Dottie, the long-faced girl from Capetown who did makeup, was by her side.

"Bollocks!"

"My maggots!" cried Cammie. "My maggots!" like Cathy cried out "Heathcliff" in *Wuthering Heights*. Cammie fell to her knees. They were all squished. She screamed, really better than Trudy did in the last scene. Dottie, who should have screamed as well, picked up the dummy, shook it, and nodded.

"Wash the buggers off, and it'll be right as rain."

Turk loaded up his handcam. "Ran over it?"

"Looks cool," Dottie said, "needs that smashed-in look."

Dottie and Turk hurried off, leaving Cammie with her tragedy. There weren't any maggots left, and the next scene was their biggie. They would be Norma Desmond in *Sunset Boulevard*. And Cammie had no maggots. She clutched her empty case and ran off.

Run where?

In search of maggots, that was where.

Cammie reasoned that finding maggots was like having sex. Sex was all over the place, you just had to hook up in the right location at the right time. But to find maggots, she needed wheels, and everyone had bugged over to scene fifty-eight. She shook her head and wiped her brow.

An SOS of horn honking caused her to whip her eyes toward the improvised gate. She squinted, and security waved at her like snow angels minus the snow. A dusty Datsun was on the other side of the barrier. A familiar Datsun, as was its owner. It was Brain, her on-and-off-again boyfriend. He had wheels. They were definitely on again. She ran to the car, one arm waving, the other hand clutching her empty maggot case. "Brain!"

Brain Smith frowned. "Hey! You stood me up."

Cammie tried, but couldn't open the passenger side. It was locked. The door was hot. "When? Where? Come on, let's go."

Brain stared across the top of the hood like it was no-man's-land. "Last week. When I left for my tour. We planned a night out. I waited."

A long sigh from Cammie, only partly made-up. "Poor Brain. I told you I had to make that party. With Karasashian."

"Yeah. Another party."

"Hey, it's networking. He's doing a zombie flick, and I had to pitch my wrangling the maggots. Try getting an agent for that. Open up. We gotta go."

"Are you going to dump me? You said I was dumpable."

Cammie's eyes feigned shock while she wondered if she could wrestle the keys away from Brain. He had height and weight on her. Cancel that. Back to womanly wiles. "I never said that."

"You texted Jasmine. She showed me."

Cammie's thoughts darkened into a class one hurricane stare. *That little snake. And she borrowed my purple ensemble.* Cammie didn't trust just anyone with purple. "She's full of it. Brain, come on. Open up."

He swallowed, expecting the worst. He got dumped like Belgium got invaded. "Cammie, do you love me?"

She pulled the door again and made a fist. "Love you? Brain, I'm nuts about you. I need you so much. I need you *now*! Open the freakin' door."

He sighed. "What do you have to do?"

"I got to find maggots."

Brain's face fell like a falling log. He pushed the lock. The doors clicked open. Cammie popped in. His car interior was in its usual immaculate state, except for binders of music, a bottle of water, and the French horn, encased and filling the backseat like a mother. Brain and his horn had that kind of relationship.

"Where are we going?"

"A place. Down the road. A lab."

"A lab?"

"Animals. Rats. Chickens. I saw it as the crew passed by. They must have maggots."

The car stopped. The traffic jam was long and pointless. This was some podunk on location in the middle of nowhere. Traffic was blocked. *Why?*

"What?" cried Cammie. She jumped out of the car and stared down the road, thrusting her arms out.

Cammie dove back into the car. "Pass 'em."

"But that's illegal. There's a yellow stripe—"

"Brain, I need maggots. Do it!"

He did, just as a semi came at them. Horns blared. He bowled around to the shoulder just as it whizzed past. "Holy…" he gasped. "I could have been… We could have been…"

Cammie stared ahead. "Wrong way. Go straight."

"But you said—"

"I screwed up. This way. Go on. The lab's down there."

Brain pulled off. A man in a rusty pick-up with odorous junk in back pointed a withered finger. "Hey! You made a U-turn! That's agin the law!"

Cammie shouted over Brain. "I'm doing a movie! Stuff it!"

Brain Smith was named for Dennis Brain, the famous English French horn player. In rural North Carolina, his first name wasn't seen as unusual. *Hey there, Brain. Why, there's Brain.*

At the conservatory, they were respectful. Normal life had other ideas.

"People look at me," Brain explained. "Down here?"

"Yeah. I remember when the unit drove past."

"So, everyone always says 'brains.' But it's singular. I always have to point that out. There's nothing here."

"Keep going. We'll see a taco stand. Then the lab." Her eyes stared ahead. She swallowed, her mouth silently making an *O* for *Rio by the sea-o.*

"People think I'm brilliant. The name. The horn. Like Einstein. What do you think?"

"It's around the bend."

"No. My name. 'Brain.' Einstein?"

"Zombies."

"Huh?"

Cammie's voice deepened and she clawed her hands. "*Braaains. Braaaaains.*"

Brain sighed. "You see. It's singular. Do you really love me?"

Cammie took a deep breath when she saw the tattered drive-in and bleached sign: Taco Mucho Macho. Then, the glass shoebox flanked by tidy scrubbed pines and a sprinkler stuttering in front. Palindrome Labs.

The receptionist had one of those eyeglass cords around her neck like librarians wore. More to the point, like Miss Tutweiler back home, who kicked Cammie out of the library for sneaking behind the restricted book stack to read *The Joy of Sex.* A deep stare came from the woman. A Miss Tutweiler stare.

"You're with a motion picture?"

"A movie," Cammie tried to control her impatience, "up the road. I need maggots."

"Are you serious?"

Cammie flashed her pass, the large plastic photo ID that got her drinks in bars and sighs from lots of people. The receptionist only raised an eyebrow, like the goon who carded her in Santa Fe.

"You are doing this in *connection* with a motion picture?"

Cammie glanced at Brain, who glanced back. There was some kind of code here, like the place was a front for something. Cammie heard a chicken cluck behind the thick metal doors. Okay, they had animals. "A movie. Motion picture. Yes, ma'am, and I'm the maggot wrangler. I need maggots. It's being directed by Stu Flemming. Won eight awards. We'll pay any price."

"Excuse me," said the receptionist. Her eyes meant Cammie and Brain were to discreetly turn their backs while the world behind the metal doors was consulted.

"Cammie?"

"Yeah, Brain. What?"

"Do you love maggots? I mean…attached to them in a…weird kind of way."

She sighed and flipped her hair. "Look. You can't love them. They only last three days once they hatch. As far as perversions go, that's not even top drawer."

The receptionist hung up the receiver, then went back to writing on her notepad. Not even a glance. Cammie and Brain approached. "Well?"

"I'm very sorry," the receptionist said, not sorry at all, "it is not our policy to give or rent specimens to the motion picture industry."

"Ma'am, come on. I need maggots. You have maggots, right?"

The receptionist sighed. "We experiment on a variety of species. Our research is vital to—"

"Please. I need maggots." Cammie whipped out her wallet. "Look, here's fifty dollars. We'll pay double. I have to have those maggots, and soon. Can I talk to someone?"

"Good day."

Cammie frowned. "You trying to flip me off?" She went to the doors and banged on them. "Hello! Hey! Open up!"

"Get away from that door!"

Cammie's face flared at the receptionist. "Look. This is important. Just sell me some maggots!"

"Leave."

"Not until I talk to who's running the place. You tell him—"

The receptionist reached in her drawer. Her hand filled with a taser. She slowly advanced.

"You are to leave now. We will not deal with the motion picture industry."

Cammie wanted to jump the receptionist, but Brain grabbed her arm.

"Don't taze me, sister," he said quietly.

The receptionist advanced. Cammie and Brain fled outside. Cammie shook her fist.

"And they're movies, you slug! *Movies!*"

The receptionist marched out, taser aimed. Cammie and Brain dove into the car and sped out the entrance, almost hitting a truck. Tires squealed. Rubber burned on the road. It was the smelly truck from before. The man looked out, and twisted his face into a prune-like rage.

"You again! Can't obey the law! Can't drive! Where you from, huh? Mars?"

"We're making a movie!"

"Don't got respect for nothin'."

Brain sped off as Cammie leaned out the window. "Ah, stuff it, ya cornpone!"

Cammie had to claw her way into the studio. Her break came when she was a stand-in. It wasn't a bad gig, the pay was decent, and you got to network as you stood in the star's place, discreetly stepping aside when it was time to do the scene. Her parents thought it an absurd way to make a living, but it was Cammie's way to the top. Her biggest gig was *The Maltese Iguana*, when she stood in for Holly Haymen. Holly never spoke to her for the entire shoot except on the last day. Holly clicked up in designer stilettos, tossed her wavy blonde hair, and looked Cammie up and down, then shrugged. "That's not the way I stand."

Brain cruised the road as Cammie checked her watch. Twenty-five minutes to go.

"Maggots," she said in melodramatic terms, "where am I—"

Brain braked. Cammie almost hit the windshield.

"What the hell?"

"Look."

Off the road, there was a tattered shop of varying sorts of lumber nailed together, with old boats and scrap metal scattered around its gravel lot. Boxes and knick-knacks clustered by its front door. It had a sagging but friendly porch. The kind of place you'd look at and whistle the theme to *The Andy Griffith Show*. Its hand painted sign cozied: Roy's Fishin' Hole.

"If it's a fishing place," Brain said, "like the one we had back home, they got all kinds of bait. Dad told me some old boys used maggots. You toss 'em on the water, and the fish—"

Cammie burst out of the car and charged through the door.

The girl at the counter was a Barbie doll surrounded by mounted fish and rows of poles, not to the mention the little glass compartments of lures. A fan hummed, its air raking Cammie's head.

"You have maggots?"

"We sure do," the girl said. "Not a lot of people want 'em, though. Now, you goin' for cat? They ain't—"

"I just want the maggots."

"Well, now carp, they're real fond of 'em, but carp ain't for everyone's taste."

Cammie held up a fifty. "I'll take 'em. All of 'em. It's for a movie."

Barbie's eyes widened. "A movie? You got the whole shebang. Roy'll be proud. I don't do a lot of sales. Guys here, they don't trust a woman with fishin' stuff."

She came from behind the counter. In her cut-offs that looked like a denim bikini bottom and shirt that was knotted above her midriff, it was easy to see why poor salesmanship didn't impede her career at Roy's. A truck pulled up. The girl held a large plastic case.

"Now, we gotta charge you extra for the—"

"I'll pay," Cammie smiled, "let's see the maggots."

Barbie opened a bucket, and squirming maggots lined its bottom.

"I think they're really gross."

Cammie grinned. "They're my babies."

"Ain't it kinda yucky, working with maggots?"

"It pays eighty a day."

Barbie's eyes widened. "That's incredible. Is there a down side?"

Cammie shrugged. "On the credits, you're listed as the Maggot Wrangler."

The screen door creaked open. Cammie swallowed and felt her hands tremble with delight as she opened the container.

"Hey. Hey there!"

Barbie and Cammie turned. Barbie's face widened into a cheerleader's smile. "Hey, Roy, I just sold all the maggots. For fifty."

Roy was the man in the truck. He snatched the bucket from Cammie's hands.

"Ain't sellin' this one nothin'. Breaks the law. Called me a cornpone."

Cammie's mouth was open, her eyes wide. "No. You...can't be Roy."

"I sure am, and Roy ain't sellin' you nothin' nohow. Get off my property."

"Look...Roy. I'm with a movie. We need maggots. I'll pay you whatever you want."

"Please, Roy." Cammie's hands opened in humble petition. "I need the maggots."

Roy's rust-stained thumb jerked. "G'wan."

"I am sorry. I am so sorry for losing my temper. And I...the studio...will make it up."

Cammie kept pushing forward, but Roy kept the bucket out of reach. "Come on, Roy. *Please.*"

"Hey, you movie lady," Roy sneered, "you mocked me. You broke the law and mocked me. Get out, and I ain't saying it again."

Cammie gritted her teeth and lunged for the bucket. "*Gimme those maggots!*"

Roy was too quick. Barbie yelped at Cammie's lunge, her arms and legs swung and circled. Why wasn't she at Roy's throat? Brain. He grabbed Cammie and wrapped his arms around her body.

The bucket safely behind the counter, Roy re-emerged with a shotgun. *The Andy Griffith Show* morphed into *Deliverance*. Cammie's fury disintegrated into fear when she heard a metallic click from the chambers. Roy and a terrified Barbie shrank in the distance like a pullback shot as Brain retreated out the door with a firm grip on Cammie.

In the car, Brain shifted back into drama.

"You take me for granted, and I came all this way to be with you. You know, Jasmine—"

"Ah, forget her. She's playing you. She just wants to get into your pants."

This perked Brain's interest. He'd never been fought over, and although his eyes expressed disbelief, a quick twinkle meant this possibility was also cool. But he switched back to outrage. "I don't know, Cammie. I drove all the way here to find out. Made a boring trip, now here I am with people chasing me out of everywhere. Out the window, I got to smell that stinking—"

It was a pungent odor of rot. They looked at each other and shouted: "Roadkill!"

Several hundred yards back was a hump by the side of the road. Brain stopped. He and Cammie dashed back up the road. It was recent. No rot. Bad. They charged back to the car and drove slowly.

Brain narrowed his eyes, singing "Dead Skunk in the Middle of the Road" under his breath.

There was one. The nose doesn't lie. But it was also recent. They crept along, waving an impatient SUV around them. Cammie felt like they were Dr. Frankenstein and Igor looking for a good, used model. Then Cammie smelled it. The Comstock lode of roadkill. Like aged cheese, only a million times worse…or in this case, better.

Brain stopped. The stink led to a decaying hump on the other side of the road. Cammie sprang up and looked over the top of the hood. She made out the squirming mass all over the fur and caved in frame of…she had no idea what it was, except now it was maggot central. And it was hers for the taking. She made a fist and jerked it down. *All right!*

A siren's whoop made Cammie and Brain look to one side while an oversized Chevy pulled off to the shoulder, a police car in back of it. It pulled directly above the roadkill. Cammie's elation switched to confusion, disbelief, then turmoil. A baby having its Christmas teddy bear snatched out of eager hands. She shook her head. "No," she whimpered, "no…"

The trooper got out of his cruiser and strolled, stern and bulky from too many doughnuts and the bulletproof vest, to the offending Chevy.

She jumped out of Brain's car and ran to the Chevy.

"You got to move the car," she pleaded. "Gotta move it now."

The trooper and his hapless victim, an unshaven man with a vulturous nose and smeared T-shirt, stared at her. "Hey," the man said to the trooper, "she with you?"

"Never mind her. Ma'am—step away. Sir, know why you're being stopped?"

"I dunno. I wasn't breaking no laws."

"Please. Please move just a few feet."

The trooper glowered. "Ma'am. I told you to step away."

"I can't." Cammie held up her ID. "I'm with the studio. We're making a movie. I need you to move the car. I need those maggots. Now."

"What the hell," the man said, "she undercover? Do I move the car?"

"You don't go anywhere. *You!* Step away or you're under arrest."

"What for? Making a movie? Making a *motion picture?* What is this place, Weirdville?"

The trooper scrunched his mouth. "You're interfering with a police officer. Now step away!"

"I need the maggots."

"You were doing forty in a thirty mile zone."

Cammie leaned into the window. "Just move the car a few feet. I have to get them. Now!"

The trooper straightened and pointed. "Is that your vehicle across the road?"

She stared. "It's my vehicle."

"Go *back* to your vehicle. *Now.* You mouth off one more time, and you're going to jail."

The trooper turned to the man. "Let's see your driver's license."

But Cammie didn't go back. She slunk down and duck walked to the front of the Chevy. She heard the trooper go back to his car to run the license. Cammie whipped out the plastic gloves she carried in her pocket and pulled them on. The stench was enough to clear out Nashville. But she was a maggot wrangler. Cammie dealt with stench.

"Damn," the driver called out. "Pee-yew. It stinks like hell."

Cammie peeked up and pantomimed for the man to drive up. He gave a hopeless shrug.

She looked across to Brain, a helpless spectator. She took a deep breath and crawled under the Chevy, seeing the mess in front of her, readying her case. Even under the shadow of the Chevy, Cammie saw she had all the maggots she needed and then some. The stench was gruesome. If it could be bottled, it could be dropped over Iran. She gripped the paws of whatever it had been, and slowly inched it forward so she could dump the little critters into her plastic case. Fortunately, the corpse held together. She saw the trooper's shoes come back to the driver's side. Held her breath. Words were exchanged. She gritted her teeth. *Closer, closer…*

The trooper's shoes clicked back to his car. Cammie inched the corpse closer…

The motor started above her. *What the…?*

The trooper called out, but the Chevy sped off above her. She bunched close, expecting to be run over or dragged. No. Just a hot sun beating on her as the Chevy squealed and zoomed off. The cruiser wailed as it followed. Cammie's heart thumped, but she didn't lose it. The sight of hundreds of maggots made her spring up and start grabbing them and scooping them into her case.

Brain came over. "Holy…I heard something on the cop's radio about an outstanding warrant, and…" he scrunched and held his nose. "Damn it, Cammie, you actually pick those things up? This is what you do?"

"This is what I do." She scooped two handfuls into the case, which filled up like a family serving of mutant fried rice. Cammie sprang up. "Let's go. We got ten minutes."

Brain sped down the road, curved off onto dirt, and honked the horn. Cammie waved her arms and got a heads-up from security. Brain's Datsun zoomed past their opened barricade.

At the set, Maggie hopped out of the car, then quickly, quietly made her way to the collection of cameras, cables, and vans. She saw actors do a heated snap-fire dialogue.

She nudged Francine, one of the assistants, and held up her case. Francine nodded. Flemming was glued to the action, his hands gesturing. *Bigger. Bigger.*

The actor's dialogue crested. They stepped away. Trudy screamed at the dummy propped up against the tree.

Flemming stood, not looking back, and gestured. *Maggot wrangler.*

Cammie charged forward, shaking maggots on the dummy until they filled it like a five o'clock rush of maggots commuting on the subway. Turk moved in with the handcam.

A relieved sigh came from Cammie. Brain snuck beside her.

"Look," he said, "I don't know about us. I mean, maggots. Are we really in love?"

"Never mind, Brain," Cammie shrugged, already thinking of her résumé presented to *Evil Maggots.* Of the shoot in Brazil. *Rio.* "Never mind love. You were a good man. Tonight, you get sex."

Brain nodded. He had come for love, but was getting sex. You made the best of things.

Cammie imagined what a hell of a bar story the last hour was going to make at the wrap party. A fly buzzed around her, perhaps a guardian angel of maggots, perhaps to remind them that they too, would get wings and live it up for a few days—that they had a crack at their own Rio.

HAPPY DAY PLAN
Harriett Ford

He opened the passenger door, and I climbed inside the snow-covered Mercedes, shivering like a wet kitten escaping from a polar bear's ice den.

"Thanks Mister," I panted. "My car ran out of gas. I don't think I could have lasted another ten minutes in this whiteout."

I turned to look at my benefactor and blurted, "You! The guy who nearly gave me a concussion at the store."

"Excuse me?" the driver said, a look of surprise on his face.

"We banged our heads together when we bent down to pick up that shopping bag you tossed on the floor," I explained. "You had a tantrum because the computer lost service and you couldn't buy that gown for your wife."

"Ah yes, I recognize you. Your hard little head raised a nice knot right here." He lifted a finger to his forehead where the knot appeared visible in the waning light.

Serves him right, I thought. I fingered my own lump and wondered if the injury would cause a black eye.

What a day. My usual plan-ahead policy had failed. I'd had enough complaints at the store to last until Bigfoot shows up to buy a bikini. The manager refused to close early, even though the Chicago weather stations repeatedly warned drivers to stay off the streets if at all possible.

By the time Mr. Boss let me go, I faced a grueling drive on slippery roads. When I turned onto Lake Shore Drive, the traffic slowed and soon stopped moving altogether. Drivers sat helplessly watching thick wind-driven powder swirl across their windshields. They ran their engines to keep warm and waited. They had nowhere to go. Icy gray waves reared up on one side and a Twilight Zone of snow-filled air whirled on the other. A queue of taillights stretched ahead as far as I could see.

Just when I thought things couldn't get any worse, my old-beater Honda ran out of gas. I half expected a little window to pop up on the dash with the words, "Your Bad Hair Day Is Now a Category Five Nightmare."

Great. I'm stalled on Lake Shore Drive. I'm out of gas. This morning it was sixty-five and sunny. I hadn't even bothered to wear a coat—another lack of plan-ahead wisdom. I'd trusted the weatherman's prediction that the storm wouldn't arrive until late in the evening. He missed it, big time. The wind chill felt like fifty below when I left the store for the parking lot. *What do I do now?* Even if I had dressed appropriately, how far could I walk?

At least I had enough juice left to answer my cell phone when Mom called.

"Jyndi! I've been so worried about you. The TV announcers are all talking about the big traffic stall—some two hundred cars already abandoned along Lake Shore Drive. They're advising motorists to stay inside their cars until a snowplow or a rescue vehicle can get to them, which they admit could take hours."

I explained my situation.

"Out of gas! Darling, you've got to get into another car. Someone will let you in."

Cheese and crackers.

I'd have to go pounding on a stranger's car door and hope for a kindly Aunt Bea instead of a Freddy Kruger behind the wheel. The marrow-freezing cold crept in at once. My breath frosted the interior of the windows. My teeth started chattering.

Okay, here goes.

I took a deep breath, steeled myself, and struggled to open the car door against the gale.

A biting blast ripped through my inadequate sweater and skirt. I waded the swirling drifts to the nearest car.

That's how I entered Mr. Headbanger's Mercedes.

Actually, I half fell inside, and it no longer mattered if he was Freddy Kruger. I figured I'd be frozen stiff in another few minutes anyway. I wriggled my feet out of my snow-filled street shoes.

Headbanger said, "I did *not* deliberately toss the shopping bag on the floor, and I did not throw a tantrum."

"Looked like it to me, mister. I guess it just jumped out of your hand." I realized he could put me out in the storm. So what? I didn't like the idea of his company anyway.

He paused and drew a deep breath. "I admit I was irritated by the store's no-checks policy. And like everyone else out here, I hoped to get home before this—" he waved a hand toward the disheartening scene.

"Yeah, well me too. If you hadn't spent so much time trying to decide between the red lace negligee and the black, I could have been home by now. Your wife certainly could have exchanged one for the other." I felt absolutely snarly.

"I wasn't buying a gown for my wife."

I arched an eyebrow. "Oh? Your girlfriend then." Now he really ticked me off. I don't like cheaters.

"I'm not married," he said. "And I don't have a girlfriend. Not at the moment."

"Really? You were planning to wear the nightie yourself? Are you a cross-dresser? We have some nice bikini panties to match."

He rolled his eyes. "Of all people to find in my car during a blizzard, I end up with Smarty Sue. No, I'm not a cross-dresser. If you must know, the nightgown was supposed to be a gift for my sister. She's getting married next week. I hoped to drop it in the mail tomorrow. Instead, I end up with no gift and a long wait before I get home."

I looked him in the eye. Well actually, the ear, because he was staring straight ahead. He had dark hair and a nice profile, manly, and rugged. He reminded me of Dennis Quaid.

Was that a tiny earring on the lobe? I looked more closely, and decided he wasn't a cross-dresser.

"Did you know you have a black mole on your ear? You really should get that checked out," I warned.

"Thank you for your concern, Miss Sharp Eyes. Are you by any chance a doctor?"

"No, I'm a clerk at the store where you threw your little tantrum. I'm also going to law school nights. My name is Jyndi Jones. How do you do, Mister...?"

"I'm doing as well as anyone stranded in this mess." He turned toward me. "Hello, Miss Jones. I'm Martin Day. You keep insisting that I threw a tantrum at the store, so it probably won't do any good to explain, but I suffered a polo injury to my elbow a few months ago. It's healing; however, a certain weakness in my hand causes me to drop things at times."

Martin Day. Where had I heard that name?

He didn't want to admit his tantrum. I wouldn't have minded his male ego so much, but I remembered how he eyed my legs a little too long. I don't like lecherous men who purchase lingerie. Did he really play polo? Or was he trying to impress me? I decided he was lying.

"You know what? You may have an injury, but you bumped me in the head and didn't even bother to apologize," I challenged.

"Apologize? You were the one who should have apologized. You're the most annoying clerk I have ever had to deal with."

"Yeah, well you weren't so annoyed when you checked out my legs, Mister Day."

"Bored is the more appropriate term. I was bored waiting for the computer transaction. I've never shopped in a lingerie department. The entire experience was unpleasant. I couldn't help noticing your legs when you climbed the stepladder to reach merchandise on the upper shelf."

Bored? The word struck a nerve. "Do you make it a habit of ogling store clerks just because you're bored?"

He said, "I wasn't ogling. I just noticed. And by the way, you have very nice legs."

Oh boy.

"Thanks. But don't bother to ask me out," I warned. "I don't date customers."

"Ask you out? What makes you think I'd—?" This time he turned a searching eye on me. After a moment, a slight grin played around his lips. A teasing look gleamed in his eyes, which I noticed were cobalt blue.

"You'd go out with a guy like me in a Chicago minute," he declared, his voice filled with cocky certainty.

I popped back, "A guy like you? Sure, if he wasn't too much like you. Sorry, Martin. I think you suffer from delusions of grandeur."

He answered, "Of course, doesn't everyone? Delusions of grandeur make people feel better about themselves. You should try it. Delude yourself into being a better clerk, more patient."

The nerve of this arrogant man. I raised my chin. "If you knew me better, you would know that I don't have to delude myself to be good at my job. I have a standard of excellence."

He answered, "I've already found out enough about you. All that I want to know."

"Oh really?" I fumed. The man annoyed me more every time he opened his mouth.

Before I could think of a smart retort, Martin cut me off. "If you will excuse me, the only thing I want to know right now is how long before I get out of here."

He turned on the radio. Chicago reporters kept running updates on the snowstorm and the big stall along Lake Shore Drive. They reminded motorists to prevent carbon monoxide poisoning by keeping tailpipes clear.

Martin drummed his fingers on the steering wheel. "Guess the meeting will be postponed. I should go over my notes just the same." He opened a leather-bound legal pad.

Fine. I didn't want to talk to him anyway.

He had something to occupy his time. I merely watched the storm. Through wind-whipped gusts of white, I could see nothing but yellow headlights and red taillights blinking like a necklace strung on black velvet.

After a long silence, my stomach growled. "Got anything to eat in here? I'm starved." I had intended to have lunch in the store, but I'd forgotten my sandwich—one more plan-ahead failure in the day.

"Oh yeah. This car has everything. I just push a button on the dash and a menu appears along with a selection of wine. How about a Polar Pizza?"

Sheesh. He was in as snarly a mood as I was.

For a moment, I almost believed his comment. I'd never been in a Mercedes before. The luxurious interior and the multiple controls and screens on the dash were mind boggling to a store clerk who drives a well-used Honda. I wondered how much he owed for it.

Martin reached across me. His arm brushed my leg and my alarm system went on full alert. He opened the glove compartment and produced a package of nuts.

"Sorry, this is the best I can do."

I tore open the package, poured out a few cashews, and handed him the rest. We sat munching in strained silence.

The wind howled and shoved against the Mercedes with invisible hands. The announcer advised Lake Shore Drive motorists to settle in for a long while.

We both groaned.

"What if they don't get us out of here for hours?" I asked, dismayed at the possibility of having to spend the night in Martin's car. "Does your car have plenty of gas?"

"I filled the tank this morning." He decided to switch to a station that played easy listening music, oddly relaxing. The sweet strains reminded me that somewhere, perhaps even now, people enjoyed candlelight dinners, danced in elegant flowing evening gowns and tuxedoes, and sipped wine beside softly glowing candelabras. My imagination pictured Martin by candlelight. He looked rather handsome in a tuxedo.

Laying his notes aside, he stretched and settled himself in the seat. "Say, it's been a very long day and it may be an even longer night. I'm really not up for conversation. I'd like to catch a little nap. That is, if you promise not to molest me."

I rolled my eyes. "Don't worry. I'll make sure to keep my hands to myself."

After a while, I also relaxed. I must have succumbed to the lulling melodies and the cozy warmth from the purring heater, because I woke to find my head resting on Martin's shoulder.

Oh horror!

I jerked upright. Martin opened his eyes.

"Pardon me. I didn't mean to sleep on your shoulder like that," I stammered.

He yawned and said, "Yeah, well I have that effect on a few women. Not most, you understand."

I started to make some snappy remark when it struck me. "Martin! Are we getting carbon monoxide poisoning? Is that why we're so sleepy?"

At once, Martin opened the driver's side door and headed to the rear of the car. The icy blast hurled snowflakes inside. I brushed them off the seat and waited. A few minutes later, he climbed back in.

"Good thing I checked. The exhaust was almost clogged. I cleared a space around it. We're okay now. I'll check it again later if we don't start moving soon."

I said, "Look, I know this isn't any fun. You're as anxious to get out of here as I am, but we're going to have to keep each other awake. So, what shall we talk about? Politics? Something serious? The Abominable Snowman's shoe size?"

"I never talk about serious topics with women I hardly know. How about Big Foot? Do you think he's real?"

"Of course he's real. I saw him at a fast food drive-thru the other day. He was ordering a burger."

Martin nodded, "Did he ask 'where's the beef?'"

"Yes. The clerk told him to just look under the pickle and he would find it," I bantered.

He grinned. "You're funny."

"No. I'm just trying to stay awake. You might as well tell me about yourself since we don't have anything else to do."

"I'm a typical American. You know. Mother, four step-dads, a half sister from her second marriage, her illegitimate son."

Sensing my dismay, he chuckled, "Not so. That's just a poke at our society these days, Miss Jyndi. My parents are still married after forty years, and I have only one sister who lives in Vermont. Oh, and a brother who's always there for me whenever he needs money."

"Are you going to your sister's wedding?" I asked.

"I plan to. My partners are hosting a theme party for one of our retiring attorneys that day. It's a gay nineties party, since the old fellow managed to practice law until into his nineties. I really should be there, at least for a while. Then I'll head for Vermont."

"One of your partners is gay and the other is ninety?" I suggested.

Martin burst into a hearty laugh. The sound of it made me want to laugh with him. I couldn't stop myself. Laughter really does good—like medicine.

After that, we both relaxed. I said, "Now, let's talk about something pleasant, like death by freezing instead of carbon monoxide. The science of cryogenics involves freezing your body before you die and then reviving you after doctors find the cure for whatever illness you had. But what if you froze to death? Could they revive you?"

Martin answered, "Pleasant subject? I don't much care for death. The hours aren't good."

I decided to get personal since I figured I'd never see him again, so I asked, "Why aren't you married?"

He said, "My divorced friends tell me that something magical happens when you live alone. All your annoying habits simply disappear."

"Do you have annoying habits?"

"None at all," he said. "I haven't annoyed myself since I was four." His eyes danced with amusement.

"What did you do when you were four?"

"I asked my mother about carrots. If they were so good for my eyes, why did I see so many dead rabbits on the road? She made me eat them anyway. The carrots, that is. I've been annoyed by carrots ever since. However, my vision is perfect. So a serving of carrots at age four must have a lasting effect."

I liked his sense of humor. I liked his laugh.

I liked his name. "Hey Martin. At some point, if you ever do get married, you could name your kids Wendy and Stormy. Perfect with a last name like Day, don't you think?"

He suggested, "How about Lucky, Sunny, or even Dusty Day?"

We continued to amuse ourselves by thinking up laughable names for a while—Sandy, Harry, or Happy Day. I liked Happy.

Then it struck me. "Wait a minute. Are you the Martin Day who owns the second floor of the Shaw and Crandell law firm in the Talbot Building?"

He nodded. "That's me. I'm a joint owner."

Wow. If I ever wanted a job at a highly respected law firm, it would be Shaw and Crandell, Ltd. What had I stumbled into? A chance connection with the one man who might make that possible, and I had tried to provoke him as soon as I entered his Mercedes.

Oops. Big mistake. Another in my avalanche of uncomfortable events.

"You're the attorney who won the famous Anderson case. What a success!" I exclaimed. "And no wonder. You could argue a case against carrots when you were only four."

"I didn't win the case alone," he answered modestly.

I swallowed. He really did play polo. He really did not deliberately toss the bag on the floor due to a bad temper.

Unbelievable. Mister Cracker Jack Attorney Martin Day.

And he thinks I'm an annoying clerk. I groaned inwardly. How could I overcome that first impression? Did I have any good points?

It took a while before I remembered that I happen to be an ace law student and that he also liked my legs. My conversational skills did not disappear entirely. I drew him into a conversation about Chicago's criminal justice system. He seemed fascinated that I could discuss fine points of law on a par with his intellectual level. His voice took on a note of respect. My confidence began to soar.

Throughout the night, we talked about many subjects and laughed repeatedly. He kept the tailpipe clear of snow. We took turns dozing a few times, but turned the radio volume up loud enough to wake the dead. We discovered we had many things in common. For instance, we both like pizza. Imagine that.

Later.

Seven hours later.

The snow stopped falling. A pale sky promised the sun would rise on schedule, and somewhere ahead the cars started to move.

I thanked Martin for sharing the warmth of his car and for saving me from waking up dead in a cryogenics lab.

He flashed a charming grin. "Well, Jyndi, this has been an interesting night. I hope you have forgiven me for not apologizing when we bumped our heads together."

Oh yeah. Forget the apology. I knew I wanted to see him again. Again and again. And not just at the law firm. I decided to push the possibility.

"Only if you promise to take me out for that Polar Pizza. After all, we never got around to talking about the Abominable Snowman's shoe size."

"Are you kidding?"

My heart sunk.

Then he added, "You deserve better than pizza for putting up with me all night. Why don't I drive you home since your car is not going anywhere without gas? You can freshen up, and I'll take you to breakfast. Then we'll come back here and rescue your Honda. And now that we've gotten acquainted we can talk about something serious."

"How serious?" I asked.

"How about coming with me to the Gay Nineties party?"

I couldn't help flashing my biggest Julia Roberts' grin. "I thought you already knew everything about me that you wanted to know."

Martin looked at me, his eyes merry and mischievous. "I know you have beautiful green eyes, great legs, and a smart sense of humor. We've just spent an entire night together, during which I've discovered there's a whole lot more I want to find out about you."

"Like my shoe size?"

"That too."

What a perfect ending to a monumentally bad day.

Happy Day?

Oh yeah. I liked the sound of that.

My plan-ahead mode kicked in.

Happy would be a little boy with dark hair and cobalt blue eyes.

KUMFUMBLED
Kathy Page

Gwen frowned slightly as she walked to the mailbox. The flowers along the sidewalk were in full bloom, their fragrance light upon the morning air and there was not a weed in sight. As she glanced at the sky, her frown deepened; just a few wispy clouds accented the beautiful blue color. With a sigh, she opened the mailbox. Darn it! Her social security check was right on time, and her new magazine subscription was there just as promised. Turning slowly around, Gwen took stock of the neighborhood activities—everything seemed peaceful and quiet. There weren't any dogs prowling for a place to dig, no little boys hefting rocks to throw at the dogs, and no one waiting to yell at the little boys.

Well, this day just couldn't possibly get any better, Gwen fumed as she marched back to the house. The cake she baked earlier for a school fundraiser had risen perfectly, her coffee-machine had clicked on at the right time, her checkbook had balanced, and her *hair looked great!* Gwen was a petite woman, always well-groomed, but casually dressed, and usually with a warm smile on her face. Laugh lines only enhanced the sparkle in her blue eyes.

Today, the smile and sparkle were missing. She had just sat down to a perfectly brewed cup of coffee when her next-door neighbor, Janet, knocked on the door. With a "Yoo-hoo!" Janet came right on in but stopped immediately. When she saw the thunderous look on Gwen's face, she gasped. "*What* is wrong? You look mad as an old, wet hen!"

"Well, I have good reason to be mad. Not one thing has gone wrong today," fussed Gwen.

"You poor thing, you really mean nothing has gone *right!* I know just how you feel. When I have bad days, sometimes I get so angry my words come out wrong, too. Why, once I said the hogs needed a sponge-bath when I meant..."

"No," said Gwen, "I *said* nothing has gone wrong, and I *meant* nothing has gone wrong!"

Janet poured a cup of coffee and sat down, a puzzled look on her face. Gwen's house was always so cozy and inviting. As she looked around at the sparkling kitchen, the herbs growing in the window, and the cat sleeping in the sunshine, she burst out, "Well, you're as crazy as a pet coon! We've been talking all week back and forth, and you haven't said one single word about anything being wrong. Seems to me like it's been smoother than a baby's bottom for you lately."

"You just don't understand," moaned Gwen as she dropped her head into her hands. "Things going right are wrong, but when things are going wrong, I can make them right. Lately, I haven't had anything to make right and that's just wrong!"

Janet sat there for a moment with her mouth open. "Kumfumbled, you are just plain kumfumbled," she finally said. "You must be working too hard or sleeping badly, maybe both. You need a nice vacation, with nothing to do. Maybe find a nice place on the beach with a cabana boy or a retreat at one of those monastery places where you don't speak for weeks, just use sign language, 'though I don't know what the sign would be for toilet paper."

"If *you* would stop speaking for a while, it would be a blessing!" huffed Gwen. After seeing the hurt look on Janet's face, she apologized. She and Janet had been friends a long time, and by now, she should be used to her friend's ramblings.

Sighing, Gwen continued, "Janet, you know that I like to be in the middle of things. I like to be involved in whatever is going on."

"You sure do! Why you're involved in almost everything at church, you cook and serve at the soup kitchen, you knit prayer shawls, you raise money for cancer, and Lord knows what-all else. You're busier than a long-tailed cat in a room full of rocking chairs! Why, everyone around comes to you when they have a problem!"

"See, that's what I mean! I have been waiting and waiting for something to go wrong so I could fix it, but nothing has! I've been moping around here with nothing to do, no problems to fix, no hands to hold—not one thing has gone wrong!"

"So let me get this straight. You *want* something to go wrong? I have known some squirrely people in my time, but Gwen—you take the nut."

Sighing, Gwen poured another cup of perfectly brewed coffee. "It's not that I want things to go wrong," she said slowly. "It's just that when things are going well, no one asks me to help with their problems. I need to be needed. I've always been the one that people come to for help. I like to take on challenges, even if I don't come out on top. It makes me feel alive and kicking when I can help someone out. Otherwise, life is just plain boring."

Janet slapped the tabletop, making Gwen jump. "Yessiree Bob, you do have a reputation for kicking butt when it needs to be kicked! Remember last Christmas when the City Council bought you those steel-toed pointy boots? Your face turned redder than a ripe tomato in August! But they sure were thankful to you for getting the city's money back from that traveling statue salesman."

Gwen chuckled and said, "Yes, and I could have used those boots when I finally tracked that weasel down. Oh, that was fun!"

"And what about that time the school needed new lab equipment and there just wasn't anybody willing to donate even a single dollar? Why, you started that Outhouse Yard Art fundraiser and had the money in no time! Of course, that's 'cause Maybelline Winchester paid extra to have that outhouse moved out of her prize flowerbed! Three different times! Oh, oh, and what about when the Kincaids had triplets, and you organized a bottle and diaper brigade? There were diapers hanging all over town! And I'll never forget how you faced down those kids who were spray painting nasty things on buildings. Why, you got them to apologize and clean it up. That took guts; those boys were meaner than a sack of rattlesnakes!"

Gwen's grin slowly died away. "But no one seems to need me anymore. Today has been the worst; usually I can at least expect something around here to go wrong. The cat gets sick, the paperboy throws the paper in the lily pond, or the milk goes bad…something! But today is just perfect. Why, there isn't even a single weed in my flowerbed! And you know what the worst thing is? I dyed my hair this morning with one of those kits from the dollar store, just knowing it would turn out horrible and look at it! It looks great!"

"Well, I'm still as confused as an orphan on Father's Day!" said Janet. "Don't worry Gwen, if it's supposed to be right it will be. Or is that, if it's wrong? I need some aspirin—I feel a headache coming on."

Gwen sighed, "Getting someone to understand what I mean is like trying to nail jelly to a tree. Oh, good grief! Now I sound like you, Janet!"

"Why? I don't have any idea what you mean!"

Gwen and Janet spent the next hour thinking about things that might need to be done. The closets were all cleaned out, the sheets were drying on the line, the church bulletin was printed, the silverware was polished and organized, and the fish tank was clean. Other than drink coffee with Janet, what was she going to do for the rest of the day? What about the rest of her life?

Janet finally said, "I think I'm starting to understand. You need things to do. If your day isn't spent like somebody trying to herd cats, you just aren't happy! Everybody knows that you're great at helping others figure out what to do—that's why they're always calling you. I don't know, Gwen. If problems aren't knocking on your door or calling on the phone, maybe you need to learn to just be happy anyway. Maybe you could learn to meditate or something. I just saw a swami, or something, on TV and he said that the secret to a calm life was to take creamed spinach…"

Just then, someone knocked at the door. *Thank goodness*, Gwen thought as she opened the door. Cindy Lewis stood there, anxiously wringing her hands. "Gwen, the worst thing has happened! The county says that our new memorial flower garden is in the way of the road expansion they're planning. They say we have to have it moved by next week! We know how busy you are, but could you chair the meeting tonight to see what can be done?" Before she could answer, the phone rang. Telling Cindy to hang on, Gwen grabbed the phone to hear that the local animal shelter was almost out of food. Could she make some calls to see if anyone would help? After writing down the contact info, she turned back to Cindy, and before long, they had the meeting planned. Cindy left in a much calmer frame of mind to make some calls.

Gwen happily grabbed a notepad and was about to start making notes when Janet said, "Hey, don't you have sheets on the line? There's storm clouds building up, and it looks like it might be a toad strangler!"

"Oh, no! If it rains, we'll have to figure out another place to hold the rummage sale. We need money from that to support the 4-H club. If it rains too much, we won't be able to transplant the flowers from the memorial garden! But those dogs and cats need food before we worry about the flowers. Janet, can you look at the weather forecast while I go get the laundry in?" A loud clap of thunder sent Gwen running outside. She gathered up all the sheets and turned around just as the cat ran right in front of her. Gwen tripped, stumbled and landed in the lily pond, scaring the goldfish half-to-death. Gwen sat there in a daze, looking at the sheets that would have to be washed again as the rain started coming down in earnest. Looking down to make sure she wasn't sitting on one of her fish, she realized that her cheap hair color was dripping from her chin onto her wet, now see-through blouse. *I'll bet I look like a drowned, "Brazen Blonde" rat!* she thought.

Janet leaned against a pillar on the back porch, drinking another cup of perfect coffee. "Well," she drawled. "Guess you're having a bad hair day after all! You have to be careful what you wish for— right now, you've got enough problems to last you for a coon's age."

Despite the hair dye running down her face, Gwen grinned and said, "Yes, and isn't it wonderful!"

MR. PERFECT
Beth Carter

Alyssa sneered into her smudged Cover Girl compact. "I hate my boring, flat hair."

"You have gorgeous hair. Why is it suddenly bothering you?" asked Maddie as she fluffed her own unruly curls.

"Um. Well. I have a date tonight."

Maddie hit the brakes and turned into a Starbucks. "Hold that thought. We're getting coffee. I want to hear everything."

Once they settled into a table with a tall skinny vanilla latte for Alyssa and a whatever-is-the-most-fattening grande for Maddie, the best friends sipped their coffee.

After one big gulp, Maddie leaned forward. "Well? Spill."

Alyssa smiled. "Okay. Okay." She cleared her throat for dramatic effect, grinned, and in a purposely calm voice said, "Tony Patoosi called and asked me out."

Coffee spewed out of Maddie's mouth.

"Shut up! You mean Mr. Perfection? Mr. Perfect Sperm Donor? Mr. I'm Cuter Than Brad Pitt? Mr. I Rival George Clooney?"

"Yes, him."

Maddie blew out her breath. She leaned back in her chair, then put her elbows on the table. "When did he call you and why didn't you tell me *immediately?*"

Alyssa smiled and sipped her latte. "I couldn't believe it either. He actually texted me this morning. Maybe he got the wrong number." She looked down at the table and ran her finger across a crack.

"Mike Patoosi did *not* call the wrong number. You're a hottie. Own it, and stop blushing for God's sake."

Alyssa felt her cheeks pinken again. "You're my best friend. You're supposed to say that."

"It's true, though. Now about your flat hair..."

"I'm calling a hair dresser right now." Alyssa plucked her phone from her purse and Googled hair salons. New Euro Hair Salon popped up first. She dialed their number.

"New Euro…" Alyssa heard a pause then something that sounded like bubblegum popping, "Hair Salon."

"Hi. Do you have any stylists available today?"

"Sure. What do you need?"

"Some volume."

"Oh." More gum popping. "Let's see. Georgina is available at two."

"Great." Alyssa gave the popper her name, phone number and hung up. She found directions for the salon on her phone and turned to Maddie. "Want to go with me? I think I'll get a perm."

Maddie wrinkled her nose. "Do they still give stinky perms? No thanks. Besides, I have a date with Pat, Ben and Jerry."

Alyssa giggled. "Let me guess. You and your cat, Pat, are going to eat Ben & Jerry's ice cream while watching *The Bachelor*."

"You got it. But call me after you're finished. I want to see your new 'do before your hot date."

At the salon, the bubblegum receptionist led Alyssa to the back of the salon. A blonde in pigtails with Betty Boop images on her apron smiled a toothy grin and draped a leopard skin cape around Alyssa. The collective images were dizzying.

"I'm Georgina. Whatcha want today?"

"I need some volume. I hate my hair."

Georgina picked through Alyssa's hair, lifting section after limp section. Her hair got straighter and oilier the more the stylist touched it.

"I'd like some soft waves. You know those beachy-type, loose waves," said Alyssa. "So, I guess I need a perm."

"A perm? Wow. I haven't done one of those in a while, but okay. You're the boss. Let me get my cart."

She hasn't done one in a while? Maybe this isn't such a good idea. Alyssa chewed on a red fingernail.

When the stylist returned with a cart filled with rainbow-colored rods, she turned to Alyssa. "Want anything to drink before I start?"

"No, thanks. I'm good. By the way, my hair curls easily. I know it looks wilted, but it's deceiving when you curl it."

Georgina nodded. "Uh huh."

What seemed like a hundred rods of every size and color later, Alyssa looked like she was ready to pose for a fifties swimsuit ad. Georgina squirted the foul-smelling solution between the rods and plunked Alyssa under a dryer with a handful of magazines. "See you in an hour or two."

Alyssa couldn't hear Georgina over the dryer. She read about celebrity break-ups, eyed the new runway collection, filled out a crossword puzzle, and balanced her checkbook. She had left her phone in the car and couldn't see a clock anywhere. Alyssa rubbed her aching neck. It seemed like she had been under the dryer forever. A sweat moustache was forming on her upper lip.

Finally, Georgina bounced back, flipped the dryer head up, and took out a rod.

"Ohhhh." She frowned.

"What?"

Alyssa could see Georgina's Adam's apple bob up and down as the stylist swallowed hard several times.

"Nothing. You're finished processing. Let's wash this solution out."

Georgina shampooed Alyssa's hair four times, scrubbing so hard her scalp hurt.

"I think it's clean," said Alyssa.

Georgina rinsed it again and furrowed her brows.

"What's wrong?"

"Nothing. Let's blow it out."

When they finally left the shampoo bowl and walked to Georgina's station, the hairdresser blocked the mirror. She turned Alyssa away from her reflection, thrusting another magazine in her hand. "Read this while I work."

As the stylist blew her hair dry, Alyssa could see frizz from the corner of her eye. She put her hand up to touch her hair and it felt like a sink scrubber. She twirled her chair toward the mirror, catching Georgina's leg and nearly knocking her over. "Ow."

"Oh. My. God. It looks like I stuck my finger in a socket. You left the rods in too long. I told you my hair curled easily." Alyssa started sobbing. Loudly. "My hair is ruined."

"Shhh. Let me work on it." Georgina opened a door and pulled out a white squirt bottle.

Alyssa took deep Yoga breaths. Otherwise, she'd kill the stylist. When she saw the bottle, she asked, "What's that?"

"A relaxer. It'll help. I hope."

"You *hope?* How long have you been a hair stylist?"

Georgina beamed. "I graduated from cosmetology school three months ago."

"And how many perms have you done?"

"You're my first! Well, besides one disaster in school."

Alyssa gritted her teeth. She wanted to punch her. "What have you done? I just happen to have a date with the most gorgeous guy on campus."

"Cool. When's your date?"

"Tonight."

"Oh. I don't think it'll relax by then."

"No kidding. Just try the stupid relaxer." Alyssa's jaw was set and tears stained her cheeks.

"Why did you leave me under the dryer so long?"

"Sorry. I was on the phone with my boyfriend. He had a fight with his roomie and needed to talk. Now, everything's okay between him and his bestie."

"Gee. I'm really happy about that. Meanwhile, my hair looks like a tumbleweed. I suppose you're going to charge me for this too?"

"Just fifty dollars. We're priced right at New Euro Hair Salon." Georgina glowed.

Could she really be this dumb? Alyssa couldn't decide if she should be mad or sad. When she finally got into her car, she pounded the steering wheel and burst into tears again. Then, she called Maddie. She told her everything through heaving sobs.

"Calm down. It can't be that bad."

"It is. Trust me."

"We need a plan. What time is your date?"

"Six."

"That gives us an hour. Meet me at Target. We'll buy you a cool hat."

Alyssa liked that idea and almost smiled. "Okay, but I'm starving."

Maddie wasn't deterred. "They have hot dogs at Target. I'll get one for you while you try on hats."

The two friends met in the parking lot. As Maddie walked closer, Alyssa could tell she was suppressing a giggle.

"Go ahead. Laugh."

"I'm sorry. It looks awful. Really, really bad." Maddie cupped her hand over her mouth.

"It's hilarious—especially since I have a date with Mike tonight."

"Crap. That's right. Mr. Perfect. Let's get a move on."

Alyssa headed toward the hats while Maddie walked to the food counter. She tried on cowboy hats, baseball caps, Fedoras, and knitted berets. Nothing hid her hair. Not enough, anyway. The frizz stuck out in every direction. In fact, most of the hats were too small because of her big hair.

Maddie chomped on a hot dog with mustard running down her arm while handing Alyssa her food. Maddie grabbed a big, floppy beach hat. "Try this one."

"Ha ha. Problem is we're not going to a beach, and we're not going to a rodeo. I'm going to look ridiculous. He'll never go out with me again."

"Yes, he will. He'd be crazy not to." Maddie looked around the aisle. "How about a headband?"

"That's like putting a skinny belt on a Sumo wrestler."

Maddie chuckled. "At least you still have your sense of humor. Come on. Just pick a hat. You've got to change. You're going to run out of time. Besides, with your hot body, he won't even notice your hair."

"Liar. But I love you for it."

Alyssa chose a burgundy beret and tried tucking her hair behind her ears. The sides bushed out like shrubs. "It's no use. I should cancel."

"You are *not* cancelling." Maddie fished in her purse. "I'm buying this hat for you, and then we're going to your house to find a sexy outfit."

While driving home, Alyssa wondered how she would face Zeus with her fried hair. She picked up her phone to cancel and then set it back in her purse. She knew this might be her only chance to go out with the one guy every girl on campus wanted to date. She decided to go for it.

In her bedroom, Alyssa pulled several shirts and jeans out of her closet while Maddie made space on the bed for herself and played fashion police. They narrowed the choices down to three—a silky ivory blouse and skinny blue jeans, a shimmery lime shirt and turquoise denim, and a black cut-out tank with white jeans.

"You look great in all of them. If you weren't my best friend, I'd hate you." Maddie threw her hands in the air. "Where are your potato chips? I've given up on diets."

Alyssa decided on the sexy black tank and white jeans and found a burgundy purse to match her beret. She added silver hoops, a chunky bracelet, and stilettos. If her hair didn't suck, she'd almost look good. Alyssa tried one last-ditch effort of pulling her tresses into a ponytail, but it ended up looking just like that—an animal's tail—possibly from a raccoon or a large squirrel. She grimaced, removed the band, and squirted more smoothing gel through her hair. It wasn't any smoother but looked shinier. Alyssa stared at her reflection and couldn't decide if that helped or drew more attention to her locks.

She glanced at the clock. It was nearly six.

"You've got to leave, Maddie. I'll call you when the date is over, which I predict will be soon."

Maddie hugged her friend. "I bet he won't even notice. You're gorgeous even with bad hair."

"You're the best. Now, go."

Ten minutes later, the doorbell rang. Alyssa's heart nearly stopped. Her feet felt like quicksand as she walked toward the door.

Mike smiled broadly, and just as quickly, his smile faded. "Well, hello—um…"

"Alyssa. My name is Alyssa." She tried to act as if nothing was wrong. "Come in."

"I know your name. You just…anyway, I made reservations at the new Italian restaurant, but I don't feel so great all of a sudden. Do you care if we go to my apartment and order a pizza?"

Jerk. He feels fine. He just doesn't want to be seen with me in public.

Alyssa's southern upbringing wouldn't allow her to confront him. She put on a brave face. "Sure, that's fine. I love pizza."

They drove in deafening silence toward the south side of town. The rich side. Naturally. Alyssa felt sure this would be her shortest date on record.

"Here we are. Make yourself comfortable. I'll call the pizza place."

Alyssa noticed Mike hadn't made much of an effort on his appearance. He wore a Nike T-shirt, worn blue jeans, and sneakers. But, then, he didn't need to make much of an effort. He had perfect genes. The perfect male. Brad Pitt's nemesis and all that. She fidgeted on the couch and noticed a baseball game was muted in the background. She wondered why he had left the television on. Probably because perfect people don't have to worry about high electric bills.

When he returned, Mike picked up the remote and unmuted the sound. "Mind if we watch the game?"

"No. I love sports," lied Alyssa. She deplored them, but as long as Mike wasn't sitting across from her staring at her Brillo pad hair, she was happy.

When the pizza finally arrived, two men walked in. One was holding the pizza and the other was Mike's clone.

Mike fished in his pocket and pulled out five dollars. He looked at Alyssa. "I'm a little short. Have any cash?"

I don't believe this. What a tightwad. He expects me to pay half the bill on a first date?

The clone pulled out his wallet. "I've got it, bro."

Mike took the pizza into the kitchen and Mr. Look-alike extended his hand.

"Hi. I'm Phil, Mike's twin, as you might have guessed." He gave Alyssa a warm smile. "Nice beret."

She felt wobbly. "Thanks."

Mike walked back balancing the pizza, paper plates, and two sodas. He looked toward his brother. "Are you staying?"

Phil winked at Alyssa. "Do you mind?"

She was relieved to have a distraction from her hair, plus Phil seemed much nicer than Mike. "Not at all."

The three of them settled onto the couch, and Mike turned up the volume.

Phil poised the pizza toward his mouth and turned to his brother. "What kind of date is this? You bring a nice woman to your apartment, serve pizza, don't have enough cash, and then watch a game? What's wrong with you?"

Mike shrugged. Then, it looked as though he faked a yawn.

"I'm really tired. After I eat, I'm turning in. Phil, will you drive Alyssa home?"

Tears stung her eyes, but she held them at bay. *What a toad. He can't even be bothered to take me home?*

"I'd be happy to escort this lovely lady. That is, if she doesn't mind."

Alyssa looked at Phil gratefully and nodded. She was afraid to speak. Afraid of embarrassing herself by crying.

Mike turned to the game and wolfed down four pieces of pepperoni pizza. He left his paper plate filled with pizza crusts on the coffee table. He stood and patted Alyssa on the shoulder as if she were his buddy. "See ya around."

After Mike left the room, Phil looked at Alyssa as if gauging her reaction. "He can be a real tool."

"I didn't even know Mike had a brother."

"That's why I moved away several years ago. Since we're identical twins, everyone expects our personalities to be the same. I'm a nice guy. He's not. I love my brother, but he can be a piece of work."

Alyssa stared at her barely touched pizza. "You *are* a nice guy. I can tell. You didn't even shudder when you saw my dreadful hair."

"What dreadful hair?" Phil flashed a movie star smile.

"Come on. I know it's horrible. I had the bright idea to get a perm today for my big date. And I just happened to be lucky enough to call a salon with a stylist who had only done a perm once in her life."

Phil shook his head. "Unfortunate timing."

Then, he dazzled her with that smile again. "I can fix it if you want. Of course, I think you're beautiful just the way you are."

Alyssa's mood brightened. "What do you mean you can fix it?"

He reached into his shirt pocket and pulled out a small pair of scissors. "It just so happens that I am a darn good hair stylist. I trained at the Paul Mitchell salon in New York City and worked at Bumble & Bumble where I had several celebrity clients before I moved back."

"No way!" Alyssa leaned back onto the worn brown couch, taking in this bit of timely news.

"Way," said Phil.

Alyssa decided Mike Patoosi wasn't the least bit cute after all. Strangely enough, Phil looked exactly like him, yet he was gorgeous. Phil really was perfect—inside and out.

BUNNY HOPS
Edgar Bailey

"Why DuPont? Why at the only, only I say, vertical escalator Metro station in the world? Even the Tibetan Metro in the middle of the Himalayas has fewer nearly vertical escalators. Do you know how many times I had to hop off trains?"

"Once?"

"Do you know what Metro Central is like at five o'clock?"

"A circus? Is it like a circus, Sharon?"

"No, a zoo; circus animals are trained. Stand to the right, walk on the left. Tourists, their baggage, and their rug rats block the escalators."

"I thought you thought rug rats *are* baggage."

"Some of them are cute. You know, with chocolate ice cream dripping off their cherubic little faces onto my shoes, cleaning their little paws by smearing them on my skirt, showing me the treasures they've found hiding deep in their nasal cavities. Nasty little *blennioid homunculus.*"

"I didn't follow all of that but shouldn't '*homunculus*' be plural? Children, right, so, is it *homunculi*? Oh, now, don't make that face. It's misplaced anger. You're perturbed with me for calling you out of your cozy little Silver Springs cocoon."

"Mary Katherine, you had to meet at the top of the one and only vertical escalator in the world *and*," Sharon emphasizes the "and" with verbal venom, "the repairs; one of three escalators working."

"First of all, it's Kathy. You're not my mother, and you're not calling me down."

"I may be—depending on the reason for this gathering."

"The reason is because we're friends; the precipitating cause is David North Bell."

"My office is on the Red Line. We couldn't meet in Crystal City?"

"Nope. I needed to shop for shoes. At Comfort Shoes and then Ben & Jerry's."

"It couldn't be any of the one hundred thirty stores at the Underground Mall but only at Comfort at DuPont Circle. Seems reasonable."

"I wanted Cherry Garcia for lunch and to people watch. B & J's is closed here now—"

"—So, you've substituted white wine—"

"—and I sat across from Zorba's Café; David and Tiffany, not her real name, more likely Dollar General or 99 Cent store, were having an intimate little *tête-à-tête*."

"Woolworth's or McCrory would be funnier."

"Only to you because you watch movies from the forties. He became a second story man."

"Second story man? You mean like a cat burglar?"

"More like a bunny burglar. No, don't look puzzled; it will all be clear in the end."

"That's what our minister always told me, too."

"He expected me to walk his bunny when he worked late. It is more than a cute little bunny—it's a giant butted lop-eared rabbit he takes from show to show. Then we were supposed to have dinner after a drink at Bardo."

"With the entry levels and undergrads?"

"The music is just loud enough to drown out the sound of cell phones. At eight o'clock, he texted me about not getting together tonight, or ever. He'd leave his door unlocked if I want to pick up my DVDs and CDs this morning."

"He broke up with a text?"

"Yes, one hundred forty characters for his 'Desperation of Independence.' But he was gentlemanly enough to follow up with an email; thereby is the second story. The thing is, he called me by his ex's name."

"Why?"

"Let me count the ways I've not been good to him: not ambitious enough, not spending enough time at his 'social' voluntary/mandatory work functions, I don't present myself as a professional. Oh, yes, the worst of all—he says I abuse his bunny."

"Is that a euphemism?"

"No. He accuses all his girlfriends of trying to destroy his rabbit; I think it's projection. He hates the bunny. His Lepus loathes him. He accuses all his girlfriends even though only one did go all Alex Forest all over his bunny."

"Passive aggressive."

"Mostly just passive."

"If the rabbit hates him, and he hates it—?"

"Why doesn't he just sell it? Donate it? Eat it? Because, like ninety-five percent of the men in DC, he's ambitious."

"Only ninety-five?"

"The other five percent have acknowledged they've surpassed their highest level of incompetence; the ninety-five are still delusional or congressmen, or both. David appeared to have interests outside of work. They were, I found out, interests he feigned only to network— kayaking with Mr. Leo, golf with Mr. Radzikowski, bunny shows with Joe Stella, *ad infinitum*. He keeps it only because Joe, his former boss, has unlimited networking potential, and he gleans a half dozen names every outing."

"That's why you were going out with him? Hobbies and interests other than work?"

"He fakes interest. He calls it '*The Taming of the Shrewd*.'"

"*Mr. Blandishment Builds His Scream House*?"

"You know if you keep making allusions to last century's movies, people will think you're strange. Quoting *The Millennial Falcon*—"

"—*Maltese*—"

"Yes, it doesn't matter because anything before 2001—"

"—another great movie before this century."

"Do you want to hear this story?"

"Only if I laugh, I cry, and it becomes a part of me."

"It is a part of you. In this town, there are ninety men to every one hundred women. We don't get the cream of the crop. We glean the leavings."

"Don't you think that's a little harsh?"

"No, not harsh, not abrasive."

"Very bitter, are you?"

"Not bitter, not sour, not acidic, but perhaps caustic."

"Caustic with cause?"

"In seven weeks of dating, we went to nine 'functions,' eight of them business related and one networking with an NGO. We went to one on short notice. We were supposed to have an evening to ourselves at the National Zoo. I dressed for it. Good walking shoes, light pants and he said to me, he actually said to me, after springing it on me that we're going to a diplomatic cocktail party, 'You're not going to wear that, are you?' in a tone I'd not heard since middle school. He, like every other professional man in DC, is only marginally human."

"That's not really the case—"

"How long have you been dating Michael? Two years? Ah, did you take Michael back to St. Paul last time you went home?"

"Michael? Oh, no. He'd talk only about the more esoteric provisions of the Affordable Care Act."

"Would you take him to your college reunion?"

"Oh, hell, no."

"High school?"

"Good God, no. That'd be worse than college."

"Would you have gone on a second date if you were both living in St. Paul? Don't answer; I can see it in your face. I rest my case."

"How many," Sharon pointed to the now empty glass, "have you had?"

"Two."

"Glasses?"

"Carafes."

"Tell me, Kathy—"

"That's better."

"Tell me the rest."

"He dropped me for the ex, the woman who emailed him ten times a day, who got plowed at an office Christmas party, totally obliterated, and then whispered to his boss that she'd like a threesome. He calls her his manic pixie, a flirty, fun-lovin' gal. He dropped the g in the email and did refer to her as 'a gal.' Now he says she's good for his career, an entirely different story than before. He said he's trading up, both his apartment, going to take the rental in Georgetown, and in his women. He talked to me before about moving but not about 'trading up' women. Look at this, Sharon," Kathy said while dropping a heavily laden Brooks Brothers bag on the table. "These are my copies."

"Yes, a shopping bag filled with DVDs. Very nice. Have you given up on dating? Is this what it's all about, Kathy?"

"No, dear, these are bunny revealed treasures. The rabbit, the one he loathes and the one who loathes him, was loose when I went to pick up my CDs. It proves you have to be smarter than the rabbit to keep it caged. David has a stuffed teddy bear in every room; I really did not notice before because of all his sporting gear, books to impress and miscellaneous feigned interests. But one in every room? All identical. And the only stuffed toys anywhere in his apartment. Bugsy—"

"—Siegel ?"

"I'm sure I'd laugh out loud if I knew who that is. He thinks Bugs—"

"Moran?"

"And again I'd laugh if I knew who that is. Bugs *Bunny* would be too obvious. Speaking of laughing, he ended his email with 'lol'—I don't know if he knows what that means."

"Lots of Love?"

"Probably 'Look Out! Loser.' Let me finish this because it all hinges on the bunny tale. Bugsy hopped up on the back of the divan, shredded the teddy's face, revealing—and here you need to give me a drum roll or dramatic organ music—a nanny cam. DVDs of all his girlfriends were behind the recording equipment on the bookcase. It appears a bad hare day occasionally can be good for morale."

"Tell me you didn't send them to his girlfriends."

"No, they're not my property. It would probably be illegal, so I just had copies made and left the originals on his coffee table, the one recommended by the deputy director of procurement at GSA, along with a copy of his email to me. Oh, yeah, I almost forgot. The DVD of his ex-girlfriend, now current girlfriend and soon to be ex again, is playing on a continuous loop in his apartment. Tiffany will probably be first in the apartment and first to throw a lamp. In those few minutes, I went through the seven stages of a breakup. Sorrow through acknowledgement in six minutes flat."

"Zero to seven in six—very good."

"Even better, I'm sending one copy to him every week for the next thirty-six weeks. I underlined two sentences in his email. One was apropos of nothing. It read 'That which does not kill you makes you stranger.' And, do you want to venture a guess?"

"He did not finish with 'Let's be friends,' did he?"

"Worse."

"What could be worse? What in the history of the world, including The Spanish Inquisition, could be worse?"

"He used the *R* word."

"*No.*"

"Yes. He wants me to be his roommate, share the rent in the Georgetown apartment, and being modern or even postmodern—a term I don't understand—not being exclusive."

"But with benefits?"

"Yes."

"Laugh out Loud?"

HAIR TO THE MAX
Lisa Ricard Claro

Libby Carter slapped the alarm clock, hitting the snooze button more by luck than design. When the obnoxious beeping stopped and silence reigned, she snuggled into her pillow, groaned, and cursed her best friend and roommate, Sunny.

"Why," Libby mumbled, "did I let her push me into this?"

Libby's orange tabby, Igor, responded with an affectionate head butt against Libby's hip. She caressed his silky coat and blinked into the early morning darkness.

"I hate blind dates, Igor. I haven't even met the guy, and he's already ruining my day."

Libby thought back to her conversation with Sunny the day before.

"Oh, c'mon, Libby," Sunny had cajoled over lunch. "Rob—you know Rob, the hairdresser?—he says this guy is great. He's never been married and—"

"He's probably gay," Libby interjected and pointed her fork at Sunny. "Like the last guy you set me up with."

"That was an honest mistake," Sunny protested. "Anyway, he's really cute and he owns his own business. And he has a cat named Ratso. How can you not want to meet a man with a cat named Ratso?"

"How? Let me count the ways."

"It's one night of your life, Lib. What do you have to lose?"

"Two hours of sleep," Libby answered now, to Igor. "Let's get up, buddy. Like it or not, I have a blind date tonight and need to dye my roots so my hair isn't two-toned."

Igor padded into the bathroom with Libby and settled on the edge of the tub while his mistress fumbled blindly in the cabinet for the box of hair dye.

"What a pain it is to stay Buxom Beach Bunny Blonde," Libby mumbled, eyeing the box. She yawned and squinted in the mirror at the dark roots sprouting from her scalp. "One of these days I'm going back to my natural color."

Half asleep, she donned the plastic gloves provided in the box of dye and mixed the chemical creams as directed. She slathered the stuff onto her roots and worked it in, then dumped the unused portion down the drain and tossed the bottles in the trash.

She shuffled to the kitchen and set the oven timer for thirty minutes, then brewed a pot of coffee. Breakfast followed, accompanied by the *New York Times* crossword puzzle, and she applauded herself for perfect timing: Her last bite of bagel coincided with the beep-beep-beep of the alarm.

Yawning, Libby returned to the bathroom and flicked on the light. "What? No!"

She snatched up the box that had contained the dye and checked the color: Buxom Beach Bunny Blonde. She stared at the picture on the box of a smiling woman who was, indeed, both buxom and blonde, then looked back at her own sticky tresses.

Black. The dye saturating the top third of her head was definitely black. The darkest of blacks. The pitchest of blacks.

"Dear God," she whispered.

She fished the bottle of hair dye from the trash and compared the color stamped on the plastic container to the color on the outside of the box: Black Beauty. What?

"No…no, no, no…" Libby groaned.

She jumped in the shower with no regard for her pajamas or water temperature, applied shampoo, and scrubbed as if rubbing out sin. Conditioner and another thorough scouring followed. Desperate, she grabbed her exfoliate cream and squeezed a generous dollop onto her hands and worked that into her scalp as well, praying the black color would fade.

"Please," she whispered, "please, please, please…"

After a thorough rinsing, Libby wrapped a towel around her head and stepped from the shower. Her soaked pajamas dripped a wet trail on the tile as she scrambled to the mirror. She steadied herself with a cleansing breath and pulled the towel from her hair.

"Noooo…" Reduced to whimpering, she further inspected herself, shoulders slumped. Some of the dye had dripped onto her face, leaving dark gray splotches on her skin—a speckled reminder that black hair dye is not for sissies. Or the sloppy at heart.

Libby the sloppy sissy stared.

The huge doe eyes of her reflection stared back.

Horrified gasps propelled themselves from her lips and hyperventilation seemed a possibility. For a wild moment she considered that passing out on the bathroom floor would be preferable to looking at her own reflection. Instead, she breathed in through her nose, out through her mouth, and flipped down the lid of the toilet seat and sat. Still dizzy, she rested her elbows on her knees, dropped her head into her hands and moaned.

"Hey, you okay?" Sunny appeared in the doorway looking way too perky in her Hello Kitty nightshirt. "You look hung over."

Libby lifted her head, bi-colored hair hanging and dripping.

"This is your fault," she ground out. "You and the stupid blind date you insisted I go on."

"Wait. What?"

"My hair! Look at my hair!" Libby grabbed the dripping mass and gave it a shake. "The wrong color dye was in the box."

Sunny's eyes widened and she covered her mouth with her hand, but a squeak escaped.

"How can you laugh?" Libby cried. "Look at me! You have to cancel this date tonight. And I have to call in sick. I can't go in looking like this."

"You have to," Sunny said. "Today is the big meeting with Majik-McClellan Household Appliances."

"The meeting is tomorrow."

"They moved it to today, Lib. Didn't you get the memo?"

"Are you freaking kidding me? Is this a joke?" When Sunny just raised her brows and bit her lip, Libby buried her face in her hands again. "Oh. My. God."

"Call in late to work. I'll phone Rob at the salon and see if he can fit you in." Sunny grinned. "You certainly qualify as an emergency."

"Are you crazy? Rob's not at a salon. He's a teacher at the beauty college. I'm not letting some first year beautician touch my hair."

"Not one of the students," Sunny rolled her eyes. "Rob."

Two hours later, Libby tucked her half-black, half-blonde hair under a baseball cap and drove to the salon. A spiky-haired redhead with Amy Winehouse eyeliner glanced up from the counter and offered an abbreviated smile.

"May I help you?"

"I hope so," Libby said. "I have an emergency appointment with Rob."

"Oh, bad luck, hon," Spiky-hair snapped her gum. "He called a little while ago. His car won't start and he's waiting on a tow." Snap. Snap. "You can see..." she tapped the keyboard in front of her and squinted at the computer screen. "Suellen. She's pretty good."

Why, Libby wondered later as she sat in the stylist's chair, did these things always happen to her? She stared at the goop in her hair. Suellen was not an instructor or a licensed stylist, but with limited time and in dire need, Libby had agreed to settle. How bad could it be?

"Well," said Suellen an hour later. "It ain't perfect, but considering how you looked when you walked in, it ain't so bad."

"Are you kidding? I look like Cruella De Vil!" Libby cried.

"Well," Suellen beamed, cornflower eyes wide. "It certainly makes a statement!"

"It's not funny," Libby growled, staring at her reflection in the ladies' room mirror. She usually loved her job as an advertising assistant here at Creative Minds, but today she wished herself anywhere else.

"I'm sorry." Sunny wiped tears of laughter from her eyes. "I know it isn't funny, but...well, it really sorta is. Your meeting is in ten minutes. What are you going to do?"

"What can I do? This is my first real shot at being project manager and look at me! As if this isn't bad enough, it's getting ready to rain, and I left my sunroof open."

"Give me your keys, Cruella." Sunny held out her hand. "I'll take care of the sunroof. You try to do something with that hair."

Libby dug through her purse and finally emptied the contents onto the counter. She snatched up her keys and dropped them into Sunny's open palm.

She blinked at Sunny with mournful eyes. "Thanks. You better hurry. It's starting to thunder."

"You're the one who better hurry," Sunny said over her shoulder as she rushed out. "Your meeting's about to start. Good luck, Lib!"

Libby stared into the mirror. She should never have gone ahead with Suellen's suggestion to dye back to blonde. The black was too dark, and the subsequent blonde dye too harsh. The result was a horror show mess. Like a train wreck or a bad B movie, no one would be able to look away.

An idea bloomed and Libby grasped it, desperate.

"That's it! No one can look away! Hair gel. I need hair gel to calm it down some."

Desperate to find the hair gel, she rifled through the things she had dumped onto the counter. A blast of thunder reverberated, and in the next second, the bathroom morphed to a lightless cave. Libby stood still as a frightened rabbit, blinking unseeing into the darkness.

"Great," she whispered.

With no time to spare, she fumbled blindly through her stuff in search of the hair gel.

"Yes!"

She grabbed the tube, twisted off the top, and squirted what felt like a good amount into the palm of her hand. She rubbed her hands together and smoothed the substance through her hair from scalp to ends. It wouldn't look great, but at least it wouldn't be exploding from her head like pampas grass gone wrong.

Done, she washed her hands and pushed everything from the counter back into her purse, feeling around the counter to be sure she hadn't missed anything. Satisfied, she forced a smile onto her face just as the lights sputtered on.

"Aaargh!"

Libby gaped at her hair, now covered with a gooey paste. She didn't need to look in her purse to confirm that she had covered her head with hand cream instead of gel. Her shoulders sagged and icy fingers of disbelief traced their way along her skin. How could this mess get any worse?

Hold it together, Libby, she told herself. *Find a way to use it.*

Libby drew a deep breath, lifted her chin, pushed her shoulders back, and marched from the bathroom toward her office. She ran into Sunny on the way.

"Don't ask," Libby said, rushing past. "Just wish me luck."

Libby hid in her office until the call came from the receptionist that the people from Majik-McClellan had arrived. She marched toward the conference room, ignoring the stares and chuckles from coworkers and focused on the task at hand: Sell the best advertising concept Majik-McClellan had ever seen and cement her future at Creative Minds.

"Good afternoon!" Libby's cheerful greeting was met with shocked expressions and dropped jaws from everyone in the con- ference room. "I'm sorry I'm late." She flashed a smile at her boss and looked away. If she focused on his horrified countenance, she'd lose her nerve.

"First," Libby said, "I'd like to thank you for coming. You're here because Creative Minds is in the running to handle Majik- McClellan's next big advertising campaign. We're excited about this and eager to show you that we're not only the right choice, but the only choice for Majik-McClellan.

"Why? Three words: Unexpected. Surprised. Riveted.

"You were all of those things when I walked into this room. Even now, your minds are working to process my appearance and you can't look away. I have your full attention. Not only that, when you leave here today, you'll remember me. That's good. Because that's the exact reaction you want from your potential customers. You want an ad campaign that is so unexpected, so surprising, so riveting, that they can't look away.

"When Creative Minds handles your ad campaign, we go all out for you." Libby pointed to her hair. "I'm not afraid to look like Cruella De Vil having a bad hair day because I'm doing it for you. And as it happens, this crazy 'do is the centerpiece of my ideas for your advertising. Intrigued?" She smiled and relaxed for the first time in hours. "I can see that you are. So, if everyone is ready, I'll get to the heart of my presentation."

"I heard you were brilliant!" Sunny gushed two hours later in the break room. "How the heck did you tie that mess of a hair-do into an ad campaign for home appliances?"

"Inspiration struck," Libby said, scratching her head, "replaced by an itchy scalp. I need to go home and wash this gunk out and see if I can find a salon somewhere to help me fix this disaster."

"You don't have much time. It's four o'clock and you're supposed to meet Rob's friend at seven."

"What? You were supposed to cancel that. I can't go on a blind date looking like this!"

"You don't have a choice," Sunny said. "The guy you're meeting is Rob's friend. You can't just stand him up, and I haven't been able to reach Rob. He never made it into the salon, and his cell is going straight to voice mail."

Libby laughed without humor. "Great."

"What about that salon at the end of the street next to the coffee place? Hair to the Max."

"We've never tried it. What if they're awful?" Libby said.

"Do you really think they could make your hair any worse?"

"Good point." Libby sighed. "Hair to the Max, here I come!"

Libby opened the door to Hair to the Max and did a double take at the man sitting behind the counter. The Johnny Depp-alike did a similar double take when he glanced up at her. By now, she was used to the wide eyes and dropped jaw that accompanied a look in her direction.

"No smart-ass comments," Libby begged. "As you can plainly see, I'm in desperate need of a quick makeover. Can anyone here help me?"

"I'm an artist, not a miracle worker, but I'll try," he said with raised brows. "Lucky for you my last client just canceled. I'm Max. Come have a seat and we'll talk."

Libby dropped into the stylist's chair with a huff. She glanced at his framed cosmetologist's license and noted the photo next to it of Max with another man, arms around each other. *Why*, she wondered, *are all the gorgeous men gay?*

Annoyed, she grumbled, "It all started because of a stupid blind date."

As she relayed the events that led to her wacky hairdo, Max's humor grew. By the time she explained how the hand cream ended up in her hair, he was laughing out loud.

"Poor baby," he chuckled. "No blind date in the world is worth all of that hassle."

"I know, right?" Libby said, happy to find someone who agreed with her. "So can you fix it?"

"You have to be out of here by six?"

"Yes. I still have to go home and get ready for my date."

"Okay," Max narrowed his eyes and assessed her hair. "Here's what we'll do."

At five minutes to seven, Libby pulled her car into an open parking space outside the restaurant where she was set to meet...

"Oh, for God's sake," she spat out. "What is this guy's name?" She fished through her purse in search of the piece of paper with the man's name and general description. For the second time that day, she dumped her purse and cursed herself for being an idiot. She'd been so caught up with her hair and the meeting that she had never talked to Sunny about her blind date. Unable to find the paper, she grabbed her cell phone.

"Sunny," she said. "Who am I meeting? What does he look like? Is he getting a table or waiting outside? Help!"

"Geez, Lib, I dunno," Sunny said. "I told you, I never got hold of Rob. But listen, I'm sure Rob must've told him what you look like. He'll be watching for you."

"And he won't find me. He'll be looking for a long-haired blonde, not a mid-length brunette." Libby lay her head back on the seat's headrest and for the first time saw humor in her day. "This is impossible. More bleach would have damaged my hair too much, so Max put my hair back to my natural color and cut off about four inches to make it look healthier. He's awesome, by the way. Max. Too bad he's gay."

"All the good ones are gay," Sunny and Libby said at the same time, and laughed together.

"Okay, well, I'm going in. I'll look around and see if I can find the guy. Wish me luck."

Libby put her purse back together and took one last look in the rearview mirror. All things considered, she had to admit she looked pretty damn good. Max had done a great job. She actually liked the color and admired the sleek fall of her hair. Maybe this date would turn out okay after all.

Two steps from the car a thunder boomer blasted and the heavens opened up.

"Oh, for Pete's sake," Libby said aloud and looked up to the sky, heedless of the water drenching her. "Really? Is this some kind of crazy test?"

By the time she entered the restaurant, her sleek hair was no more. A glimpse in the huge mirror behind the hostess station told her that Cruella De Vil had been replaced by Drowned Rat.

She gave the restaurant dining room a cursory once-over so it wouldn't be a lie when she told Sunny she looked for the guy but never saw him. There was no man sitting alone, and she used that to assuage her guilt about running away. Turning to leave, she bumped into—

"Max!"

Max ran a quick hand over Libby's drenched hair and burst out laughing. "Lady, what have you done to my masterpiece?"

"I thought I made it clear at the beginning of our relationship that there were to be no smart-assed comments," she laughed up at him. "Can you even believe it? I got caught in the rain. Today is the worst hair day ever."

Max's espresso eyes caught and held Libby's. "It's actually pretty great from where I'm standing."

Libby's heart skipped a beat. Was he flirting?

"Why don't we get a table?"

"Uh," Libby gulped. "I'm supposed to meet someone. And you're...? Right?"

Max grinned. "Catholic? Hungry? Give me a clue."

"There was a picture of you with...a guy. I just assumed..."

"Kid brother," Max flashed a smile that melted Libby's bones.

Color bloomed up her neck and into her face. Speechless, she blinked at Max and wished herself away to a quiet beach where she could stick her head in the sand.

"You look so miserable," he chuckled. "I can't tease you anymore. When you came into the salon earlier and told me your tale of woe, I knew immediately who you were. It's a small world, Libby. As it happens, we both know Rob. I'm your blind date."

"If you're teasing, I'll strangle you." Libby narrowed her eyes. "And I'm not joking."

"Would I tease about something like that after the bad hair day you've had?" His tone was serious, but his eyes smiled into hers. "Besides," he lifted a handful of her sopping tresses, "you need me."

Libby raised a brow and pretended to ponder her choices.

"Is it true you have a cat named Ratso?"

"Well, yeah. Ratso rules."

"In that case," Libby said, "this date is on."

She smoothed a hand over her dripping 'do and grinned. She had a new account on the books, had found a great stylist, and a drop-dead-gorgeous man who liked cats.

This had turned out to be a great hair day after all.

CURSE OF THE CAT'S PAW
Mary Ellen Martin

"What does it do?" I asked.

"It broken."

"I see that, but what does it do?" Again, I reached for the paw on the small plastic cat on the restaurant counter. It was white, with small flowers all over it, and a Cheshire grin. One paw was upraised in a waving sort of gesture. I pushed the paw down, which bounced back up, but nothing happened. No meow, no toothpick or candy, no cheesy Confucius quotes.

"It broken." The young waitress handed me my change and another fortune cookie. She grabbed two menus and motioned to some customers behind us. Clearly, with the bill paid, neither we, nor the cat, were very important anymore.

As Shari and I stepped from the dark lobby of Wong's into bright sunshine, she started laughing. "Boy, you're pretty dumb. How many times did she have to say, 'It broken'?"

I chuckled. "A lot, apparently."

Okay, I have to admit what ensued might have been my fault. As our shoes crunched on the gravel parking lot, we began to mimic the waitress's accent.

"Women who eat in cheap Chinese restaurant pay later," Shari said.

"Confucius say: broken Chinese cat mean happy dog," I answered.

"Confucius say: if dog broke cat, that was not Schezwan beef," Shari intoned.

Both of us started laughing. As we walked to my car, we passed a door that led to the kitchen. The screen door was open, presumably to attempt to keep the kitchen cool.

A cook overheard us and came to the door, yelling at us in Chinese. Shari and I looked at each other, and hurried back to the car, grinning. I had forgotten to crack the windows, and the car's interior was broiling hot and stuffy.

"Ugh, hurry up and get the AC going. My face is gonna melt," Shari complained.

"Maybe you should use less makeup," I said as I turned the ignition. Nothing happened. I turned the key again. And again, nothing happened.

"Oh no, no, no," I whispered.

"What the hell?" Shari asked. "It was fine an hour ago."

"Yeah, I know." I tried again. "Crap." I leaned my head on the steering wheel. Shari looked at me.

"How much did you tip our waitress?"

Thank God, my phone was charged. A tow garage was right down the street, so it didn't take long for them to get my car. Unfortunately, my only help was my ex. He picked us up and took Shari to the club where she dances. Andrew grumbled the whole time until Shari got out of the car, mumbling about houses of sin and hellfire. I smirked as Shari put a little more swing in her hips as she walked away from the car.

"So, what happened? Did one of her 'clients' trash the car?" I rolled my eyes.

"What happened to 'judge not'? And no, it wasn't trashed, it just died. And thanks, by the way." Andrew said nothing.

The ride to the bank where I work was tense. It was hard to tell which made the car colder, his working AC, or his attitude. Ex-husbands were just great that way. It made me wonder why he chose to stay in Reno. But he wouldn't leave, so I was stuck.

On my next work break, I checked the recent calls on my phone. The car garage, the doctor's office, a couple of numbers I didn't recognize, and Shari. Naturally, I called her first.

"I got fired!" She wailed. Or whined. Her voice sounded odd.

"What? Not possible. You're the best dancer they've got."

"No, you don't get it," she sniffled. "My heel broke in the middle of my act and hit some guy in the eye. He was drunk, tried to grab me, and the bouncer rearranged his face. But in the scuffle, my nose got broken. I'm at the clinic right now. Can you come get me?"

"Boy, it's a bit early in the day for that, isn't it? And I don't have my car back yet. I will call the garage next and get back to you." My phone buzzed. "Oh crap, that's the doctor's office. I need to go."

"Ms. Paulsen, this is Dr. Witt's office. I'm sorry to tell you your test was positive, and you need to come in right away for follow-up."

I frowned. "What are you talking about? What test?"

"Ms. Paulsen, I'm talking about your recent physical. Your blood work came back. I can schedule you for—"

"Look, are you sure you have the right person? I haven't seen the doctor in over a year."

"Is this Rhonda Paulsen?"

"Yes."

"Birthday April 1969?"

"No."

"Oh, um," stammered the woman. "Well, I apologize for the confusion. Do you think you could verify your contact information with us? You'll need to come down in person, so we could see your ID and match it with the information we have on file."

I groaned inwardly. "Look, my car is in the shop. I'll get there when I can. But it sounds to me like the only verifying you need to do is check your phone numbers." I hung up on her. The garage was next.

"Yeah, Ms. Paulsen, this is Don at the garage. We've got your car here, and it's got a busted fuel pump and a dead battery." I reached for the antacid in my purse when he told me what it would cost to fix it. Great, I'd have to hit my ex-husband up for money, again. Shari would normally be my go-to girl for this stuff, but since she was now out of a job, Andrew was my safety net. I was in serious trouble.

My boss, Mr. Ryerson, walked by the break room door tapping his watch and giving me a pointed look. I nodded and rose, just as my phone buzzed in my hand again, this time from my son's school.

"Ms. Paulsen, we've been trying to contact you. Your son, Matt, is in the office. We think he has head lice, and you need to come get him right away."

Before I could stop myself, I threw my phone down and shouted at the ceiling. "Doesn't anyone understand I don't have a car!"

When I opened my eyes, four coworkers were standing in the doorway, staring at me. "What?" I demanded. "I turn into a lunatic under stress. Sue me." I grabbed my phone, still intact, and told the receptionist I would try to get there as soon as I could. I sank down into a chair and tried counting to ten, not knowing whether to laugh or cry.

My coworkers had not moved from the doorway. Embarrassed, I tried to wave them off. "Sorry, been one of those days. I will be out in a sec."

One of them, Johanna Chen, looked at the others. "Can you guys stall Ryerson? I'll stay with Rhonda." I smiled my thanks to Johanna as the others left.

"Thanks. I don't know what you can do, though." I relayed everything that had happened. It was hard to believe it only started two hours ago.

"Hmm, I must admit, karma has its sights set on you today. What did you do?"

"Huh?" That's me, witty as ever.

"Well, the only explanation I can see is the universe is getting back at you for something. What happened today?"

I thought. "Well, nothing, really. This morning was normal. Breakfast for me and Matt, getting to work, normal morning. Things didn't hit the fan until lunchtime."

"What happened at lunch?" Johanna asked.

"Nothing. We ate, got yelled at by a Chinese cook—"

Johanna sat up. "Where? Where did you eat?"

"Wong's, down on Third Street."

"*Ai ya,*" Johanna whispered. "What did the cook say?"

"Johanna, you're freaking me out. He was yelling in Chinese, so I don't know. And then, my car breaks down, Shari loses her job, I'm getting false positives on tests I never took, and now my son..." I put my head in my hands. "What else could go wrong today?"

Johanna sat back and looked at me. "Don't challenge the universe like that. It will take the dare. And I don't like Wong's. I hate their feng shui."

"Yeah, the décor is tacky, but it's the only cheap Chinese food in town that doesn't make me sick."

Johanna smiled. "It started there, you need to finish it there."

"What are you talking about? Finish what?"

"You need to finish whatever karma started at that restaurant." Johanna knocked on the fake wood table. "Your Western superstition would say you walked under a ladder. I think you've been cursed."

"Don't be ridiculous. A Chinese curse? Please. Food poisoning is usually the only curse I get." I rose and splashed some water on my face in the sink.

Johanna handed me a towel. "If you think about it, you will realize something was different about today. Something out of balance. When you find it, you can fix it. Then, things will be better."

"Johanna, I don't believe in Chinese magic, or superstitions for that matter. I couldn't write a sitcom episode better than the day I'm having. But thanks for listening. By the way, can I borrow your car?"

After some fast-talking with Ryerson, I drove off in Johanna's Saturn. It was much nicer than my car. Let's face it, a Pinto would be better, the way today was going. I walked into the school office, and did a double take on the receptionist. Why was she familiar?

I looked to where Matt was sitting. The bench he and two other kids sat on was covered with a sheet. All three looked pretty glum. I walked to Matt and peered closely at his head. I was afraid his blond hair would make spotting the nits difficult, but in fact, there was no trouble at all.

"Who says he has head lice?"

"The school nurse, of course. Today she's checking the fourth and fifth graders," the receptionist said.

"Uh huh. And how old is the school nurse?" I asked.

The receptionist looked confused. "Um, close to retirement age, I think. Why?"

"Yeah, and when is the last time she had her eyes checked? These aren't nits in his hair. It's rice."

"There was a food fight in the cafeteria," Matt said.

The receptionist began to look around at the other office workers. "Um, I'll get Mrs. Rabe, she's the principal. She can explain it to you."

"You do that. I bet she can tell the difference between nits and rice." I looked down at Matt and gave him a hug. "A food fight?"

"Yeah, it was so awesome, Mom! Jason Posey started the whole thing. He said he saw a food fight on TV yesterday."

"Swell." I turned as Mrs. Rabe came out of her office, followed by a boy covered in food. I could barely see the boy's dark skin through all the muck. Mrs. Rabe pointed at a chair next to her office door, and the boy sat down, making faces at her back.

"Ms. Paulsen, I can assure you the school nurse is very competent at her job, and we'll have to ask you to take your son home and get treated."

"I'm sorry, Mrs. Rabe, but I have to disagree. Before I worked in a bank, I was a beautician, with plenty of experience dealing with head lice. This is not it. Take a look."

Mrs. Rabe, looking hesitant, leaned over my son's head. Her eyes widened. She then reached over and touched Matt's head. The receptionist gasped. Mrs. Rabe looked at the other two children. "None of them have lice. Incredible. Sally, call the parents back and tell them they don't need to get their kids." The receptionist turned to the phone, and then paused as the office door opened and more adults walked in.

"What's this about my kid having lice?" blustered a father, whose son tried to shrink into the bench he was sitting on.

"And what is this about my daughter starting a food fight?"

Mrs. Rabe blinked. "Mr. Posey, can we please step into my office—"

"No, I'm not Posey, I'm Carhart. That's my son, Nate, right there." He pointed to the other boy sitting with Matt on the bench.

Mrs. Rabe turned to Sally, one eyebrow raised.

"Um, oops," Sally said. "I must have gotten all the parents confused, between calling for Jason's parents and the head lice kids, I..." she trailed off and swallowed, her eyes huge.

I couldn't help it. I started laughing. This whole day had been too much. And to see it happening to someone else, well, I couldn't stop laughing. My belly began to hurt, and I leaned on Sally's desk. I finally realized why she looked so familiar, and laughed even harder.

"Sally, didn't I see you at Wong's for lunch today?"

"Yeah, what does that have to do with anything?"

"Did you touch the cat on the counter?"

"Yes, I did."

I wiped my streaming eyes and gave Matt a hug, flicking a couple bits of rice out of his hair. "I'll pick you up after school, kiddo. And Sally, good luck. You'll need it."

I picked Shari up at the clinic. There was a small bandage on her nose, and both eyes were black. She was limping, due to wearing only one spike heel. Someone had loaned her some scrubs to put over her skimpy bikini, which was her dancing outfit. She wore a black leather jacket over the scrubs. I gave her a hug. "Take that other shoe off before you break your ankle. Are you going to be okay?"

"I think so, but you wouldn't believe the day I've had. Can we head back to the club? I need to give Chris his coat back."

"Yeah, but there's somewhere else we have to go first. And if we're keeping score on today's disasters, I think we're even."

I explained to Shari everything that happened to me after lunch, and my conversation with Johanna Chen.

"So, what, we go back to the restaurant and, like, fix the karma? Do you even hear yourself right now?" Shari asked.

"I know, I know. Stop touching that. This isn't my car."

"But it's GPS!" Shari squealed. "And satellite radio!"

"Would you pay attention? It all started right after lunch. I don't know, maybe we offended someone, and need to apologize. That cook did overhear us talking."

"I repeat the question," Shari said. "Do you hear yourself? This is completely stupid. I'm not going in there with you."

"Hey. I'm grasping at straws here. Everything is falling apart, and I will do anything to fix this, and you're coming with me. Because you were there when all this started. Unless you don't want a ride to the club?"

Shari stuck her tongue out at me before opening the car door. "And when things keep going downhill, you'll still look like an idiot."

"And you'll still look like a raccoon. C'mon, let's go."

The lobby of the restaurant was blissfully cool and dark. I gave my eyes a few minutes to adjust. Everything looked exactly the same. There was a large picture on the wall to the left of three Chinese girls sitting under a cherry blossom tree. To the right was the counter, with the stupid broken plastic cat and the till. On the floor, to the left of the entryway to the dining room, was a small plastic Buddha. Electric candles were on each side of it, and a small vase of fresh flowers was right behind it.

One thing that was missing today was the grapefruit. All the times Shari and I had lunch here, that Buddha always had a large grapefruit in its lap. Except for today, apparently. I tried to remember if the grapefruit had been there when we came in at lunch, but honestly, I had taken the thing for granted in my quest for Kung Pao chicken and Schezwan beef.

Shari and I looked at each other, and then at the cat. Why on God's green earth anyone would pick that for a decoration was beyond me. Shari reached out to touch the cat's paw. I felt my heart suddenly speed up, and I started to sweat.

"Don't."

She rolled her eyes. "Seriously? A plastic flower-covered cat that doesn't do anything?" She reached out again, and I grabbed her wrist.

"God, don't!"

Shari looked at me. "Uh, Rhonda, are you okay? You're pale." I began pacing back and forth, racking my brain.

"No, no, I am not okay. Okay, let's think this out. What did we do, exactly?"

Shari squinted, and winced, touching her nose. I only felt a little sympathy, and it was overshadowed by panic that something else might go wrong. It could happen.

"Um, we came in. Our waitress showed us to the table."

"Right," I said. "We ordered before she could hand us the menus, and then you went back to the lobby—"

"—To go to the bathroom," Shari said.

"Yeah. We ate, we paid, we made fun of the waitress, got yelled at by that cook, and then all hell broke loose." I rubbed my eyes. "But I was the only one who touched the cat, not you. So why did you have trouble today?" I mused. "Because you were with me?"

Shari shrugged. "Beats me. I can barely breathe right now."

Damn and double damn. I did not want to have to do this. Taking a breath, I rang the small bell on the counter. Our waitress from earlier came out, and I got ready to grovel.

Before I could say anything, she pointed at us and started shouting in Chinese. A little bit of English was mixed in, and it sounded like she said, "You steal offer! You steal offer!" She whirled and went back to the kitchen area, where more shouting could be heard.

What the hell was that about? I looked at Shari. "You asked me earlier if I tipped her. Did you steal the tip?" Shari shook her head and adjusted her grip on her bag.

The waitress came out again, accompanied by the old cook we had seen at lunch. He started yelling at us in Chinese, and I looked at our waitress.

"Look, we don't understand what happened. Just tell us why you're upset, and we can apologize. Or leave a better tip. Whatever will make this bad karma, or whatever, go away. Please."

The woman glared at me. "You get curse because you steal offer!"

I sighed. "Look, I don't know anything about any curses or anything stolen. I'm not Indiana Jones, so I have no idea what you're talking about. All I know is bad things happened the second we left. Tell us how to make it right."

The waitress pointed at the small Buddha on the floor, and then at Shari and me. "Give back offer."

I looked at Shari, stunned. "This all happened because of you? You stole a damn grapefruit? This whole time I thought it was because I touched that stupid cat! But it wasn't because you were with me that your day sucked, it was because I was with *you* that *my* day sucked." I couldn't believe it. Shari shook her head, her black eyes enormous.

"I can explain, really." She looked back and forth between the waitress and me. "When I went to the bathroom, I saw the grapefruit there. I knew I was going to get fired today, even before the fight happened. I get feelings about things, okay? It happens a lot. So anyway, I grabbed it, thinking that was going to be my dinner tonight. I mean, come on, I didn't think anyone bought into this crap."

I face-palmed, if only to keep from slapping the snot out of Shari. "Why didn't you tell me you thought you would get fired?"

Shari glowered at me. "Oh, sure. Tell Miss Stable Banker that her bar dancer friend can't keep a job. But after what happened to your car, I couldn't ask you for help."

"That's weird, because I thought I was always asking you for help," I said. "But this isn't going to be me fixing this, it's you."

Shari sighed and reached into her bag. "Fine. Here." She pulled out the grapefruit and gave it to the waitress. "I told you it wasn't about the stupid cat."

The waitress grabbed the grapefruit and said something to the cook. He muttered something in response and shuffled back to the kitchen. The waitress placed the fruit on the small dish in the Buddha's lap and turned around. Shari and I took a step back involuntarily. Rather than say anything more to us, she retreated to the kitchen as well.

"Huh, what do you make of that?" I said.

Shari placed her hand on my shoulder. "You think they'll let us eat here tomorrow?"

CRUMBLE
Michelle Tom

"I can't marry you, Ned. It would be impossible."

"Why not?"

"For a lot of reasons."

"Name one." Ned stands defiantly, arms akimbo.

Because you have small hands and lady hips. Because you were meant to be a fling. Because you're staring at me like a petulant child, and your big cheeks are still flush with the arrogant pride of getting down on one knee. After two months.

I sigh. "Your mother."

"What about her?"

"She grates."

"What? Cheese? Carrots?"

"Nerves, Ned. Nerves." I want to leave, but I can tell Ned will not let up easily. The small kitchen of his apartment feels like a lung collapsing, the air stagnant and heating up by degrees each minute. Two droplets of sweat, perfectly symmetrical on either side of Ned's broad forehead begin to grow larger and larger until they form parallel trails of perspiration that flow down in front of his ears like translucent sideburns.

"My mother grates nerves?" A familiar look of confusion warps Ned's face so it looks even more childlike. He shakes himself. "But, you wouldn't be marrying my mother. You'd be marrying me." He steps forward to grasp my hands, and I quickly put them behind my back.

"That is just one reason."

"Do I grate nerves?"

"You're more like a zester. You know, like lemon peel."

"Zest?"

"Yes, Ned." I sigh again, and guilt begins to creep in. I unfold my hands from my back and take his little, clammy ones in mine. We stand, facing each other, a few feet apart like we're about to sashay down the room in a Virginia reel. "Zest. It's great, but—" I hesitate.

Ned gulps, and I can tell this is finally sinking in.

"Two months, Ned. It's only been two months."

"Sometimes you need only two months."

"And sometimes two months can be a lifetime." His eyes are welling, and I cringe as tears join the sweat cascading down his face. "You will be fine." I smile up at him, and he begins to sniffle. I grab a Kleenex and hand it to him. "You will be fine," I say again, but he just rubs his nose with the tissue and acts like I'm invisible. The guilt grows, and I start to feel panicky. "Please, you'll be fine." I hesitate. "I want to always be friends." I say the lie, hoping the guilt will stop its steady progression throughout my body. "You are important to me." That sounds genuine enough. And "important" has many meanings.

Ned finally looks at me again, and I see that his brow is furrowed. *So we have moved on to anger. Good. I suppose.*

"I hope my mom tromps you in the contest."

"*What?*"

Ned's expression mocks me, as if I am suddenly the one totally off kilter. "The coun-try fair. The pie con-test." He says each word slowly, enunciating the syllables as if I have to read lips rather than listen.

The black guilt recedes, and fiery anger, something I'm far more comfortable with, burns the peripheries of my vision. I speak through gritted teeth. "Ned, I don't care if your mother *tromps* me in the pie contest. I'm entering to honor my mother, her memory." I will not cry.

"And my mother always beat your mother at every country fair."

I'm not sticking around for this anymore. I turn from Ned and grab my pie from the table. I came over that morning to show it to Ned, apple with a sugar crumble, a variation I've been working on all summer. Since I got back home from my first year at college, back to an empty house that my mother used to fill with cold lemonade and cookies and joy.

"Bye," I say, and *tromp* through the back door, banging the screen door on my way out.

My nose close to the pie, I inhale whiffs of cinnamon and butter. The frayed edges of my nerves begin to even out, and thoughts of Ned and his ridiculous proposal already begin to fade. I get to my car, a rusting white Civic. But it looks funny. With the utmost of care, I place the pie on the roof of the car, and then begin to inspect the vehicle. It's lopsided. The right rear tire sits flat in the gravel, and I see the head of a nail poking out of the cracked rubber.

"Great," I mumble, and instinct drives me to turn around toward the house again. Ned is standing at the kitchen window. His front hair is matted and wet from sweat, but he just stares at me. No way am I going to ask him for help.

I pull my cell phone from my purse and dial my sister. She rarely answers. It rings and rings and then goes to voicemail. Her pert voice comes on, and then the beep. "Kara, it's me, Aline." I hear tense curtness in my voice. Kara doesn't call back when I sound annoyed, so I take long breaths and deepen my tone. "I've got a flat tire and need to get to the fair for the contest." I glance at my watch. "It starts in twenty minutes. Can you come pick me up? I'm at Ned's. Outside." He's still staring at me through the window, and I'm pretty sure he knows about the tire. "Thanks, bye."

If Ned doesn't know about the tire, he definitely knows something's wrong.

I text Kara with the same message, but time is already running out. I scroll through my phone contacts. There's no one. Why did I come back here this summer? I could have stayed in the city, taken more courses, or gotten a job. All my high school friends were out seeing the world, *tromping* through Europe or volunteering with orphans in Africa or something like that. I came home. To bake. And honor my mom's memory. And summer in my childhood home one last time before my sister and her husband move in and overrun it with their four kids, three dogs, and bunny rabbit.

A glance at my watch tells me I have seventeen minutes. I shake myself, kick a rock in the driveway, and grumble loudly. Sometimes a throat just needs to make noise. Ned's away from the window now but not coming out of the house. I would steal his car. If he had one. My gaze wanders to the shed, and I resign myself to what I must do next.

I pry the old wooden door open and extract the rusted out Schwinn Ned uses to carouse about town when he's not mooching rides off his friends. There's a big wire basket hooked to the front, a bit effeminate for a boy's bike, but right now, I'm not one to judge. The tires are firm. I place my pie in the basket, hop on, and I'm fifty yards down the street before I hear Ned yelling at me from his drive.

It's a mile and half through neighborhood streets and then a short stretch downtown before I reach the fairgrounds at the end of Main. Canned music penetrates the air, and the old Ferris wheel, red and yellow, teeters on its axle.

My cell phone rings just as I'm setting down the bike. I balance the pie with one hand. "Kara," I say through gasps of air. My dress is soaked through with perspiration, and I imagine my brown hair is looking an awful lot like Ned's matted mess right now.

"I'm at the fair," Kara says, and sure enough I can hear the tinny music twice, once in real time and the second only a split moment later through the receiver. "Do you still need me to pick you up? I didn't get your message until just now."

"It's okay," I say.

"What?"

Now is not the time to tell my sister she's as flaky as dried coconut. "I'm here. Do you know where they're setting up for the pie contest?"

"The main bandstand. Actually, I'm there already. And everyone else is here too."

"Great," I mumble and walk through the crowds, dancing on my toes to avoid jostling my pie. In the distance, I see my sister waving her hands about. Sunlight glints off her rhinestone rings, and I walk toward the beacon.

"Thank goodness," she says once I finally reach her, and together we flip our cell phones shut. She points to a long table. "You're over there, next to Ned's mom."

"Great," I repeat. If I say the word enough times, it will come true, right?

Kara's expression grows curious. "Why isn't Ned here?" She finally starts taking in my disheveled appearance, connecting the dots. "What happened?"

"Long story." I squeeze her arm and walk toward the table and Ned's mother.

For a five time, all county, pie baking winner, Ned's mom is…unexpected. She's in her mid-forties with bleached out hair, tan leathery skin, and two friends from the doctor she enjoys putting on display for all to see. Today, she is dressed in a short pink mini skirt with ruffles and a striped fluorescent tank top. In honor of the occasion, her two-inch long fingernails are painted with stars and stripes.

"Mrs. Honer," I say in greeting as I place my pie down on the table.

"Ned told me what you did." Mrs. Honer pulls a long thin cigarette from a box on the table and places it between her thinning lips. She never lights them, just lets them sit there for a while, chewing on the end and sucking on the filter until it is mashed up and soggy.

"Or what I didn't do," I say.

"Hmmmph." Mrs. Honer crosses her arms over her chest.

"We've only been seeing each other for *two months*," I say. I want to shout it, *Two months!* But reason doesn't seem to matter much with the Honers. It must be a genetic predisposition. Along with pretending not to listen.

The judges begin to make their way down the table. Each contestant introduces her pie and works feverishly to stand out, crack a joke, and flirt with Mayor Thornton, the one male judge. The pies are cut with delicate precision, and the judges make a show of lifting their forks to their noses before tasting each piece of pie, rolling each morsel around in their mouths to gauge the flavor like a sip of wine.

I glance down at the table. My pie suddenly looks ordinary, brown, and bumpy with the crumble starting to get soggy on top. My gaze shifts to Mrs. Honer's pie, and I can't keep my jaw from dropping. It's blackberry with a thin glaze and a twisted lattice top. Little sugar florets dance along the edges like fairies, and I see that she has sculpted a little white butterfly to perch in the center of the circle. It's breathtaking.

"And what do we have here?" The booming voice of Mayor Thornton jolts me from my pie trance, and I look up at three rather round faces, each smiling with warmth and the satisfaction that comes from eating pies for a job.

"Uh, I'm Aline Thompson," I say, and my voice sounds flat. "This is an apple crumble based on a recipe my mother made up."

"Who's your mother?" The rounder woman looked at me expectantly, but before I could answer, the other woman whispered quickly in her ear.

"Ah, Shalene's daughter," the round woman says. "We were all sorry when she passed. Such a kind woman."

"Thank you," I say. I reach forward to begin cutting the pie, but a bump from behind makes me lose my balance. My right arm jumps forward to catch myself on the table, but instead of grabbing the table, I hit the pie. Like in slow motion, it flits off the table, a little UFO of apple, crust, and brown sugar. And then *plop*. The pie lands face down at the feet of the judges, who stare at it with perplexed expressions, as if it were some little green alien standing there waving hello.

"Uh…uh…uh…" I am without words. I scramble under the table, turn the dish over, and begin scooping the pie contents back into the tin. "Do you—do you—" I can't finish my question, and clearly, they *don't*.

"So sorry dear," the round woman says, and she bears a pitying expression. "Perhaps next year."

They move on to Mrs. Honer who expresses mock sympathy for my situation and then begins to recite a poem about her pie. The judges smile and nod enthusiastically.

I'm still sitting on the floor, the pie pan and its contents next to me. All I can do is stare up and watch the contest unfold. I should get off the stage, go home, but I seem frozen to the spot.

The judges continue to move down the line, and Mrs. Honer looks down at me. "Better luck next time."

"Right."

"Ned will be so surprised about what happened."

"Somehow I doubt that."

"Would you like a piece of my pie?" Mrs. Honer lifts the confection to show me her tart, perfectly intact save the one missing sliver she has served to the judges. "It's delicious." Her eyes twinkle, and my gut clenches as bile makes its way up my throat.

"Ugh, no," I say. "No thank you."

"Suit yourself." Mrs. Honer shrugs.

The judges finish up with the contestants and spend a few moments conferring in the corner. I see Kara trying to make her way through the crowd, but I shake my head, and she stops. Any sympathy right now would put me in a pool of tears.

Mayor Thornton taps at the microphone, a wide smile across his politician's face. He greets the audience, talks about how each and every pie was exquisite in its own way. *An exquisite mess.* I look at my crumble still sitting on the floor next to me, and I can feel my eyes beginning to water.

"And, now," Mayor Thornton pauses as a drum roll begins from the side of the stage. "This year's winner of the Kade County pie contest is…"

Mrs. Honer already wears a plastic smile on her leathery face.

"Georgann Booth! With her peaches and cream!" The audience breaks out in cheer, and I feel the applause rumble through my chest like a powerful wave, washing away my insides until they are shiny and new again.

I scoop a small bite of apple crumble from the dish and place it in my mouth, licking each sticky finger as I relish the swirl of tart and sweet on my tongue. Delicious.

HAIRSPRAY
Linda Fisher

It was never a good sign when the phone rang before daylight. Velda almost didn't answer it when it raced through her mind that today was her tryouts for *Hairspray* at the local theatre. She had primped to the nth degree, even digging out her large pink brush rollers and risking dark circles under her eyes by sleeping on them. She had applied an avocado mask to help offset the fitful sleep she was expecting after a twenty-year hiatus from sleeping on hair rollers.

She grabbed her glasses from the nightstand and stared at the caller ID. Mattie. What the heck could her ding-a-ling daughter want this time of day? That girl was so scatterbrained that her life was nothing but a series of crises. She had always been the squeaky wheel—causing more chaos than Velda's other three children combined.

"Holy crap," she said aloud although the only being to hear her was Sassy, her calico cat. Sassy lazily opened her eyes and turned around with her butt almost in Velda's face. She pushed the cat away and grabbed the phone. "What now?" she croaked.

"Mom, why do you always assume the worst when I call?" Mattie said in the little girl voice she used when she needed a favor.

"I know you didn't just call to chat at this time of day since you know I'm never out of bed until eight o'clock."

"Okay. I'm desperate and need a really big favor."

"Spit it out."

With Gatling-gun speed, Mattie pleaded her case. "My car won't start and Carter needs to be at school early for basketball practice. Could you please, please take him? Coach won't let him play even if he's five minutes late. He has to be there in twenty minutes and Triple A won't be here in time for me to take him. You can go as you are, Mom. You just drop him off in front of the gym. Please? Carter is so upset he's already thrown up on his shoes."

Velda could have told Mattie no, but she couldn't stand the thought of Carter being upset. His mother was so unreliable that at eight years old, Carter had developed an anxiety disorder.

"Tell Carter I'll be right over," Velda said. She jumped out of bed and grabbed her purse. As she passed the patio doors on her way to the carport, she noticed it was pouring rain. Whatever happened to gentle showers? It seemed like it was drought or downpour, just as willy-nilly as you please.

She pivoted and stepped on Sassy's tail. The cat yowled and ran like Velda had deliberately trounced on her. "Geeze Louise, Sassy! Why are you sneaking along behind me?"

She opened the closet door and pulled out her rain slicker. She felt in the pocket and there was an old-fashioned plastic rain bonnet. She fanned the plastic open, slapped the pink polka-dot bonnet on her head, and firmly tied it under her chin. She put the yellow slicker on over her green and orange plaid pajamas. She glanced down and noticed that from habit she had slipped on her house shoes—the ones with the duck heads on the toes. Well, at least they matched her slicker.

Five minutes sailed by while Velda was dinging around, and the thought of her grandson anxiously waiting put her in panic mode. She rushed to the door and as soon as she grabbed the doorknob, she realized her hands were empty. Where had she put that purse? Her eyes raked the room, but she could not remember where she had set it down, and it was nowhere to be seen. Oh, well, she didn't have any time to spare, so she grabbed the extra set of keys from the rack beside the door. Keys in hand, she sprinted the short distance from the door to the carport.

As soon as she pulled up in front of Mattie's house, Carter darted toward the car, yanked open the door, tossed his backpack in the middle of the backseat, slid in, and buckled up with the speed of the very, very young.

Velda peeked between the seats to make sure he was safely buckled in. "Good morning, Carter."

"Mornin', Grandma Velda. Is that your Halloween costume? I'm going as Batman. What are you anyway, a Martian? That's a cool outfit, with your helmet and the green face and all."

Velda took a peek in the rearview mirror. Holy cow! It's a wonder she hadn't scared the kid out of a year's growth. She did pretty much look like a little green woman. "Yep. Martian. That's what I am."

The drive to school was short and Velda pulled into the circle drive where parents, or in this case a grandma, could stop long enough to drop off their little ones. Carter yelled a thank you and jumped out of the car. Velda watched him run toward the building thinking that something was wrong.

The crossing guard impatiently waved her on and scowled at her for taking more than her allotted time. She slowly inched forward trying to figure out what was bothering her. Just as Carter reached the double doors, Velda noticed that he didn't have his backpack. She glanced back and sure enough, it was in the backseat.

She slammed the car into park and grabbed the backpack. The crossing guard was yelling at her now. "Ma'am, you cannot park here! Your car will be towed. Immediately."

Geeze, what a blustering fool. There's no way a school could have a tow-truck on retainer. Velda jumped out, glaring with all the power of her green face. "My grandson needs his backpack," she said in the no-nonsense voice she used in the days when she taught school.

She stomped through a mud puddle, soaking her favorite house slippers and the bottom three inches of her plaid pajamas. Still she held her green, rain-bonnet covered head high as she scurried up the sidewalk with all the dignity she could muster.

Velda wasn't confident that she would be allowed inside the school, and had no idea how she would get the backpack to Carter. She looked up to see Carter barreling back through the door.

"Grandma! I forgot my backpack."

Velda held out the backpack, and Carter gave her a quick hug before he pushed open the doors to go back inside the building.

Velda reached up to brush away a tear and realized her facemask was melting. Her tender feelings vanished when she saw the security guard behind her vehicle, eyeballing her license plate while he talked on his phone.

"Hey, big jerk! What are you up to?" Velda was a woman on a mission, and she was apparently targeting the crossing guard who stood at least a head taller and was twenty years younger.

The guard quickly held up the stop sign.

Before she could help herself, Velda stopped dead in her tracks. A stop sign meant stop.

The crossing guard backed slowly into the street without looking right or left. He held the sign like a shield. He was apparently petrified by the green-faced woman.

As soon as the guard had moved away from her car, Velda shook herself off and slid behind the wheel. She pulled away from the curb, intent on driving home and preparing herself mentally and physically for the play tryouts.

She saw the flashing lights behind her before she heard the siren. "No good deed goes unpunished," Velda said as she loosened her seatbelt to find her license and insurance. *Oh, crap,* she thought, *now he'll give me a ticket for not wearing my seatbelt.* She frantically tried to hook the belt and looked up when she heard a tap on her passenger side window. She rolled the window down.

"Ma'am, don't you ever wear your seatbelt?" he asked.

"I always wear my seatbelt!" Velda protested.

"Then why were you trying to fasten it when I walked up."

"Because I unfastened it to get the insurance card out of the glove box, and then realized you would think I wasn't wearing it."

Apparently, that sounded stupid enough that the officer seemed satisfied.

"Ma'am, have you had anything to drink this morning?"

"No officer, I haven't had anything to drink this morning...not even coffee." Velda handed over her insurance and registration. "I forgot my purse at home this morning," she said. "I *do* have a valid driver's license."

"I'm not sure I would be able to identify you by the picture on your license. Do you know why I stopped you?" he asked.

"No, I don't. I wasn't speeding."

"The crossing guard at the school said you parked in their unloading zone against his directions to the contrary."

"Guilty as charged. My grandson forgot his backpack and I knew I had to catch him before he got inside. They won't let anyone inside the building—not even harmless grandmothers."

"Ma'am, you shouldn't be near a school in costume—it makes everyone nervous these days."

"I beg your pardon? What do you mean 'costume'?"

"Well, you know," the big man stuttered, "like the green face and weird headdress you have on. If you don't mind me asking, what *is* that thing on your head?"

"It's called a rain bonnet, young man." Suddenly, she recognized Sammy Stucker from her fifth grade class. Thank goodness, the name on her registration was her married name. She was always proud of her looks and youthful appearance.

"Stand up straight, young man. It is so unattractive when a young person slumps!" The words came out automatically.

"Uh, uh, yes ma'am!" The officer straightened to his full height.

"Now, give me back my registration and spend your time more productively than harassing grandmothers."

The officer's face turned red with embarrassment. He handed Velda her paperwork, tipped his hat, and said, "Have a good day ma'am. Drive safely." With shoulders squared, he headed back to his patrol car.

Velda glanced at the digital clock, and decided if she hurried, she would have plenty of time to get ready for the audition. She stepped on the gas. Mr. Sammy Highway Patrolman was still behind her, but he wouldn't be bothering her again anytime soon.

A short thirty minutes later, Velda was dressed in her skinny jeans and wearing her highest heels. She had teased her hair and shellacked it with a generous coating of hairspray. Velda admired her reflection in the mirror. Yes, she certainly had the right look for the part of Velma Von Tussle in *Hairspray*.

The cell phone rang just as Velda pulled out of her driveway. She saw the call was from Mattie.

"Oh, Mom, I just remembered that today was your big audition. I hope taking Carter to school didn't cause you to be late or anything."

"Of course not, dear. It wasn't any problem at all."

"Just wanted to wish you luck...I mean...break a leg!"

Velda was still smiling when she walked into the theatre. Her smile faded when she saw Sammy Stucker reading for the part of Edna Turnblad. As soon as Sammy finished reading the part that John Travolta made famous, he walked over to Velda and shook her hand.

"It is so good to see you again Miss Beaman. You look fabulous, and not a day older than when I was in your class."

"Stand up straight, Sammy," she said with a smile.

"Everyone calls me Samuel now," he said. "And that is the second time I've heard that today. The first time was some crazy lady with a green face, wearing this helmet thing on her head, who said it wasn't a costume."

"Oh, Sammy," she said, playfully tapping him on his arm, "I see you have the same wild imagination and still tell the funniest tall tales."

AUTHOR BIOS

EDGAR BAILEY, born a North Carolinian, is a Missourian by choice. Raised in various states and in one territory, he was privileged to attend eight schools in his first twelve years of education. He has held the obligatory unskilled and semi-skilled jobs as an undergraduate ranging from hospital attendant, short order cook, cashier, and file clerk before settling into the exciting world of Information Technology.

"The Interior Minister's Address" won second place in 2009 at Missouri Writers' Guild contest in the short science fiction/horror category. He has written short plays for concert performances at the University of Missouri and very short plays for Turner Hall River Rats for the Arts.

BETH CARTER is the author of two children's picture books: *What Do You Want To Be?* and *The Missing Key*. She was published in *It All Changed In An Instant*, a collection of six-word memoirs, alongside famous authors and celebrities, as well as *Six Words At Work*, another memoir collection. Carter was also published in two anthologies: *Echoes of the Ozarks, Vol. VI* and *Vol. VII*. Carter writes women's fiction, romantic suspense, picture books, short stories, six-word memoirs, and haiku. Carter has received awards for her writing. She was in marketing for over twenty years and was previously a bank vice president. She lives in the Midwest and is a member of Ozarks Romance Authors, Sleuths' Ink Mystery Writers, and Ozarks Writers League.

Follow her on Facebook at Beth Carter or Author Beth Carter, or her blog at http://banterwithbeth.blogspot.com.

C J CLARK, an award-winning author, writes short stories, novels and poetry. She has been published in *The Storyteller*, *Mobius The Poetry Magazine*, *Pegasus*, *Pasque Petals*, *Back Home Magazine*, and more. Her novels *Wyoming Dreamer* and *Marry Me Under the*

Mistletoe are available online. She is currently working on her third novel, writing contest entries, judging contest entries, and giving attention to her nine cats, two dogs, and a husband.

STEVEN CLARK has written several novels, and two of his stories have been published in *Black Oak Review*. His first novel, *The Green Path*, will be published this year by Black Oak Press. Steven lives in St. Louis, and his play *The Love Season* won a national award in 1985.

LISA RICARD CLARO is a freelance writer living in the Southeastern United States. Lisa's articles, essays, and stories have been published in newspapers, magazines, and online, as well as in multiple anthologies. When not writing she enjoys family time, visiting with friends, reading, and deciding what to write next.

For more of Lisa's writing please visit her blog, *Writing in the Buff*, at www.writinginthebuff.net.

MARY ANN (MAYA) CORRIGAN lives in Virginia, just outside Washington, DC. She grew up in New York City and earned a PhD in English from the University of Michigan. She taught courses in nonfiction writing, detective fiction, and American literature at Georgetown University and other colleges. Currently, she works as an instructional designer for online courses and as a fiction writer. Her essays on drama have appeared in five anthologies. Her recent short stories include "Chimera" in *Chesapeake Crimes 3* and "Delicious Death" in *Chesapeake Crimes: They Had It Comin'*. Her website, www.mayacorrigan.com, is devoted to the fine art of mystery writing.

E. B. DAVIS, beach author/bum, lives in the Washington, DC, Virginia suburbs and longs to live at the beach. She is a member of the Short Mystery Fiction Society, Sisters in Crime, and its Guppy and Chesapeake subchapters. Her short stories have appeared in online magazines and in print, including other *Shaker of Margarita* anthologies. "Lucky In Death" appeared in *Chesapeake Crimes: This Job is Murder*. *Fishnets*, a Guppy anthology, will include her short story, "The Runaway," soon to be released by Wildside Press. "An

Acidic Solution" was published in August 2012 in the anthology, *He Had It Coming.*

She blogs at http://writerswhokill.blogspot.com.

LINDA FISHER, Mozark Press, is the project leader and editor of *A Shaker of Margaritas: Hot Flash Mommas, Cougars on the Prowl,* and *A Bad Hair Day.* She was editor and project leader of *Alzheimer's Anthology of Unconditional Love.* She has published four books of essays from her award-winning Early Onset Alzheimer's health blog. She has been published in *A Cup of Comfort, Chicken Soup for the Soul,* other anthologies, and online publications. Linda has won awards and prizes for her stories and essays. She is a member of the Missouri Writers' Guild, Ozarks Writers League, and the Columbia Chapter of the Missouri Writers' Guild. She blogs at http://earlyonset.blogspot.com and her websites are www.lsfisher.com and www.MozarkPress.com.

HARRIETT FORD is a veteran reporter, award-winning author of numerous short stories, three novels, and the editor of a historical essay collection. She is an inspirational speaker and currently lives near Branson, Missouri.

Visit her website at www.deniedevidence.com.

KARIN L. FRANK'S poems have been published or are forthcoming in the *Rockhurst Review, Taj Mahal Review, I-70 Review, Mid-America Poetry Review, Little Balkans Review, Coal City Review, Kansas City Voices, Asimov's, Tales of the Talisman, Dreams and Nightmares, Cost of Freedom, Storm Country,* and *Free Wheeling.*

In April 2012, her first book of poems entitled: *A Meeting of Minds* was released. Except for the illustrations, it is entirely a work of speculative poetry.

Her prose has been published or is forthcoming in *Kansas City Voices, Chicken Soup, A Shaker of Margaritas: Cougars on the Prowl,* and through *PenTales,* with a simultaneous release in a Swedish journal.

Her website, wolfweyr.com, currently tells the story of a dysfunctional family through the eyes of their dog. Readers can also follow her haiku and senryu @KLFrank1.

CATHY C. HALL is a writer from the metro Atlanta area. Her essays, articles, and short stories have been published in both adult and children's markets. She's currently working on several novels, and would probably be finished if not for a succession of bad hair days of her very own. You can learn more about Cathy at cathychall.wordpress.com.

THERESA HUPP is an award-winning author from Kansas City. She was a Midwest Voices columnist for *The Kansas City Star* in 2010, and has worked with *Kansas City Voices* literary magazine and its publisher, Whispering Prairie Press, as assistant prose editor, secretary, treasurer, and president.

Theresa has been published in *Chicken Soup for the Soul* books and in *Kansas City Voices*. Her anthology, *Family Recipe: Sweet and saucy stories, essays, and poems about family life*, is available in paperback and in ebook formats. She is currently working on a series of historical novels about life on the Oregon Trail.

Theresa is a member of the Kansas City Writers Group, Oklahoma Writers Federation Inc., and Write Brain Trust. Follow her blog, Story & History, at http://mthupp.wordpress.com.

JODIE JACKSON JR. and CAROLINE DOHACK are journalists and co-workers at the *Columbia Daily Tribune* in Columbia, Missouri, where Jodie is the *Tribune's* county government, health and environment reporter. His freelance work includes a feature in *The Bugle* about elk restoration in southeast Missouri. Jodie, who married his junior high sweetheart thirty years ago, grew up on the northern cusp of the Ozarks in Maries County. Jodie's personal blog, *Jackson's Journal*, is a memoir-in-progress. Caroline is the *Tribune's* lifestyle editor and an adjunct instructor at the Stephens College School of Design & Fashion. She grew up on a goat farm in the hills of southeast Missouri. She writes about country life and assimilating to city living on her blog, *Riding in Cars with Goats and Other Stories*.

Jodie and Caroline routinely write parodies and songs about their co-workers for the Tribune Christmas party. This is their first short story collaboration.

MARY LAUFER is a freelance writer, substitute teacher, and new grandmother living in Saint Cloud, Florida. Her stories have been published in *Women's Words*; *Her Story: What I Learned in My Bathtub*; *Prizewinning Stories;* and in several issues of *Chicken Soup for the Soul*, *A Cup of Comfort*, and *Patchwork Path*. Her poems have appeared in magazines, newspapers and anthologies, including *Proposing on the Brooklyn Bridge*; *Hunger Enough: Living Spiritually in a Consumer Society*; *Hello, Goodbye*; *The Dire Elegies: 59 Poets on Endangered Species*; *Bombshells: War Stories and Poems by Women on the Homefront*; *Beautiful Women—Like You and Me*; *Living Lessons;* and *Cradle Songs: An Anthology of Poems on Motherhood* (Quill and Parchment Press, 2012).

SUZANNE LILLY writes lighthearted stories with a splash of suspense, a flash of the unexplained, a dash of romance, and always a happy ending. Her short stories have appeared in numerous places online and in print, and she has placed and received honorable mentions in writing contests. Her debut novel is *Shades of the Future*, (July 2012, Turquoise Morning Press) followed by *Untellable*, (February 2013.) She lives in Northern California where she reads, writes, cooks, swims, and teaches elementary students. Follow her on Twitter, Facebook, and her blog at http://www.teacherwriter.net.

MARY ELLEN MARTIN has been previously published in *Barren Worlds* and *A Shaker of Margaritas: Cougars on the Prowl*. She has also written for *Idaho Magazine*. When not writing, Mary Ellen referees impromptu wrestling matches between her sons. She and her family make their home in North Idaho.

CAROLYN MULFORD started writing while growing up on a farm in northeast Missouri. After earning degrees in English and journalism, she served as a Peace Corps Volunteer in Ethiopia. There she became fascinated by other cultures. She has followed those interests by traveling in seventy countries and by editing a United Nations magazine in Vienna, Austria, and a national service-learning magazine in Washington, DC. As a freelancer, she wrote hundreds of articles, five nonfiction books, and countless other materials. She now lives in Columbia, Missouri, and focuses on fiction. Her novel for young readers, *The Feedsack Dress,* became Missouri's Great Read at the 2009 National Book Festival. In her first mystery, *Show Me the Murder* (Five Star, February 2013), a wounded ex-spy returns to her Missouri hometown to relax and heal. Instead she must adapt her skills to reveal an old friend's murder.

BETSY MURPHY lives in Columbia, Missouri, where she is a part-time professor of economics and math by evening and an observer of the absurdity of life on Earth by day. She has written articles on the economy of the U.S. and Canada for a research publisher, as well as several study guides for distance education courses, but of late has been hankering for her own ISBN number. She is currently working on a satirical novel about a centuries-old gang of middle-aged women who ride around Kansas on Vespas while painting out suggestive billboards, rigging county elections, and restoring their own brand of culture to the befuddled Midwest.

LINDA O'CONNELL, is an accomplished writer and seasoned preschool teacher. A positive thinker, she writes from the heart, bares her soul, and finds humor in everyday situations. Although she has won awards for poetry, prose, and fiction, she considers herself an essayist. Her stories appear in fifteen *Chicken Soup for the Soul* books, *Voices of Autism* and *Voices of Breast Cancer*, several Adam's Media anthologies, HCI Ultimate series books, and numerous *Silver Boomer* books. Her work can be found in regional and national publications: *The Writer's Journal, Reminisce Magazine, Sasee, True Love, Joyful Woman, Thriving Family*, in literary journals, and online.

The ocean tugs on Linda's Midwest soul with the same intensity that the moon pulls the tide. She and her husband, Bill, vacation at the beach every summer.

Linda blogs at http://lindaoconnell.blogspot.com

KATHY PAGE dabbles in many things, writing being one of them. She also enjoys participating in the local community theatre, reading, painting, traveling, and spending time with family and friends. This story has quite a bit of Kathy's life in it. While it didn't start out that way, sometimes stories just take on a life of their own.

SIOUX ROSLAWSKI is a freelance writer, a third grade teacher, a consultant for the Gateway Writing Project, a dog rescuer for Love a Golden Rescue, and a member of Saturday Writers. Her memoirs have been published in *Chicken Soup for the Soul* anthologies, as well as in *Sasee* magazine. Currently, she is working on her children's book, *A Home for Always*. Sioux is proud to be one of the five founding members of the WWWPs—Wild Women Wielding Pens. Her weekly musings can be found at http://siouxspage.blogspot.com

HARRIETTE SACKLER is a longtime member of the Malice Domestic Board of Directors and serves as its Grants Chair. She is a past Agatha Award nominee for "Mother Love," her short story that appeared in *Chesapeake Crimes II*. "The Factory," which takes place in turn of the twentieth century New York City, appears in *Chesapeake Crimes: This Job is Murder*. "Fishing for Justice" will appear in *Fishnets*—a Sisters in Crime Guppies anthology to be published shortly. An avid pet lover, Harriette is vice president of House with a Heart Senior Pet Sanctuary. Harriette lives in the DC suburbs with her husband, Bob, and their five pups. She has two married daughters and loves thoroughly spoiling her two grand-babies, Ethan and Makayla.

Harriette is a member of Mystery Writers of America, Sisters in Crime, Sisters in Crime-Guppies, and the Rockville Writers Group. Visit Harriette at www.HarrietteSackler.com.

ROSEMARY SHOMAKER believes reading *is* freedom. The written word—and then her bicycle, and then her car—gave her tastes of freedom that she'd otherwise have missed as a child and as a young person. As an adult, she continues to value the power of the written word to free people from boredom, from anguish, from ignorance, and from limitations.

Ordinary situations are highlighted in her stories that focus on those odd or funny details often hidden by the obvious. She's a government data and policy analyst by trade, an urban planner by education, and a long-time Virginia resident by choice. She's circulating her short stories more widely these days, even beyond her friends and critique group. Her first novel edges toward completion.

MICHELLE TOM, a teacher in Menlo Park, California, spends her summers baking, writing, and running. She has taken several writing courses with Stanford Continuing Education and enjoys transporting herself to new worlds through fiction. She and her husband are enjoying their plants and pristine couch for a few more years before they have children. This is Michelle's first publication.

Made in the USA
Charleston, SC
09 November 2012